THE MINISTER'S HAUNTING

(As told by the minister's wife)

by M. Sue Alexander

SUZANDER PUBLISHING, LLC
The Minister's Haunting
FIRST EDITION 2017, USA
Copyright © 2017 by M. Sue Alexander

Cover Design by Ron Watson
Author Photo by Janet Barnett

SUZANDER PUBLISHING, LLC
VANLEER, TN 37181
www.resdawn.net

Other Books by Author

Resurrection Dawn 2014 Series

Book 1: Resurrection Dawn 2014
Book 2: The Christian Fugitive
Book 3: Rebels in Paradise
Book 4: Veil of Lies
Book 5: The Anointing
Book 6: Countdown to Justice
Book 7: All Rise
Book 8: Unlikely Suspect
Book 9: Lethal Snapshot
Book 10: Purgatory
Book 11: April Fool's Day
Book 12: Reign of Errors

Single Titles
Encounters of the God-Kind
Tomorrow's Promise

E-Books Only
Adam's Bones (e-book only)
Out of Time: The Vanderbilt Incident (e-book only)
The Forum (e-book only)

View Sue's website: www.resdawn.net

Author's Comments

In *The Minister's Haunting* the names and descriptions of the family members have been changed to protect their privacy. Although the county and town in middle Tennessee where the family dwelled is not named, the description of the early 19th-century farmhouse is accurate as well as the paranormal activity observed within its walls. This story based on a true haunting is wrapped around fiction and not meant to glorify demonic activity, rather to expose its existence. Hopefully, readers will keep an open mind to the possibility of spiritual entities dwelling alongside humanity.

1

MY NAME IS ANNA BROOKE MCLAUGHLIN and I come from a family with a long history of Christian faith. My husband is a Methodist minister, and a really good guy. I was married and divorced before I met Jeremy. We soon realized our common roots solidified our relationship. We both had grown up in Christian families and attended church in small Tennessee towns.

In some ways, Jeremy was my second savior. No one would ever replace my devotion to Jesus Christ or his love for me.

My first marriage had bombed after only a few years of trying futilely to keep it intact. I came away from the relationship bruised and ashamed of failing. But with the task of mentoring a young son in the ways of Christ, I was forced to carry on the best I could. As a single parent, I completed my education and earned a masters degree in education. Eventually, I had the financial means to raise my son alone, but I was lonely for a soul mate.

Plus I realized a male presence in our home would mellow out my strong will to keep my young son safe from a dangerous world. To have Samuel always lean on me would prevent him from becoming the man God desired. I couldn't let that happen.

When I first met Jeremy he was single, thirty, handsome, and ethically responsible. I quickly recognized there was no one who could better help me raise my son responsibly than a Christian pastor. We dated, fell in love, married, and began our adventure.

As a faithful minister's wife, I was accustomed to moving every few years. Methodist leadership felt that congregations needed to experience change. And a new pastor motivated them.

But, as always, each move meant uprooting our family and reestablishing new friends in an unfamiliar location.

Eventually, we had two sons of our own. Life was excellent and I was joyful. As a wife and mom, I tried to make life easier for my family. Jeremy and I had been married ten years when he was assigned to a church close to the Cumberland Plateau where the landscape melds into the mountainous Appalachian terrain.

By that time, our youngest son, Jamie, was born.

It was only a couple of months before Jeremy would begin work at his new church. We began house hunting since no parsonage was provided for us. We had to buy or rent a house.

After viewing numerous properties in and around the town where our new church was located, we came away disappointed. By this time, weeks had passed and we were weary of our search for a permanent shelter. Already June, a short summer lay ahead before we had to make our transition into a new community.

Our two older boys, Sam and Benny, would need to register for next year's school term. Plus, I was giving up my teaching job to make the move. And coming out of a brand new parsonage with all its modern amenities, Jeremy and I couldn't imagine living in anything less comfortable. We became anxious over the move.

Praying for guidance while biting our nails, I convinced Jeremy to let me investigate properties for sale outside the county where our new church was located. I Googled online properties and found a house I believed would satisfy our family's need for space and a list price close to what we could actually afford.

I immediately fell in love with the exterior of the two-story, ninety-year-old clapboard farmhouse fit with window dormers and an old-timey porch stretching around one side of the house.

The floor plan had a formal living and dining room, a study, master bedroom suite and kitchen, all on the lower level. Three bedrooms and a full bath were located on the second floor.

At my prompting, Jeremy contacted the listing agent to preview the property. On our appointment day, I'd arranged for my Aunt Lily in Hendersonville to look after our three boys since she was my closest living relative. It was just me and Jeremy on our excursion into the beautiful Tennessee countryside.

In my estimation, we were a happy, contented family with the normal challenges of transition, though I could tell my usually joyful husband was stressed over the move. For me the change provided an edge of excitement in contrast to life's sometimes humdrum routine. I was convinced that purchasing our first house would be a rewarding experience and worth every effort.

The quaint farmhouse on three and one-half acres was a good twenty miles from the nearest town and even farther from our church. Jeremy realized if I landed a teaching job, we would both have to spend a lot of time and gas money on commuting.

However, he was game to consider purchasing this property based on my estimation that the house possessed real character.

Ha! Had I known what our family would experience while living in the antiquated farmhouse, I never would have lifted my eyes to view the property on that magnificent June day. The malicious haunting about to accost us would eventually test our sanities, sometimes even our faith. But, how could I have known?

The listing agent met us at the house.

We pulled in the driveway, killed the motor and climbed out of the suburban. A frumpy woman with golden hair hustled out the front door with a broom in hand and muttered, "Oh, hi, folks, I'm Sally Simpson. You must be the McLaughlin's!"

We stepped closer. "Yep, that's us," Jeremy said.

The listing agent parked her broom against the porch siding.

"Oh!" Sally's murky gaze swung my way. "I hear you're in the process of moving." *Not a question*, so I kept silent.

"Yes, we are," Jeremy erupted. "Thanks for meeting us. My wife really likes the outside, could we see inside?"

No-nonsense Jeremy, let's get to it. I smiled to myself.

"That's why I'm here." Sally blurted out, appearing slightly nervous as her dusty gray gaze skittered between us. "Had to sweep away the cobwebs, you know." She spontaneously laughed.

Unfortunately, the internet pictures had failed to spotlight the house's minute flaws. The exterior sadly needed updating, its white siding deteriorating and its green dormers peeling paint.

But for me, I was enticed by its charm—like the house was calling out for my help. So dismissing any shortcomings, I managed to view its possibilities with some TLC.

Hadn't God given me a second chance at a better life?

Uncannily, I was drawn to this house like no other place we had ever lived. In a way, restoring it would be a pleasure. Plus, I'd always been a history buff and loved being around old things.

Jeremy had agreed that our family needed four bedrooms. Here, our rambunctious growing boys would have their own space. Besides, country living would be an exciting experience.

"Who owns this property?" I asked Sally as we idly stood at the front door waiting to be shown inside. I knew if I could talk to the lady of this house, I would learn a lot of intimate details.

"The owners prefer to be anonymous," Sally curtly replied; plump fingers entwined in her blond curls dancing in the wind.

Odd, I thought then said, "Oh," and tossed Jeremy a look.

Not knowing what to make of Sally's comment, I hitched a breath and questioned the former owners need for secrecy.

"I suppose they worry prospective buyers might contact them and bypass the agency," Jeremy offered. "Did they say why?"

"Why?" Sally was about to croak. "No, and if I knew, I would not be at liberty to disclose their reasons, Mr. McLaughlin."

"It's Pastor McLaughlin," Jeremy corrected Sally.

The wind rustled the bushes as the awkward moment slid past. "It's really not important," Jeremy interjected.

I tossed him a look that said, *oh well . . .*

"What are we waiting for?" Jeremy asked. "It's possible we might not like the house—I mean, it might not suit our needs."

Sally's global gray eyes squinted more from Jeremy's response than the twinkling bright sunlight. She had one thing in mind: the commission she'd collect from the sale. I understood perfectly.

Though it was hot standing on the porch, I didn't make a move. Summer was coming on early and strong. Heat prickled underneath my arms as sweat ignored my antiperspirant.

"Can we see inside now?" I prompted Sally, promising myself I would look around first and ask questions later.

2

READY TO PROCEED, I pressed the doorbell to the house and discovered it didn't work. Jeremy smiled an *I-told-you-so* as I winched at its failure. *Mark that one up for repair.*

Taking a few steps to my right, I peeked around the corner of the porch and spied another door leading inside the house and learned from Sally-the-Saleslady it opened into the dining room.

In case of fire, plenty of exits, I mentally noted.

Back at the door, Jeremy and I stepped into the foyer. Through a wide hallway that ran some sixty feet, I viewed the back porch. The layout was a basic standard farmhouse plan.

From the dusty wood floors, and musky odors seeping from the wallpaper, this house had apparently been vacant for awhile.

A little AC would attack that problem.

Bent on liking the house, I refused to allow a little thing like stinky odors alter my first impression. Plus the hardwood floors were in reasonably good condition. I smiled to myself.

A little polish and they'd shine like new.

Through a second door, to my left, I spied an ample-sized living room. Against the wall opposite the windows stood a charming brick fireplace closed off with pine paneling and flanked with built-in bookshelves. Ample light pierced the room through the two thick-glassed windows with broken lead weights.

Something Jeremy could fix for me.

It was odd, but I felt like this old house and I were having a conversation. One side of me noted the flaws, the other ignored them. And I was surprised how cool the air felt indoors. Many souls had enjoyed hundreds of hours in this very room.

If walls could talk, what stories would they tell?

I crossed the living room and entered a spacious add-on with built-in bookcases against the inner wall, perfect for storing our boys' numerous toys and books. The carpet could use a shampooing and cobwebs with dead spiders clogged the corners.

Nothing that a good cleaning won't correct, I decided.

The three of us traipsed back through the living room and crossed the hall to the compact study, featuring its own fireplace. Pairing with the living room, the study had two windows facing the porch, offering charming views into the wooded front yard.

One negative I did note. Like many older homes, the rooms were traditionally boxy. However, the twelve and fourteen-feet ceilings in the house compensated for any claustrophobic issues.

Taking a shallow breath, I began placing our furniture in each room as Sally quietly led us through the house, carefully noting anything of interest on my handy yellow pad. I'd ask my questions later after we'd finished seeing all of the property.

Halfway down the hall I spied a carpeted staircase leading up to the second floor. "What's up there?" Jeremy asked.

"Three bedrooms, a full bath and some storage," Sally replied. "There's a description sheet in the kitchen."

"Good, we'll take a look when we get there," he said.

Oddly, I felt a connection to the house—like I'd been there before. Smiling at my silliness, I listened as Sally droned on about the property's many unusual amenities. We passed a laundry room tucked inside the wall opposite the base of the stairs.

Hearing the old pine floors creak beneath my feet as I trailed after Jeremy and Sally only made the house seem more mysterious. The last room on our left at the end of the long hallway was a master bedroom suite. We stepped inside.

"Where's the closet?" I asked Sally.

"On the other side of the bathroom," she replied, pointing through an open door. "As you know, with no indoor plumbing, outhouses were common in the past. At some point, space was created for a full bath by walling off a portion of the master bedroom. I'll show you." Sally led us deeper into the suite.

Okay, sacrificing bedroom space for a modern bathroom was a necessity, I concurred. As if already owning the house, I began positioning our four-poster bed against one wall and our oversized dresser with tall mirrors against the other wall absent windows.

Without using a measuring tape, I was reasonably certain our antique armoire would fit in the space next to the bathroom door. Any lingering negatives dissipated as I glanced through the picture window at the colorful summer foliage and rolling hillsides.

"This is so lovely," I uttered. And at that moment, I knew that sleeping in this lovely historic bedroom would feel right. More and more, I envisioned our family living here.

"Nice," Jeremy commented regarding the large master closet, visualizing how his Sunday suits would nicely fit inside.

"As you can see," Sally pitched, "the owners spared no expense in updating the master suite." She hugged her notebook to her chest. "Do you have any questions thus far?"

"I don't," I said, casting a look at Jeremy.

"What's over there?" Jeremy pointed across the hall.

"The kitchen," Sally replied. "Come, I'll show you."

Fully updated, the kitchen featured a bay-window with a breakfast nook large enough to accommodate our round table with six chairs. Stately oak and mulberry trees, various species of flowering plants, plus three large pear trees, stood in the backyard.

The kitchen cabinets, countertops, and stove were all new. This was mama's space. Although a skilled French teacher, cooking was my forte. I loved trying new recipes and canning fruits and vegetables—somewhat a lost art in modern society.

But thanks to my Great Aunt Lily, my sister Becca and I were trained cooks while Aunt Lily's society-driven niece, our adorable mother, proved to be un-trainable. I often kidded I inherited Aunt Lily's cooking gene from way back. Mom was a good mother, but she resisted anything she deemed as "real work'.

Having chaired many community organizations over the decades, Mom had lived a pampered life until my father died one year ago. Unlike her I was drawn to tradition and strived to be all things to our family. My musings ceased as we passed through a short hallway with a pantry on my left and a door to my right.

"Where does that lead?" I asked Sally.

"Down to the cellar," she replied.

"Can we take a look?" Jeremy asked.

"Not today, too many live spiders," Sally replied.

Disappointed, we trailed her into the dining room, noting a wall of exterior windows and a door to the side porch extension.

The room was papered with a tiny rose pattern I'd seen in magazines that featured the remodeling of old homes. The space would easily accommodate our large dining room furniture.

Through the closed French doors I spied the study. We had come full circle. As we walked, we stood in the foyer again.

Jeremy inquired about the three upstairs bedrooms he saw listed on the flyer. Sally said, "Follow me, folks, and you'll see."

I was the first to reach the top stair landing, interested in seeing if the bedrooms had enough useful space to accommodate our boys' furniture, clothes, and electronic gizmos. However, the add-on playroom downstairs would take care of any overflow.

Ahead of Jeremy and Sally, a bit too anxious, I turned left and walked half way down the hall toward the front of the house, realizing I was standing directly over the hall downstairs.

I opened a door on my right and stepped inside a bathroom.

My gazed at an old-fashioned tub seated on plump sculptured iron legs and a single sink against the wall. Behind a short wall was the commode. A modern shower stall stood against the far wall. Jeremy grabbed a look at the bathroom then followed me through a door into an adjoining bedroom. *Doable*, I thought.

"There's plenty of room for Benny," I said to Jeremy then excitedly crossed the wide hall. "Jamie can have this bedroom." He was our youngest, a toddler. While I mentally placed Benny's and Jamie's furniture in their bedrooms, Jeremy agreed they would enjoy staying upstairs. Sally-the-Sales lady smiled sweetly.

At that end of the hall at the front of the house was a large closet perfect for storing our seasonal decorations and our several Christmas trees collected over many holidays. Turning left at the end of the hall, we entered the third bedroom.

"This is perfect for Sam," I commented.

"Nice," Jeremy piped, hands locked at his back as he rocked on his brown leather loafers, his thoughts pensive and private.

Nice? I was beginning to think my husband had no other adjective to describe his feelings about the house I loved when Sally signaled for us to head on back down the stairs.

"Do you have questions?" Sally inquired of us.

"What's down in the cellar?" Jeremy asked.

"Storage space," she replied. "It's always cooler down there during our hot summers. But it doesn't freeze in the winter."

"I know you said there were sneaky spiders, but I'd really like to take a look anyhow." He trudged down the long hallway, passed through the kitchen and paused in front of the cellar door.

"Shall I go down by myself?" he asked Sally.

"Sure." She seemed reluctant. "But be careful."

Opening the door, Jeremy descended into the dark space.

"Be careful, honey!" I called out, visualizing black spiders trapped in massive sticky webs. A light turned on.

"You want to take a look, too?" Sally stared at me.

"Not me, too clumsy." I excused myself from the adventure.

When Jeremy came back up he brushed off his hands and said, "Cellar's dry as a bone so we won't have a mold problem."

I knew that mold spores were dangerous to human health.

"Okay, let's take a walk outdoors." Sally exited through the side dining room door, down some steps into a mushy grassy yard.

"What are those monuments?" I pointed to two good-sized structures at the front of the yard near the paved road.

"Oh, those were the original posts flanking the dirt road that led up to the house," Sally explained. "The granite side-posts by driveways were a carry-over from the days of mansions."

Humph. Jeremy shrugged. I offered no comment.

As we walked around the right side of the house, I felt a cool breeze as we passed under the gangly branches of a huge tree.

Well-maintained bushes and flowering plants hugged this side of the house where the porch wrapped around. I realized gardening was a priority for the former owners—which made me question why they were selling. June in Tennessee was outrageously beautiful. I glanced around, taking in a huge breath.

Being here felt right, wonderful, refreshing. The sun was warm to my skin, yet the stirring breeze was cool and infused with perfumed plant odors. Why give up such a wonderful property?

Hindsight that thought should have been a warning.

Like opening a magic window, I turned around and took in the scenic view of the lush, rolling countryside behind the house. The hills were gloriously adorned with green growth and colorful flowering bushes and trees. I was falling in love with the old farmhouse and its setting. I wanted very badly to make it ours.

But could we afford it?

Jeremy and I would have that discussion. We were near the end of our tour and I wanted to scream, "Buy me this house!"

Surprising me, my husband quietly asked Sally, "So . . . what's the best price you can give us?" His engaging eyes were wide.

My heart took a leap and I silently prayed for favor.

Sally Salesperson quoted the list price but I knew from our online viewing that the property had been on the market for months. Surely, the owners would look at a reasonable offer.

Jeremy thanked the realtor as we stood in the front yard. "Brooke and I will talk about making an offer and let you know."

"Good, but don't wait too long, the sellers are anxious."

Ah . . . I thought; *a clue to entice us.*

The First Year in the House

3

BACK AT AUNT LILY'S Jeremy and I discussed purchasing the house. First of all, he had reservations that we could not afford the list price. Plus making the needed repairs was a figure yet to be determined. I listened and tried to be patient.

But I badly wanted to live in *that* house.

Jeremy was uncertain if driving everyday to church for forty-five minutes was something he wanted to do. As I listened to why we shouldn't own the house, I carefully planned my rebuttal.

"I really love this house, Jeremy." My blond shoulder-length curls bounced as I became animated and excited over owning our first property. "Don't say no yet. In some ways, this old relic feels like my dream home. I know that sounds silly."

I giddily laughed, batting my blue eyes nervously while foolishly keeping my fingers crossed behind my back. But in the end, I knew it would be Jeremy's decision. His rugged good looks, dark hair and eyes, and athletic stance, left me feeling weak in the knees. Ultimately, he was the head of our household.

After considering our family's needs, he would make the right decision. Of that, I was confident. But it never hurts to pray.

Before the day was out we were back home in our parsonage. The following nights over supper, we discussed the pros and cons of owning the farmhouse. Utilizing a detailed printout Sally had provided, we began calculating the costs of necessary repairs.

I tried to be patient but it was difficult. Ultimately, I realized I would need a teaching job if we owned this house. The additional household income would solidify Jeremy's decision to make an offer on the property. We were running out of time.

"I'm pretty sure if I apply I can get a teaching job at the local high school near the church." I fortified our financial position. "With my extra income, can't we afford this lovely house?"

"Okay," Jeremy half-heartedly agreed, "you're the woman of the house and I trust your judgment. If you really want this property, and you get a job, then I'm willing to make an offer."

"Great, honey!" I ferociously hugged him. "You want regret it, I promise." My mind was already engineering repairs at warp speed, so anxious to move in that I could almost taste it.

The following Monday, Jeremy visited the First Methodist Church in Roland while I packed our belongings in preparation to make the move. Two weeks zipped by. I spoke with the county superintendant of schools and learned there was a French position open at the high school located in the same town so I applied.

As promised, Jeremy proceeded with assessing the possibility of purchasing the house of my dreams based on my getting the teaching job. My application was accepted and I was set to begin teaching in the fall. We were ready to submit a contract.

After a professional inspection and quotes from repair services, we made an offer to purchase the property. Surprisingly, the owners accepted. We told our former church members goodbye, shed a few genuine tears, moved into our historic home in early July, and began planning for a new and exciting future.

* * *

Our boys were thrilled with their second-floor bedrooms. And, as anticipated, our bedroom furniture fit perfectly in the master suite. While I unpacked the kitchen, Jeremy claimed the study for himself and began organizing his books on shelves.

The following week he went to work at the church. Alone with the boys in our new environment, I measured the windows downstairs for custom drapes. I already had comforter sets with matching curtains for the two older boys' upstairs bedrooms and a twin set for young Jamie's room. So they were set for the year.

By the third week in July, I was picking and canning pears from our three trees in the backyard. I stored dozens of pint jars in our ample pantry alongside the canned tomatoes, squash, and okra. The house was a joy to manage and I never tired.

Our two older boys played endlessly outdoors in the backyard from sunup to sundown. Jamie, barely two, I kept close to assure he stayed out of harm's way. The weeks passed quickly.

Meanwhile, Jeremy concentrated on his new position as pastor at the historic downtown United Methodist Church.

But all was not to remain serene. We hadn't been in the house five weeks when both Jeremy and I were awakened during the wee hours of the morning by a clanging doorbell.

Startled, I sat straight up in bed.

"What is that noise, Jeremy?"

He shrugged and rolled over, facing me.

"It sounds like a doorbell."

His sleepy eyes came half way open as he pushed up on an elbow. "Can't be, it doesn't work, remember?"

"I guess not." The clanging stopped.

Sleep quickly reclaimed Jeremy but unfortunately not me. Fully awake, I pattered down the long hallway in the dim moonlight and glared at the cantankerous rusted doorbell.

What else could make a sound like that?

Shaking my head, I went back to bed.

Two nights later, we were both awakened by the clanging sound again. *Ridiculous!* I leaped from the covers while my sleepy husband ignored the problem. Yawning, I ventured upstairs to see if either of our older boys were awake and on their computer.

Both were soundly sleeping, as well as Jamie.

Puzzled, and somewhat rattled, I shook my head and went back downstairs to bed. Then it happened again, later that week.

"Jeremy, I swear I'm going to call a repairman tomorrow and have him take a look at that blasted doorbell. There must be a short in the wiring that's causing it to go off during the night."

18

"Um . . ." he said, turned over and snorted.

But as sunrises will accomplish, the shadows of the night diminished as daily routines required my attention. The repairman recommended by an elder in our church was unfortunately not available to check our cranky doorbell for another two weeks.

I had no recourse but to patiently wait. However, when the bell ceased to wake me at night, I considered cancelling our appointment with Mr. Lawson, despising to spend money on more repairs. But Jeremy insisted that he take a look. The last thing he wanted was an electric spark to start a house fire.

August arrived and life in the McLaughlin's household moved forward without a hitch. In-service training for teachers came the second week. Sam was pre-registered at the junior high school, and Benny would attend the elementary school next door. I had enrolled Jamie at a local daycare center, so our family was set for another school year and adventures into many unknowns.

School began the third Monday in August. Jeremy turned up the AC to save on our electric bill, locked up the house, and we all piled into our Chevy Suburban to begin our respective adventures in a community that did not yet know us. But I was confident we would all adjust and soon become a part of the social fabric.

On following Saturday, Joseph Lawson showed up promptly at ten a.m. to check out our unscheduled clanging doorbell.

"Thank you for coming, Mr. Lawson." I greeted him at the front door. "This rusty old doorbell is giving us trouble."

He leaned forward to examine the bell case as I pointed to the rusted button on the outside panel. "If you can't fix it," I said with conviction, "We'll replace it with something shiny new."

"Okay." Joe held up his metal case of tools and crookedly grinned. "If I can't fix it, it can't be fixed." He stepped inside the foyer and spread a protective cloth over my polished pine floor.

"Just need to take the bell apart and see for myself." He looked at me for permission to dismantle the bell cage.

"If you need me, I'll be back in the kitchen."

"Is that homemade vegetable soup I smell cooking?"

"Sure is." I smiled at him. Somewhere between fifty and sixty, Joe has a pleasant grin to match his twinkling lemony eyes.

"My wife's a good cook, too." He tore the bell apart.

"I have plenty soup, so you'd like to take some home."

"Sure. Mrs. Lawson would love a sampling."

"Okay, I'll get out of your hair so you can finish up."

"Thanks." Joe centered his mind on his work.

Earlier, I had chopped the vegetables—potatoes, onions, carrots, and celery—and tossed them in the boiling pot of water with a pint of salty beef broth. Adding a package of frozen peas for green color, I poured in a quart of red tomatoes Aunt Lily had canned and given us. The sumptuous odor seeping from the cook pot was enticing. Then I started making buttermilk cornbread.

Being a Saturday, Jeremy was out in the backyard trimming the bushes while Sam played kickball with Benny in the clearing. Jamie was on the floor next to my feet, a kitchen cabinet door open as he retrieved metal pans and banged them together.

"Jamie, that's enough!" I scolded my toddler as he slobbered, gibbered and kept on banging pans.

Swiping my sweaty brow, I removed the metal spoon from my steaming soup. "Mrs. McLaughlin?" Joe called out to me.

I stepped in the hallway and glanced down the hall toward the front of the house. "Yes, Mr. Lawson?"

"Can you come here a minute? Need to show you som'in."

"Sure." I glanced down at Jamie, engaged in play. He wasn't going anywhere so I hurried down the hall to the foyer.

"Can the bell be fixed?" I queried Mr. Larson, gathering my apron in my onion-glazed hands while scrutinizing the bell cage.

The puzzled expression on Joe's face was troubling. "You say this bell went off during the night?" He frowned.

"Yes, five times in the past month, always at night."

"Well, that's really odd." Joe's eyes squinted as sunlight pierced the front door's beveled glass insert. "Ain't no electrical wires attached to this doorbell, so going off is impossible."

I was dumbfounded. "Are you positive?"

"Yeah, do you want me to wire the doorbell?"

"No, I'll purchase a new one."

"That's what I'd do," he said, a grin spreading.

"We'll get to Lowe's sometime next week," I decided. "Could you possibly come back a week from today and install it?"

He thumbed through his small calendar notebook.

"If you can't, it's okay. Jeremy can probably find someone else who has the time to do it." I waited for his decision.

"No, no, I can come back." He smiled. "Same time . . .?"

"It's a date." I smiled back. "Thanks a bunch."

"No problem."

As Joe packed his gear and headed out to his truck, I called out, "Wait, Mr. Lawson. Take home some of my soup!"

"Oh, yeah, almost forgot." He flung his metal case on the open truck bed and faced me. His overalls were a size too large, suggesting he'd recently lost weight. "Thanks a bunch."

"Wait right there!"

After taking up a quart of soup in a glass bowl with a lid, I carried it out to Mr. Lawson's truck. "You can return my bowl next Saturday when you come back to install our new bell."

"Sure. And thanks again." He climbed in his truck with the soup, placed it on the floor beneath the passenger seat, cranked up the motor, and cautiously backed out of the gravel driveway.

"Brooke?"

I turned around. "Jeremy."

"What did Mr. Lawson say about our doorbell?"

"Hold that thought, I need to check on Jamie." I hurried into the house, hoping our son hadn't wandered out the back door.

4

AFTER LUNCH, WHEN our older sons settled down in the playroom to watch an old *Raiders of the Lost Ark* movie, I told Jeremy what Mr. Lawson had said about the ringing doorbell.

"That can't be true, Brooke. Are you sure?"

"I'm only repeating what he said."

In a disbelieving manner, Jeremy took out his tool box and dismantled the bell case. When he spied the dangling unattached wires inside the bell case, uneasiness settled into his expression.

"I know," I said. "It can't possibly ring."

"Do you think we imagined hearing it clang?"

I huffed, "Both of us at the same time?"

"This just doesn't make any sense."

"No, it doesn't," I agreed.

Unable to process what we were told and verified by Mr. Lawson, we let it go for the evening and went to sleep.

With three boys in the house, life resumed at a normal pace. Monday, the last week of August, the day started off with a lightning storm. Jeremy went to the church while I dropped our older boys at their respective schools. Jamie loved his daycare and I was pleased. It freed me to teach French without worry.

However, I had difficulty getting the sound of the gonging doorbell out of my thoughts. What both Jeremy and I simultaneously heard was impossible and I began to question if we had a poltergeist in residence. At that idea, I giddily laughed.

The boys enjoyed their school classes and quickly made friends. We had an open-door policy at our house, so Sam's friends frequently visited. Benny met a boy his own age who lived next door and they often rode horses. Jamie our toddler was easy, always underfoot but good-natured. Life was beautiful.

As promised, we purchased a chocolate lab for the boys.

Boomer stayed outdoors most of the time, utilizing a deluxe doghouse for his sleeping quarters. Come winter we'd need to bring him indoors during freezing temperatures. If potty-trained, he could have lengthy visits. No bother really, rather a joy.

I was far too busy mothering my boys and teaching school to dwell on the unique noises plaguing our house, often referring to them as "bumps in the night." With the new bell, I slept fine.

Our family attended church services on Sundays and Wednesdays and any special Bible studies or social activities.

In early September I joined the adult choir since music was second nature to me. Skilled at playing the piano and singing, I had even written a few of my own compositions, though I scarcely shared them with anyone. But that secret was soon out.

"Hi, my name is Alice Jacobs," a woman near my age introduced herself one Sunday after the service.

I smiled. "I'm Brooke McLaughlin."

"I know." Alice chuckled. "Word gets around that you're an accomplished musician and singer. I'd love to hear you play."

"Did Jeremy tell you that?"

"Oh, no, it wasn't Brother Mac!" Alice said. "My husband Willard is on a committee with the church secretary's husband Carl. He mentioned to Willard that Janice told him you were a gifted musician." She lolled her head. "Word gets around."

The church grapevine . . . I graciously thanked Alice.

"We should get together for lunch one day soon," she said.

"It will have to be a Saturday. Weekdays, I teach school."

"Saturdays aren't a problem." Alice nodded. "Willard and I have no children at home so he often plays golf on weekends."

"Okay, I'll check with Jeremy and we'll set a Saturday date."

My first new congregational friend, I thanked God.

Whether at church, shopping for groceries, or milling around in stores in town, I found the locals friendly, gracious and most helpful. Our family was warmly welcomed into the community.

However, in light of our ongoing home repairs, we had not yet invited our new friends over to view our property, although we'd passed around our pictures at church. All in good time. . .

Thank God, with the new doorbell installed, our first annoying problem with the house went away. September passed in normal fashion, except for the changing landscape foliage to radiant colors and the cooler weather blowing across Tennessee.

October came in blustery and stormy as cooler arctic air fronts moved south out of Canada and shoved Tennessee's southern Gulf flow of warm air out of its way. With the holidays approaching, I removed our fall decorations from storage and decorated our house in Halloween orange and black in anticipation of trick-or-treaters on the thirty-first.

Meanwhile, Jeremy stacked two bales of hay on the front porch to support the large pumpkin I'd purchased at Kroger's. Sam and Benny talked endlessly about what kind of ghoulish costumes they wanted to wear to the Fall Fest at their schools. Jamie only screamed over their excitement as I rode with the flow.

Unbeknownst to us, the second round of the unbelievable was about to occur. It seems odd how weird things happen during the middle of the night. Two nights before Halloween, Jeremy woke up hearing an eerie voice calling out "Daddee . . . Daddee!" Startled, half sitting up in bed, he nudged me.

"Hmm . . ."

"Wake up, Brooke. Did you hear that?"

"What?" I rolled over and glanced at the clock. *3 a.m.*

"Daddee . . . Daddee . . . !" The voice echoed its eerie message again. "Who is that?" Jeremy's eyes squinted at me.

"I don't know, I'd better check on the boys." I threw off the covers as simultaneously my bare feet hit the cold pine floor and I raced down the hall like a fireman on call, my heart thudding.

Mounting the stairs two at a time, I was afraid it was Benny since he occasionally had nightmares. But his bedroom door was open. He was asleep, snuggled up with his fluffy teddy bear.

I checked on Sam and Jamie. They were also fast asleep.

False alarm . . . I ventured back downstairs. By this time, Jeremy was fully awake with our bedroom light turned on.

"Is something wrong with one of the boys?"

"No, they're sleeping." I wearily climbed into bed.

"Then who called out to Daddy?"

I shook my head, no answer available.

"Let's try to get some sleep," I advised.

He turned out the light and we snuggled under the covers. It was just another "bump in the night."

Two nights later, our congregation celebrated Halloween by sponsoring a Harvest Festival. The advertised event was held in the paved parking lot behind the church. Daylight Saving Time was in effect so darkness descended over the town at five p.m.

We headed off to church in Jeremy's Suburban, our family appropriately dressed for the occasion. Sam was debonair in his spiffy pirate's outfit while Benny was dressed as a scarecrow with loose hay poking out everywhere. Young Jamie wore a pumpkin suit that I had picked up cheap at a local Good Will Store.

Brother Mac, as our congregation had dubbed him, wore his "holy" blue jeans, scruffy boots, and a heavily lined flannel shirt. He looked silly in a squashed straw hat. I was the Singing Nun.

La, la, la, la. I gaffed like a goon.

It was a joyous event our quaint community of common folks with religious preferences immensely enjoyed. Volunteers had loaded their truck beds and open car trunks with healthy treats and snacks for all ages to sample. Meanwhile, the good fellows of our congregation cooked hotdogs over gas grills for everyone.

Our youth minister, with the help of several teens, handed out bookmarks with information regarding the dates and times of our church services while other youths organized games for the younger children. It was a high gala evening. *All Hallows Eve.*

No person of race, color, religion, or creed was turned away from our church event. I suspect we catered to a few atheists and witches, were the truth known. And no one went away hungry.

Surrounded by stacks of hay, fake cobwebs infused with oversized rubber spiders, and dozens of carved orange pumpkins, I handed out the cold drinks and bottled waters to guests.

Just as the crowd began to disperse in the parking lot, a full moon peeked through the gathering clouds and cast its hazy orange glow over our town. The night was nearly breathless.

A cool breeze kicked up dust and debris while we were closing out the event and cleaning up the parking lot.

God's Presence was powerfully present as I silently thanked Him for His gift of grace and abiding love. Our family had been guided to this location. Individually, we each had a divine purpose to fulfill. Because of Jeremy's ministry, people would draw closer to their Creator. And to me, that was the purpose of living.

5

MONDAY FOLLOWING HALLOWEEN came on like a damp hangover following Sunday's hard rain. Our family's normal routine resumed. The workweek went forward without a hitch.

Sleep, eat, dress, hurry and go! Work, work, work!

In the back of my mind I began to think of the holidays looming before us. If plans panned out, I would have my family over during the Christmas holidays to view our farmhouse makeover. But I would not, under any circumstances, share with them the creepy events that had shaken Jeremy and me.

Nor would we ever tell our boys.

Friday evening, the first weekend in November, the bizarre happened again. Exactly *3 a.m.* As if on cue, I was the first to awaken. Then I nudged Jeremy. "Wake up, sleepyhead."

We both heard the eerie voice cry out for daddy. "Do you think we have a ghost in this house?" I voiced my concern.

"Brooke, you know I don't believe in supernatural stuff like that." Jeremy left the bed and pattered barefoot into the bathroom. I heard the commode flush before he returned.

"I'm not sure it's wise to ignore what's happening," I said.

"Ignore the spooks?" He rolled over in the bed, his back shutting me out. "Ignore them and they'll go away."

I was uncertain that was true.

"Jeremy?"

"What?"

"Tomorrow, I'm going to the county courthouse and find out as much as I can about this house and its former owners." I was determined to get to the bottom of the trauma we were experiencing. "I refuse to be terrorized by the unknown."

Jeremy shrugged. "Okay, love, but keep me out of it."

"Wait!" I started. "You've heard everything I have! That makes you a part of this haunting, if that's what this is."

He offered no response.

"Don't tell me you're not part of this *thing!*"

Jeremy rolled over and cradled me in his arms.

"Brooke, some things are best left alone. No matter what you find out, we can't explain what happened."

I only glared at him, a chill spreading over me.

"And just so you know, we're not moving out."

"Go back to sleep. I'll deal with this problem myself."

We were up early Saturday morning. Jeremy stayed with the two youngest boys while I took Sam with me down to the county courthouse. "What are we looking for?" my thirteen-year-old nonchalantly asked, limber fingers surfing his new iPhone.

When I stopped walking, Sam did, too. "What, Mom?"

"Shut off that phone and concentrate on business."

"What kind of business?" He head-tossed locks of brown hair off his forehead and glared at me like he was lost in space.

"Sam! I need your help in finding out who lived in our house before we did." I ripped his iPhone from his hand.

"Why is that important?" He reclaimed his phone.

I glared at Sam. "Son, aren't you the least bit curious?"

"No." He rolled his eyes and resumed surfing the Web.

A chip off the old block, Sam had his daddy's lazy hazel eyes and stocky build. Five feet four inches tall at puberty, I knew he would exceed my first husband Bill's height. But full grown, he would be shorter than me since I was five-foot ten.

"Sam . . . ?"

"Huh?"

"Trust your mother for once and be a sport."

"Seriously . . .? Can we get hot chocolate when we're through at the courthouse?" He pocketed his phone after turning it off.

What a relief not to compete with modern technology.

"Sure, why not?" I mussed his hair with a hand.

"Stop, Mom!" He warily glanced around.

"Don't want to be seen with mama?" I teased. "Tough luck, buddy, you're on my payroll. That means you work for me."

Inside the courthouse we learned from an employee that any information pertaining to the original owners of our property would likely be stowed in boxes in the courthouse archives.

Seriously? My thoughts mimicked Sam's former comment.

Next I learned the public could only visit the archives during the week between one and four p.m. *Dilemma, dilemma . . .*

If I came back to the courthouse one day next week after school hours, Jeremy would need to pick up the boys from their respective schools then Jamie at daycare and take them home.

He already wasn't gung-ho on my wily detective work.

"Are we gonna get hot chocolate now?" Sam asked, bringing my thoughts into focus. "A promise is a promise," I returned.

We exited the courthouse together and found a coffee shop on the square. Missy Pollard owned the Coffee Shack. We ordered our beverages and I paid the tab. Missy told me all about how she came to own the shop. We were home by lunchtime.

I rested after lunch, mulling over the idea of ghosts sharing our space. Before I would have an opportunity to gather facts on the history of our house and its owners, another episode was crouching. Some spirits might be friendly, but ours weren't.

One week night, a few days after my trip to the courthouse, I woke up cold and discovered my blanket lying on the floor at the end of our bed. As I reached for the cover, Jeremy woke up.

"Did you kick off our covers?" he sleepily inquired.

"No, and I'm freezing." I got out of bed to get the blanket.

Jeremy pattered into the bathroom to take care of business then came back to bed. I held tightly to the covers.

"What if neither one of us kicked off the covers?"

"What?" Jeremy opened an eye.

A bizarre conclusion was tripping though my mind.

"They did it," I uttered before thinking.

"What did you say?" He sat straight up and glared at me.

"Nothing, go back to sleep," I muttered.

It took me a while to relax enough to sleep again, a childhood prayer floating through my skull for our family's protection against God-only-knows-what. Then sleep captured me.

A few nights later, about to drift off to sleep, I felt the covers beginning to slide away from my body.

This isn't happening, I told myself. *Get a grip, Brooke.*

Yet, I sensed an evil presence as the covers continued to slide down the length of my body and tumble onto the floor at the end of our bed. Was I dreaming? I listened to Jeremy's faint snoring as he peacefully slept beside me. Or simply lost my mind?

Grumbling to myself, I recovered our covers from the floor and held to them tightly to my chin until I fell back to sleep.

I decided not to mention the incident to Jeremy when morning arrived. Resuming my normal routine, I fed my family breakfast, packed the boys' sack lunches, and we all headed off to our daily responsibilities. With a renewed interest in our unseen guests, I vowed to work out a time to visit the county archives.

Somewhere, reasons for the abnormal occurrences were tucked away in the history of the house and its former residents. My investigation at the courthouse would require my taking a personal day off work, or waiting until the winter semester break.

Another weekend rolled around and my sister Becca phoned after lunch on Saturday. She was driving up from Birmingham with her husband Gary to spend a night with us. After we finished talking, I found Jeremy in the study reviewing his Sunday sermon.

"We're having guests," I informed him.

"Who's coming?" He set aside his sermon notes.

"Gary and Becca," I replied. "She just called to tell me."

"Isn't it kind of spur of the moment?"

"Yes."

Not enthused with the idea, he continued reading while I launched into a cooking mode, peeling a dozen potatoes to be buttered and smashed. I doctored a large pork loin with Cajun seasoning and salt, breaded it with flour and seared it in an iron skillet. Adding a package of brown gravy and a cup of chopped onions, I placed it in the oven to slow cook for our evening meal.

While the potatoes boiled, I uncapped a quart jar of canned green beans while eyeing the backyard through the window.

Benny was tossing a football with another third-grader in his classroom. It was an enjoyable crisp November morning. Sam had gone to see a basketball game with a friend, and Jamie was playing at my feet when Jeremy appeared at the doorway.

"Hi, did you finish your sermon?"

"It's set, unless God advises me otherwise," he replied. "I thought Gary and Becca were coming Thanksgiving."

I shrugged. "Plans change."

I traipsed into the dining room and removed my antique tablecloth from the middle china cabinet drawer.

"Would you rather they didn't come?" I asked Jer.

"You know your family is welcome." He trailed me into the dining room. "It's just that Becca didn't give us much notice."

"If I know my sister," I returned, "she probably wants to discuss a family matter with me. I'm sure it's no big deal."

"She could have done that over the phone."

"Do me a favor, Jer? Check on Jamie. He's on the kitchen floor playing with my pots and pans," I said. "I don't want him wandering outside without warm clothes and supervision."

My mind was half on Jamie and the boys out back, the rest on preparing for our guests while questioning Becca's sudden visit.

"How do you know that?" Jeremy asked me.

"Know what?" I unfolded my grandmother's tablecloth and checked it for stains. If it needed washing, I'd have to do it now.

"That your sister is coming here specifically to discuss a family matter with you?" He explained his question.

"Sisterly intuition, I suppose." I laughed. "We've got this ESP thing going. Why else would she surprise us with a visit?"

"Are you going to tell her about what's happened?"

"Oh, the bell and the other stuff that's bothered us?"

"Brooke! I would rather no one knew," he said.

"Oh." *So now he was a believer?*

"I'm just saying . . ." Jeremy leaned against the doorjamb with arms candidly crossed, coffee-colored eyes burrowing into me like sharp arrows. "Seriously, Becca will think we're nuts, Brooke."

Jamie toddled into the dining room on wobbly legs and held up his small hands to Jeremy. "Daddee . . . Daddee . . ."

His face turned white as a sheet. For a brief second I thought my husband was going to faint. "Are you okay, honey?"

He nodded as he picked up our youngest.

"We can't let what we don't understand destroy us." I reminded myself more than Jeremy. "Jamie's salutation isn't an omen. He was just calling for his daddy." Case closed.

"Just so you know, Brooke . . ." Jer's chilly gaze captured me. "I still believe there's a reasonable explanation for everything spooky that's happened. We didn't just fall off a turnip truck."

"I know that." I locked blue eyes with his brown. "I'll keep our secret, if that's what you want. Besides, Becca will be far too busy telling me about her latest drama to get a word in edgewise."

I hoped that was true, trying to reassure him.

"Just so we're clear on the matter, Brooke."

"As a bell," I said, regretting my misguided cliché.

Back in the kitchen, I tossed a stick of butter to melt in a hot black iron skillet before adding half a cup of brown sugar. Then I placed a prepared pie shell over the melted sugar and added four cups of our freshly chopped apples, topping it with a second shell.

"You and Becca are close." Jeremy drove home his point. "I know how hard it is for you to keep secrets."

Really, are we still talking about this? I turned around and faced him. "I heard you the first time, Jer." I waved my spatula at him. "Tonight, we are going to have a delicious meal and a nice visit with my sister and her husband. So just chill out, will you?"

He nodded and parked Jamie on the kitchen floor then ventured out the back door to check on Benny and his buddy.

Still, the clanging bell we heard from a disconnected bell cage lingered in my thoughts, ringing like a warning of worse to come.

* * *

Becca and Gary arrived at six o'clock that Saturday, and we all sat down at the dining room table to a meal I had prepared for royalty. The conversation was light and fun and the younger boys acted silly, often prompting laughter from the four adults.

After Becca helped me clear the table and load the dishwasher, I put Jamie down for the night just after eight thirty while Benny rode with Jeremy to take his friend home.

Alone in the living room with Becca, I longed to share what Jeremy and I had experienced in the house. I suppose she sensed something amiss because she looked at me strangely.

"What's going on, Brooke? You seem a bit off tonight."

Off? I'm way over the edge, I thought to myself.

Gary came into the living room and sat down in a wingback. "Am I interrupting girl talk?" he queried, looking directly at me.

"No," I replied. "You're welcome here."

"You might be," my sister told Gary, tossing a look.

"Talk about blunt!" He laughed then said, "Jeremy seemed unusually quiet at supper, is he okay with us being here—I mean since it was such short notice?" His honest question lingered.

Always the socially sensitive one of the pair, Gary wouldn't hurt a fly's feelings. He was a really good guy, an architect by trade. A gift to their marriage, he balanced out my flamboyant sibling who resembled my mother far more than I did. Sad to say, Becca was sterile, but they had discussed adopting a baby.

"No, Jeremy's fine," I uttered. "He's just preoccupied."

"Is his work going well?"

"No, that's not it." I clammed up.

"Good," Gary said. "Glad to hear it."

"Did you bring clothes for church tomorrow?" I inquired.

"We came prepared." Becca fidgeted with her neck scarf.

"Good," I said, "Jeremy will be pleased." I noticed how my sister periodically glanced at Gary, as if to enlist his permission to tell me something. "Okay, guys, why are you really here?"

Becca's gray-green eyes shot to Gary again, really scaring me.

"What? Just say it!" The untold mystery was unnerving.

"I, uh, didn't want to, uh, tell you over the phone," Becca stuttered. "Mom's cancer is back. I thought you should know."

The news was shocking. Our mother was in her early sixties, far too vibrant to die. She'd been diagnosed with breast cancer three years before and had a double mastectomy followed by aggressive chemotherapy. Those closest to her assumed the cancer had been permanently arrested. We were all wrong.

The only other older relative left on our side of the family, besides my two sisters, was my elderly Great Aunt Lily—who was a godsend. I wished I had her shoulder to cry on right now.

"Why didn't Mom call me herself?" I burrowed into myself, a bit wounded to hear the news through an advocate.

"She didn't know how to tell you," Becca explained.

"Because she thinks I'm so fragile!" I angrily uttered.

"Don't be mad, Brooke." Tears nested in Becca's eyes, her perfectly applied makeup splotching on her cheeks.

"She's afraid I'll fall apart, is that it?"

Why is it people who know me best view me as weak? I'm stronger than anyone might think. I was hurt, and it showed.

"I'm sorry Mom feels that way." Becca empathized with me. "You know Mom, she's her own person."

Delivering the horrible news wasn't easy for Becca. I apologized for my remark. "My emotions get the best of me."

"I understand, Brooke, you have a right to be upset."

I nodded then asked, "How long does Mom have?"

"She refuses to have chemo again."

"That's not an answer, Becca!" I fought tears and fear, inhaling the residual odors of cooked pork and onions.

Cancer: that dreaded disease that had stampeded through our family from generation to generation. When would it be my turn?

"Doc Crosby told Mom she had less than six months."

"He's not her oncologist!" I blurted out.

"Mom's chemo doctor sent the report over to her primary physician, Doc Crosby, and he told her," Becca explained.

I said nothing to reveal my frustration with the situation.

"She seems to be taking it pretty well," Becca said.

I'm not. Breath left my constricted lungs.

"I'll call her tomorrow," I told Becca, aware Mom was probably already in bed. Atlanta was on Eastern Standard Time.

Tomorrow: when I have my emotions under control.

Becca nodded. "Just don't break down, okay?"

"I won't!" I snapped. "Stop pampering me!"

The living room was like a death trap it was so quiet. Dad had been dead barely a year from a heart attack. Now, I was losing my mother. Complicating matters, the holidays lay ahead and Jeremy expected me to help organize a big Thanksgiving bash for our church then decorate our home for a traditional Christmas open house. He wanted our congregation to feel they were part of our lives. I wanted that, too. But how could I fake jolly under the weight of impending death? I couldn't. I was falling apart.

It isn't fair, I told God. *Don't do this to our family.*

"Did you talk to Beverly yet?" I thought to ask Becca.

"No. Cell phones don't always work in Africa," she replied.

"Too bad, Beverly needs to know that Mom is sick again with cancer. I want her to come home." I needed family support.

Beverly was a chip off my daddy's side of the family. He had travelled extensively to many countries before he married our mom. Memorabilia from all over the world showcased his office desk and filled the bookshelves. Beverly was like a Christopher Columbus, always looking for a new and exciting adventure.

Me, I never understood their wanderlust.

"I left Beverly a message at her apartment in London," Becca interjected. "I don't think she'll call back anytime soon."

"Why not—she's not our sister? Not part of this family?"

"Brooke, I don't expect her to come to Mom's funeral."

"That isn't right!" I spewed. "It's disrespectful."

"Beverly's a free spirit, what can I say?"

With no solution to the problem, Becca and I ended our discussion concerning our baby sister's abandonment of family.

Jeremy returned with Benny around 9:30 p.m. and I shared with him Becca's unwelcome news about my mother. He expressed regret, gave me a sympathetic hug, but could not alleviate the sorrow dragging me down to Ground Zero.

I had never been one to view the cup of life half empty, but today it contained only dregs of bitterness. We all said our goodnights and went to our respective bedrooms. As I tried to fall asleep, I realized Becca was grieving, too. Her response to Mom's news was far less vocal than mine. Then I prayed.

* * *

Gary and Becca left to go home right after church on Sunday. And truthfully, I was glad our family was alone again. Jeremy was emotionally and physically exhausted and slept for hours during the afternoon while I read my Bible, prayed, and attempted to cope with Mom's news. I had a husband, three children, and a promised new puppy coming on Santa's sleigh at Christmas.

Boomer was Sam's dog, Benny insisted, and wanted his own.

I needed to stay strong. People expected that of me. I was a pastor's wife, a teacher, a sister, a daughter . . . and I was alive and well. It was not my time to die yet. For that, I thanked God.

Let the dead bury the dead, the Bible says. *Life is like a vapor . . .*

6

THOUGH I'D PROMISED myself that I'd check out the county archives to investigate the history of our mysterious talking house, it seemed that other things far more urgent impeded me.

Thanksgiving was five days away. Since nothing supernatural had occurred in our home recently, I was reconciled to the idea that whoever was taunting us had decided to give it a rest.

Eternally, I prayed.

At my prodding, on Sunday afternoon Jeremy dragged out of storage our huge boxes of Christmas decorations, most of which I'd received from Mom after Dad passed. Since Beverly had no interest in domestication, Becca and I split Mom's gift equally, agreeing to share with Beverly later, should she change her mind.

I had called Mom the day after Becca went home. Though I did my best to offer encouragement, she'd apparently given up hope of recovery. She'd even planned her own funeral, picked out her attire, casket and flowers, and added her name to Daddy's tombstone. I just couldn't handle the drama so I tried ignoring her brave positive platitudes. *Death comes to us all. Right . . .?*

Thinking of spirits moving on after death, I could not wrap my head around the idea that a few angry ones still lingered in our midst. I recalled some theories tossed around concerning ghostly activity among the living. Some people theorized the spirits were people who had died under traumatic circumstances, and found a reason to haunt the living while resolving personal problems.

Like, who murdered me? I'll get you in the end.

I mused over my morbid imagination.

Avid spiritualists suggested disembodied wandering spirits lingered at their death sites; thus the haunting of a cemetery, a house where a murder occurred, or even an old World War II building. Ghost hunters had a field day using their sensitive electronic instruments looking for the so-called "hot spots" or doorways to the Hereafter they believed existed at these sites.

Some biblical theologians thought demons were behind these supernatural events. In the Bible, the writer of Genesis 6 recorded that the sons of God intermarried with the daughters of men and produced a race of giants that altered human genetics. Some speculated that God destroyed the first world with a flood to cleanse it from sin and these genetically altered individuals.

Only the good man Noah and his family survived.

Mentioned in the Bible that God had granted Satan and his minions power over earth's airways prompted some biblical scholars to suggest that these disembodied spirits were possibly those giants in the Bible. No mention of demonic possession in the Old Testament, Jesus Christ was the first to cast demons out of sick and mentally ill people. I needed to sort out what I believed about ghosts. This was all heavy thought for a country girl who'd gone to church all her life. Pushing aside the unsavory subject, I decided to turn our lovely farmhouse into a storehouse of Christmas decorations. No storefront in town would compete.

Decorating was my way of overriding negative thoughts of my mother's impending death. Some days, it didn't work. Other days, I found joy in the season. Today, I felt hopeful.

On one side of our long hallway on the main level, I placed decorative pots of live red poinsettia. I wrapped a garland of fresh pine greenery around the staircase banister then added bunches of red Holly berries. Jeremy installed a ten-foot live fir in his study between the front two windows. We strung hundreds of white glittering lights then added antique gold-and-red ornaments.

In our living room, we erected a ten-foot cedar that Jeremy cut down on our property. I decorated it in royal blue lights and shiny silver ornaments. On the fireplace mantel rested layers of fresh pine greenery with large cones, upstaged only by a row of tall glittered white candles. I even put down a brand new red rug.

A tree was tucked in one corner of the kitchen bay window next to the breakfast table. In addition, each of the boys had table trees in their bedrooms. Every nook and cranny had a decoration.

The dining room was covered with my mom's antique lace tablecloth and a leafy Christmas decoration sat smack the middle.

I hung a huge wreath of fresh berry holly on our front door and the outside windows were ringed in twinkling white lights. Anyone driving up to our house might think Santa lived here.

I smiled at our creations. We were a magazine picture ready to be taken. Nope, just the ordinary McLaughlin's!

Every day when I came home from school that last week in November and opened the front door, I was met with the lingering odors of fresh-baked sugar cookies and extinguished scented candies. Those symbols of Christ's birth helped me deal with the idea I would soon attend my mother's funeral.

Then Wednesday before Thanksgiving arrived. Mentally and physically exhausted, I ordered a Kroger turkey with all the trimmings to accompany my sweet potato soufflé and green bean casserole. After all the decorating, planning and cooking, our quaint family of five celebrated the holiday absent of family.

Beverly was still overseas in Africa while Becca and Gary spent Thanksgiving weekend with his parents in Florida. And Mom was too sick to travel. So Jeremy and I approached the weekend with the intent to rest from our busy schedules.

However, I managed to take advantage of the Black Friday store sales and shopped for Christmas gifts. But our parental lethargy did not impede the enthusiasm of our two older boys who wanted to see the latest scary movie on Saturday.

Me? No way would I view a horrifying sci-fi movie. It was the last thing on my agenda as I flopped down in the living room recliner. "Jeremy, will you take the boys to the theater?"

I couldn't muster the energy to wiggle my little finger.

"Sure, Brooke," he said. "Just sit by the fire and rest."

7

DECEMBER MOVED FORWARD and I placed an Open House invitation in our church bulletin for the second Sunday. I received great responses and anticipated a lot of preparation forthcoming

Sensing my frustration over my mother's cancer, Jeremy insisted we hire two school cafeteria workers to assist with setting up extra tables, serving the food, and cleaning up afterwards.

Too weary to decline, I welcomed the help.

Keeping my French students focused on studying for midterm exams was a huge challenge. American children of all ages were counting the days until school was out for Christmas.

Actually, I was, too. There's something really special about an American Christmas. The holiday atmosphere was frosty and our quaint Middle Tennessee town twinkled in colored lights. Families bustled about the streets, admiring store window decorations and sampling the specialty foods offered by local vendors. Wee ones took the opportunity to sit on Santa's lap.

Hardly anyone I came across spoke of anything other than their plans for Christmas, where they were traveling, who they were seeing, and the gifts they'd purchased for others.

As the big day approached, conducting classes seemed an impossible task. Monday afternoon before our scheduled open house, I came home exhausted from the work day. My husband recognized I was burnt out with teaching and empathized.

"Hard day at school . . .?" he asked as I sat Jamie down on the floor and handed him a coloring book with a pack of crayons.

Jeremy had picked up Sam and Benny at their respective schools and beat me home by a good hour. The house was awfully quiet. "Where are the boys?" I asked, concerned.

"Out in the shed completing a project," he replied. "Let me try again." He chuckled, arms crossed as he leaned against the kitchen cabinet. I stared at him, glassy-eyed, in need of caffeine.

"Your day . . . how was it?" he asked again.

"Awful, if you're looking for the truth. How can I possibly teach my students French when their minds are on Christmas?"

I plopped my satchel of lesson plans on the floor beside Jeremy's comfy chair in the living room. "How was yours?"

He grabbed my arm and pulled me into his lap. "Forget about school and try to relax." He kissed me sweetly.

Bent on complaining, I fussed, "Mid-terms are next week and half of my French students will probably fail."

"It's not your fault, Brooke," he countered. "Look, honey, you teach. But you can't make students learn."

I shook my head. "I know you're right. I'm far too intense these days." I flattened my body against his wide chest. "We still have a lot to do to get ready for Sunday," I reminded him.

"Last time I checked we were in good shape."

"I guess I want everything to be perfect."

"Perfection is a mirage. We'll make do."

"Okay." I popped up. "Guess I'd better prepare supper."

"Need any help?" he asked.

"No, I'm just warming up leftovers. Hopefully, my beef roast is done in the crock pot. You read and relax."

"Hey, you," he called out to me. "I rented a Christmas movie for the boys to watch tonight." I recognized that gleam in his eye. "I thought we'd have some quiet moments by firelight."

That romantic twinkle in my husband's eyes told me he needed some tender-loving attention. "Sounds like a winner."

"Leave Jamie in here with me," he said.

"Thank you." I ambled down the hall to the kitchen.

I tried to remain positive as our family sat around the supper table and shared the week's life experiences. After Jeremy helped me clean up the dishes, he started the boys' video upstairs and we sat on the sofa facing the fireplace, gazing at the Christmas tree.

"Are you happy living here, Brooke?"

"I love living with you and the boys," I said while staring at the colorful foil-wrapped presents under the tree. "What's not to love about Christmas? The boys are ecstatic. Everyone's joyful."

It wasn't actually the truth. While everyone around me anticipated celebrating Christ's birth, I was privately grieving over losing my mom to cancer. But I didn't want to drag Jeremy down with me. So I tried to act joyful. Later, when the video ended and we'd tucked in our boys, we made amazing love. Jeremy and I both needed a human touch, life was always so unpredictable.

Wednesday night at choir, I was asked to do a solo in the Christmas cantata. Begging off, I claimed my voice was scratchy from lingering allergies. Actually, I didn't feel like singing.

As much as I longed to visit Mom, I couldn't until school let out for Christmas. Sunday arrived, the day of our open house.

After church, we purchased the boys Subway sandwiches and drinks then rushed home to turn on the lights and set out the prepared food. As Jeremy predicted, our Christmas open house came off successfully. Over two-hundred souls passed through our front door between two and five p.m., smiling, laughing, eating and drinking, greeting one another warmly.

When the last guest departed around 5:30 p.m., the cafeteria workers we'd hired began cleaning up. I was exhausted, but pitched in anyhow. Jeremy and the two older boys helped.

* * *

School break came on the third Friday in December. Jeremy closed down the church staff early and picked up the two older boys at their schools. I brought Jamie home with me.

Whoopee! The boys leaped for joy and tossed their books aside. I was thrilled but less vocal about it. The boys went upstairs to play video games until I called them down for supper.

At the kitchen table, Jeremy said a blessing over our spaghetti and meatballs. We were all hungry and ate ferociously.

"How was your last day at school, son?" I asked Sam.

"Fine. . ." he reached for a roll and slathered it in butter.

Fine? I gave Jeremy a look that something was amiss.

"Did something bad happen, son?" the good pastor asked.

Sam shrugged. "I guess I just don't fit in."

"What do you mean?" I started, truly surprised. Our son was Mr. Personality wherever he went. How could anyone not accept him? Well, that was a mom's perspective, of course.

Sam's shoulders slumped. He was clearly unhappy.

"Tell us what's wrong, Sam," I said.

"Well, some of the guys in my class are experimenting with pot and, uh, you know. . ."

"No, I don't know . . ." I chimed in.

Sam's liquid hazel eyes shined in the overhead light.

"I don't do drugs," he said.

Jeremy said, "We know that, son. We're proud of you."

"Do these boys go to our church?" I asked.

"Some do," Sam reluctantly replied.

Benny put down his fork, big ears attentively listening.

"Your Mom and I are so proud of you for exhibiting strong Christian principles," Jeremy said, eyeing me for help.

"Do you want to tell us who tried to give you drugs?"

"No, Mom!" He angrily tossed his napkin aside.

"This is pretty serious, Sam." Jeremy intervened. "I understand why you won't snitch on your classmates, but. . ."

"But what . . .?" He frowned. "I should anyhow!"

"Would it help you to know we'll be discreet?" I said.

"What's discreet?" Benny piped from across the table.

"Not now, Ben." Jeremy shushed him.

"Tattling doesn't win me any friends," Sam declared.

"What's pot?" Benny asked. "Is it what you cook in, Mom?"

Sam chuckled at his brother's comment as I said, "Some teens think it's cute to smoke weeds that make them drunk. Jesus doesn't want us to mistreat our bodies." I looked at Jeremy.

"Sam, the Holy Spirit indwells us so we can choose to live holy lives. Drugs will mess up your mind so you should never accept an illegal substance someone offers you," Jeremy warned.

"The only medicine you should ever take is what the doctor prescribes when you're sick," I fearfully pointed out.

Sam nodded, rolling strings of spaghetti around his fork.

"Okay, we trust you, son," I added.

"I still don't understand," Benny piped.

I would have a private discussion on the subject of drugs with our thirteen-year old Sam, hoping he would give me the names of those users. Their parents should know before something terrible happened to them. The temptations teens experienced today were far worse than when I was their age. God help them.

The weekend passed with lingering issues.

Monday evening I was about to crawl into bed when I heard footsteps down the hall. Sam peeked into our bedroom.

"Mom, are you asleep?"

"Thinking seriously of going," I told my eldest.

"Can we talk?"

I sat on the side of my bed, bare feet dangling. Jeremy was in the bathroom grooming for bed. It was getting pretty late.

"What do you want to tell me, Sam?"

"Something weird just happened."

"Care to elaborate?"

I listened as Sam told me he was watching TV in his bedroom when something touched his leg. "What do you mean, Sam?"

"I felt something touch my leg, Mom."

My heart caught in my throat. "Did you see or hear anything, Sam?" I asked. He shook his head no. "Then go back to bed."

"I'm pretty scared, Mom."

"Nothing is going to hurt you, son."

"Are you sure, Mom?"

"I'm sure." I spied my husband coming out of the bathroom and said to him, "Sam has a problem, Jeremy."

"What kind of problem?" He looked at Sam.

He went though the same spiel. When he'd finished, Jeremy locked eyes on me first then Sam. "I'll go up and check out your bedroom," the good father said. "You wait right here with your mother until I get back." He sped off like the Energizer Bunny.

Jeremy found nothing disturbing in Sam's bedroom; no spooks in his closet. He checked the windows and they were locked down. When he came back, he offered to sit with Sam in his bedroom until he fell asleep. Sam agreed and they went up.

But that wasn't the end of the taunting.

* * *

Monday before Christmas, I woke up to blood-curdling screams echoing through the house. Sloughing off the covers, I sat strait up in bed and looked at the bedside clock. *Midnight.* Then I heard the thudding footfalls of running feet down the hall.

Do we have an intruder? Our security alarm had not gone off.

Sam stood at the threshold of our bedroom, his expression drawn and face washed out white. "I'm not going back up there!"

"What's happened, Sam?" Jeremy was out of bed and pulling up his pants. It was cold in the house, the icy wind howling outdoors as snow heavily fell over Middle Tennessee terrain.

Half under the covers, I shivered as Jeremy walked over to Sam and embraced him. "Did you have another nightmare?"

"It wasn't a dream, Dad, it was real"

I knew exactly what Jeremy was thinking. *Has another strange event spooked Sam?* I was out of bed by that time and worried.

"Jeremy, talk to Sam about what happened before you go upstairs to take a look around." I considered that the wind may have rattled the panes and spooked our teen. Inevitably, the invisible hand that touched him last week was a real concern.

"Okay, I'll be back shortly." Jeremy nudged Sam across the hall toward the kitchen. "Wait!" I grabbed my furry housecoat. "I'm going with you. I want to hear what happened, too."

The cold floor creaked beneath my bare feet as I slipped on my robe and slippers. "How about I fix us some hot chocolate while Sam tells us what spooked him?" I immediately regretted using that terminology the instant it rolled off my quick tongue.

"Are you afraid for Dad to go upstairs?" Sam asked me.

"Of course not," I replied. "We just all need to chill out."

Sam was trembling. We sat around the kitchen table sipping on hot cocoa as he explained what happened thirty minutes before. "Dad, I woke up cold." His hazel eyes skittered to me.

"I'll turn up the heat," Jeremy said. "Then what happened?"

"I wasn't dreaming, Mom, I swear." Sam clasped his hands on top of the table. "The covers on my bed moved."

"What do you mean?" I glanced warily at Jeremy.

"I felt someone tug at my covers," Sam said. "Someone I couldn't see." Sam's eyes were huge with recall.

I nodded, blinking. *They weren't finished with us yet.*

"Maybe you only imagined it, Sam." Jeremy tried to gloss over the incident. "Too much caffeine, maybe . . .?"

"I'm not crazy, Dad! Something pulled my covers off."

All went silent in the kitchen. I touched Sam's hand.

"Mom," he said, "the door opened by itself and something grabbed my leg." It was obvious Sam was terrified.

Hearing something, even seeing something, was different than *feeling* something. The idea that some ephemeral identity could touch my child was unacceptable. Should I just tell Sam what happened to me, about the covers coming off my bed?

"Well, whatever made you feel like that is gone by now." I joined Jeremy in the ruse. I didn't want our boys to know what unknowns Jeremy and I had experienced. I couldn't bring myself to terrorize Sam even more. "Dad will tuck you in bed, son."

"I'm not going back up there!" he exclaimed.

"Okay, Sam, you sleep with Mom and I'll sleep in your bed."

"What do you think it is, Mom?"

"I don't know, Sam, but I intend to find out."

It took me another hour alone in my bed to settle down. I feared the entity that had touched Sam would come at me. I prayed the Lord's Prayer over and over until I dozed off.

Then nightmares trapped me in a deep dream state.

8

TUESDAY MORNING, WE woke up and realized a ferocious snowstorm had descended upon Middle Tennessee during the night and dumped six inches of pristine white snow over the landscape. Joyfully, the sleds came out of storage and the boys practiced their sledding skills on the hilly slopes behind the house.

County and city roads were iced over, mountain passes closed to traffic. No one was going anywhere until the snow melted.

I was in the middle of my third cup of morning coffee when Becca phoned mid-morning to cancel their Christmas visit with us. Apparently, the Deep South had shared our weather event.

I was disappointed, but understood. With Jeremy's parents vacationing in Switzerland in December, and my Aunt Lily visiting a friend in Florida to experience Disney World, we would celebrate Christmas without our extended family around.

Before Becca ended our call, she reported that our mother looked terrible and was declining fast.

"I intended to visit Mom over Christmas holidays, but I don't see how until the roads between here and Atlanta improve."

"I'm sure she understands." Becca empathized.

"Did she ask specifically to see me?"

"I don't think Mom wants visitors," Becca sullenly replied.

"Not even her daughter?" Mom took pride in the way she looked and dressed. Death put a real damper on her social life.

"Don't take it personal, Brooke."

How else could I take it?

I promised to mail Becca and Gary's presents when I could get to the post office. By late Wednesday, the air had warmed and the snow began to melt. Jeremy and I were set to visit Mom.

But she died late that day: *Wednesday, Christmas Eve.*

I was devastated by the news. There would be no Christmas celebration for our family tomorrow. I refused to celebrate life and open presents when my mother lay lifeless in a morgue somewhere. Disappointment clouded the older boys' faces but they were respectful of my grief. My pastor husband, paid to attend the sheep of his congregation, was clueless how to comfort me. And my guilt over not visiting my mom was overwhelming.

Why hadn't I gone to Atlanta the moment I heard she was sick again? I needed to tell her in person how much I loved her. Did I truly believe Death could be kept at bay indefinitely?

I was so foolish. And now it was too late. The tears came in torrents, the emotional draining even worse. I was a bad daughter, or so I believed. I beat up on myself for hours.

Becca had emailed me the funeral arrangements. A mortuary in Stone Mountain, Georgia, was preparing her body for burial. She would be driven in a hearse to Henderson, Tennessee, viewed by relatives and friends at the local funeral home then lowered into a plot of ground at the family cemetery behind the Methodist Church. She'd rest beside my daddy until all graves were emptied for the final inauguration of Jesus Christ's return to earth.

At that thought, my human spirit was as barren as the dead vegetation ravaging our once beautiful yard. With both parents deceased, my sisters and I were left at the helm to guide our families the rest of their way through life. Then it would be our children's turn, and so on, something I didn't want to dwell on.

I wondered if Beverly would show up for Mom's funeral.

* * *

I refused to celebrate Christmas on Thursday. Our presents remained unopened under the decorated trees. Our boys cried with disappointment. To compensate, I fed them sweet goodies and tried to help them understand the time for celebration wasn't now. Grammy had passed. And we should respect that. Next

49

week, we'd have just as much fun. Honestly, I was unsure if next week would be a good time, either if this heaviness didn't pass.

"I'm sorry you didn't see your mother before she passed." Jeremy empathized as I donned a black skirt and sweater for my trip to West Tennessee Friday afternoon. "Will you be okay?"

"I'll get there."

"I wish I could go with you."

"Sam and I will be fine." I planned on driving our Chevy Suburban since it had four-wheel drive and was more reliable on slick pavement than our four-door Malibu. "Oh," I had a sudden thought, "what about the puppy we promised Benny?"

"I'll tell him we'll get him one in the spring," Jeremy decided. "A pup will fare much better in warmer weather."

"He'll be so disappointed, Jer. It's a Christmas promise."

Our aging Boomer lazed around the house like a couch potato, a constant reminder to Benny that he wasn't a pet owner. Sam ignored his dog for the most part, spending time with friends.

"Who would've thought Christmas would turn out like this?"

"Don't obsess about the puppy, honey. We'll get Benny a gerbil with a cage. Jamie will love feeding the little critter."

"Please no! They look just like white rats."

Jeremy hugged me. "We'll celebrate Christ's birthday when you and Sam get back from your mom's funeral. Anyhow, the boys have already sneaked a peek at half their presents and suspect what's in the rest. They understand more than you think."

"Christmas will never be the same for me again."

"Honey, you can't think like that."

I could and I did. I slipped on my ankle-length, black woolen coat then put on my black leather gloves. "Do you mind checking on Sam to see if he's packed and ready to leave?"

"Sure." Jeremy went upstairs while I traipsed down the long hallway toward the foyer, boards creaking beneath my booted feet.

We had a solid marriage but I didn't like keeping secrets from our children. At some point I needed to tell my firstborn *everything* weird that had happened since we moved into the house. I hoped learning about our haunting would not skew Sam's view of reality. Like it or not, we lived on the precipice of the Twilight Zone.

No longer could our uninvited guests be ignored. Certainly, they weren't ignoring us. I was ready to go on the offensive.

I stood at the front door impatiently waiting for Sam when I spied Jeremy trotting down the hall toward me.

"He's almost ready, honey. Just a couple of phone calls he wants to make to some friends. Sure you're okay?"

I nodded, anxious to get on the road.

"Maybe I could find someone else to do Barry's funeral service tomorrow," Jeremy said. "I should be with you."

My eyes alighted with surprise. "No, Jeremy, you can't disappoint the Claytons." Mom wasn't the only one who had died Christmas week. "At this late, date, they'll have trouble finding another pastor to perform Barry's funeral on Saturday."

Their sixteen-year-old was killed last Saturday when he lost control of his new open-bed red truck and plummeted into a ravine after drinking too much alcohol at a teen party.

I could tell Jeremy was torn. He looked more like a confused teenager than a staunch pastor with the backbone of a Paul of Tarsus. "Look, honey. I know you want to come with me," I said. "But the Claytons will be crushed if you back out on them."

He nodded, head drooping as his eyes dragged the floor.

"Too bad you're not two people." It was my poor attempt at defusing his guilt. "As a good shepherd, you have a responsibility to your flock. I respect you for caring so much."

He glanced up at me. "Barry was a good kid, just got off track with the wrong friends." Excuses didn't bring him back.

Nothing I said would alleviate the grief his parents and our congregation were experiencing. Barry's new Ford truck was a Christmas gift from his grandparents. Too much material blessings too soon hurt our young when they lacked maturity.

"Mom . . .?" Sam called down from the upstairs landing.

I walked down the hall and glanced up at him.

"Yes, Sam. Is there a problem?"

"Yeah, there is," he scowled.

"We have to leave soon. I don't want to drive after dark."

He stood on the top landing in his sock feet. "I can't find my new brown loafers," he complained. "Have you seen them?"

"Look in the box at the top of your closet."

Had Sam forgotten his mom was a neat freak, preferring things in their proper place? The kids made their own beds every morning, a parental requirement. Dirty dishes went in the sink.

"Okay, I'll look." Sam pattered out of my view.

Hearing Sam's footfalls as he stomped down the stairs in his leather-soled loafers somehow reminded me of the night he came to our bedroom complaining that *something* had pulled off his bedcovers. I was grateful nothing bizarre like that had happened since and that Sam was once again sleeping in his own bed.

We walked together to the front door.

"I'll put your bags in the car."

Jeremy opened the door and stepped out into our snowy lawn, a melting slush as I stared at the beveled glass in our front door, warm inside and dripping melting ice on the outside.

A couple minutes later, shivering, Jeremy came through the door and stamped his wet feet on the floor mat.

"Be careful out there, it's pretty slick."

I stared pensively at the beveled glass in the door then uttered, "It's almost like the door is crying, isn't it?"

Jeremy squeezed me harder. "Look, love, I'll see that Barry is properly buried tomorrow then I'm driving to Henderson."

My gaze widened. "Oh, Jer, are you sure?"

"Yep, it isn't right for you to bury your mother alone."

"Sam will be with me." But I was relieved he was coming. "What about the boys?" Benny and Jamie couldn't stay alone.

"You worry too much about everyone, Brooke."

"I know." It was a mother's job.

"I love you so much, Brooke. You're my heart."

We tenderly kissed. "You're the spark in my life," I said.

"What kind of spark?" Sam had overhead the remark.

I turned around and faced him. "Hey, buster, watch it!"

Sam wore the brown woolen topcoat we gave him as an early Christmas present. His brown hair was gelled to perfection. He was a handsome teen growing into a mature man.

"Take care of your mom," Jeremy told Sam.

"Who's the spark?" he curiously asked again.

"Oh, your mom was just teasing me, Sam."

"Who will keep Benny and Jamie if you drive to Henderson tomorrow afternoon?" I asked Jeremy. "With people traveling to see their families over Christmas, finding someone to stay with our boys won't be easy. Stay home, we'll be fine."

"Let me handle this, Brooke. Go now."

I glared at my husband, always a detailed person in charge of situations. "I can handle this Brooke, trust me."

I nodded, grieving too hard to argue.

"I'll arrange for Jamie to stay with Allison Kane." His jaw was firmly set with resolve. "You know how she fusses over him during Children's Hour. Benny can come with me."

I nodded my consent. Allison was a widow who'd been a member of our church for twenty years, an empty nester who seldom saw her only son who resided in London, England.

It was time to get on the road. I dreaded viewing my mom in her funeral attire, an outfit she'd picked out months before. A blue polyester dress with white lace trim, her best color, she always said—which made me wonder what I'd wear to mine.

"I'll keep my cell phone on tomorrow," I told Jeremy. "Call me when you get close." I turned and walked with Sam to the car.

While driving west on Interstate 40, I thought about our ghosts, and promised myself I'd get to the archives and research who originally owned our property. These spirits were not our friends. God help us, they would not chase us out of *our* home!

9

THE INTERSTATE WAS layered with an antifreeze treatment, so our trip to Henderson, Tennessee posed only minor problems. A truck loaded with frozen vegetables had upturned on the west side of Nashville and held up traffic for an hour. Fortunately, Sam and I arrived at the tail end of the problem and slowly followed the accelerating traffic until we reached a safe interstate speed.

"Sam, I don't want you to get upset when you see your grandmother in her coffin." I tried to prepare him.

"I'm okay, Mom."

"Death is a perfectly natural way to enter through Heaven's door." I soft pedaled the death experience.

"Those people in our house don't think that."

I let Sam's statement marinate in my thoughts for a minute. "Exactly, what are you saying, Sam?" I looked over at him.

"Don't play dumb, Mom! We have ghosts in our house and you know it!" Sam exclaimed. "They are mean and angry, and I'm afraid we're invading their space. They're pushing back."

Pushing back? My eyebrows arched at his wisdom.

"They can try to scare us, but they can't physically hurt us."

"Why not . . .?" Sam shot back. "What if they want us to become like them? What if they think we belong to Death?"

I didn't know how to answer Sam, to give him relief from his fear. *Dear, Jesus, help me*, I prayed for guidance. *I don't want any of my family to suffer because of what's going on in our house.*

I recalled how insistent I'd been about purchasing this property. But how could I have known *they* were there?

Were they wooing me into their lives from the beginning?

Then I said to Sam: "Ghosts, spirits, evil or otherwise, can't kill us because we belong to Jesus. The Bible says *He*, meaning the Holy Spirit, is greater than any force of nature in this world."

"Then why does HE allow them to live in our house?"

It was a valid question, one that was above my motherly pay-grade. Fortunately, we came upon the exit that would lead us into Henderson. "Can I get back to you on that?" I queried.

Sam only shrugged his shoulders and stared out the window at the drifting snowflakes the size of nickels. Beautiful, serene: a sharp contrast to the insecurity jolting inside of me.

I had no answer to Sam's question without gathering more information on the house. You can't fight what you can't see unless you know what's driving *it*. Or *them*; or whatever was disturbing our peace. I shoved the house out of my thoughts.

Once we were in Henderson, I drove straight to the funeral home guided by GPS. I locked up the SUV and we went inside. Parking our coats and my satchel purse on a vacant chair near the front of the viewing room, we tentatively stepped toward the silver-coated coffin, my eyes spotting Mom's bleached blond hair.

As my hand rested on Sam's back, I gently nudged him forward, dreading the moment her deadpan eyes met ours.

She is not there, I reminded myself.

"Do you think Gram knows we're here?" Sam asked.

Why are questions from the young and inexperienced always so hard?

"The Bible says when we are absent from the body we are present with Jesus. Your grandmother wouldn't want us to feel sad for her. She was a faithful saint, and is in heaven with God."

"How do you know that?" Sam asked.

"Godly wisdom," I offered.

Mom looked waxy white and cold, although her cheeks were unnaturally flushed with pink blush. Hands with manicured nails rested on her stomach over a beautiful pink silk dress with delicate lace ruffles. From the expression on her embalmed face, she'd just gone to sleep for the night and was enjoying a pleasant dream. I wanted to cry but I didn't. But Sam did and that hurt worse.

"It's okay, son, Gram's in a good place."

But I wasn't, conflicted over the supernatural events taking place in our house. I wanted Jesus to come down and straighten out our guests. Either take them on to heaven or boot them down to hell. At this point I didn't care. My only concern was protecting my children. "Anna Brooke!" I turned around when I heard my name called. My Great Aunt Lily shuffled toward me using a crooked wooden cane. She's been offered wheels many times by caretakers and turned them down, claiming she had two perfectly good legs to walk on, refusing to be seen as an invalid.

"I wondered if you would come," I told my elderly aunt as I leaned over and hugged her. "How was Disney World?"

"I think Donald Duck can wait another year to entertain me." She laughed. Like my mother, Lily was from Italian stock and a good four inches shorter than me. Almost every female in the room was shorter than me since I'd inherited Amazon genes.

"Who brought you here, Aunt Lily?"

"Baby Jack," she replied. "He's over there."

My gaze followed the direction of her bony finger. Baby Jack was forty-five years old, Lily's grandson by her deceased daughter. She never quit calling her relatives by their childhood names.

"Oh, I see him." I waved at Jack.

"Your sister Becca is here somewhere." Twinkling blue eyes glanced around the funeral parlor. "Lots of folks knew your mother and loved her. They came by earlier to sign the register."

I loved her, too. But did she love my sisters more?

"Did you look at the registry yet?"

"Only a glance," I replied. That's how death went. Sign in, shake a few hands, take a quick look at the corpse, and move on to the side of living. Death would come soon enough.

"I'm surprised the funeral was so soon," I commented.

"Some distant relatives from Kentucky couldn't make it any other day but Saturday," Aunt Lily explained. "Another visitation is scheduled 1 to 3 p.m. tomorrow, prior to the service."

"Jeremy's coming, if he can find a sitter for Jamie."

"Good. I know you'll feel better with him here."

"I think Sam and I will find the kitchen and have some refreshments." It was after eight p.m. and we hadn't eaten anything substantial since late morning. "Want to join us?"

"No thanks, I'll find Becca and tell her you're here."

Sam and I maneuvered through the dwindling crowd. A funeral home hostess directed us down a staircase to the kitchen. Several people passed us coming up. I didn't know any of them, and if they recognized me, they didn't acknowledge it.

The basement kitchen was bright in contrast to the upstairs viewing rooms. Half a dozen relatives and some of Mom's friends were milling around, snacking on goodies and talking.

Tables with chair were scattered about the room.

Sam got in line in front of me and we waited our turn to grab a fork wrapped in a paper napkin and a plastic plate. Some older ladies from the First Methodist Church graciously served us.

I wasn't very hungry, but I knew I needed nourishment. Sam, a growing teen, overfilled his plate. I selected a couple of salads.

We sat down at a table with two male teens.

Always friendly, Sam struck up a conversation with the local boys as I quietly sipped on my hot coffee.

"Hi, I'm Sam McLaughlin." He offered a handshake.

I'd seen Jeremy make that same introductory gesture numerous times. Sam was learning all the right social skills.

Would he eventually become a minister of the Gospel?

As conversations around us faded, my thoughts turned to the subject of salvation. Jesus Christ was our Savior. He died once for all on the cross, offering His blood as a holy sacrifice for all people, past, present and future. But with evil spirits taunting us, would Sam always accept the Bible as the infallible truth?

I shuddered at the idea Sam would look for answers elsewhere—like delving into New Age thought or reincarnation? I prayed our boys would not be led astray by false ideology.

But to be honest, the haunting I'd experienced in our house—the clanging broken doorbell, a young girl's cries for her daddy, an unseen hand stripping away of my bedcovers—those experiences had begun to erode my Christian faith. I realized the spirit world was far more complicated than I imagined. Did an unseen door exist between the dead and the living in our world?

Suddenly, noises became alive to me. *Huh?*

"Are you okay, Mom?" Sam asked.

"Yeah, I am. Did you make a new friend?"

"Yep, he's a distant cousin, fourth or fifth, best we could count." Sam smiled. "It's so cool meeting our family."

I laughed. "I'm so glad."

After eating from the table of plenty, Sam and I went back upstairs to the viewing room. Several more people were there.

Gary stood idly by Becca as she shook hands with people who had come to pay their respect. Sam and I joined them.

"I wondered where you were," Becca whispered to me.

"Didn't Aunt Lily tell you we were snacking in the kitchen?"

"No, I guess our paths didn't cross."

"Sam, you don't have to shake hands with everyone unless you want to." I nodded at a vacant seat two rows back.

"Okay." He retrieved his iPhone and walked away.

Drafts from the vents chilled me. I shivered and took a deep breath, shoving aside depressing thoughts of ghosts. Today's grief was enough to endure. I wanted the funeral over with.

"Sam's growing up fast," Becca noted. "He'll be graduated from high school and out of the house before you know it." She shook hands with a golden-haired woman in her nineties.

"I don't know half these people," I whispered.

"So pretend." Becca greeted each kind soul with a smile as they passed by and morbidly stared into our mother's coffin.

The line to view Mom died down around 10:30 p.m. and the funeral parlor slowly emptied. She had more family and friends than I realized. In a way, children never get to know their parents until they're deceased. Then it's too late to get answers. History flows backwards with all the questions a child neglected to ask.

"Did you know Mom sang in the choir when she was young?" I asked Becca as we stood beside her coffin.

"No, who told you that?" Becca asked.

"Her third cousin, Craig something," I replied.

"Someone told me she was one hot mama."

We both laughed, welcoming the emotional release.

"I need to find Sam and head to the motel," I said.

He had moved to a corner at the back of the viewing room, playing a game on his phone. "I'm ready to leave, son."

He yawned, tugged on his topcoat and we headed out the front door to the SUV. When we'd checked into our motel room, I phoned Jeremy. "How did the viewing go?" he asked.

"Good. Well, good as could be, considering the sad occasion." I fell silent then added, "I miss you."

Sam grinned at me then walked into the bathroom.

"Did you meet anyone new?" Jeremy asked.

"Many," I replied. "I talked with Baby Jack for awhile. He drove Aunt Lily over for the visitation. She had a grand time."

He chuckled. "Are you at the motel?"

"Just got here," I replied. "Sam's taking a shower."

"Well, don't hold your breath for warm water."

"Sam did great tonight, made me proud. He even made a new friend and met some distant relatives," I offered.

"I guess your kin have aged a lot since you've been away."

Since graduating high school, I'd been disconnected from Henderson for decades. By choice, I realized.

"How are Benny and Jamie making it?"

"They went to bed hours ago, exhausted from playing with those blame cars that run on batteries around the house," he said.

"I thought you threw the cars away."

"I did then dug them out of the trashcan—hey, have you seen a recent weather report?" Jeremy changed the subject.

"Yes, tomorrow's going to be sunny and warmer."

"Good. How was your drive to Henderson?"

"Better than expected. No problems on the interstate except for a short delay due to an overturned truck."

"I'm glad you made it safely."

I yawned. "Sorry, I'm really tired."

"Are Gary and Becca staying at your motel?"

"No, they made other plans."

Silence ruled the moment.

"Look," Jeremy said, "Barry's funeral is late morning, so afterwards I'm driving over to Henderson in the Malibu with Benny and Jamie. We'll be there before the funeral at three."

"Jeremy! I don't want Jamie at Mom's funeral!" He was too young to understand the sadness and crying that would take place.

"It won't be a problem, Brooke. Sam can watch the younger boys at the motel while we attend the funeral and burial."

"I thought Allison Kane was keeping Jamie."

"She's sick with the flu," he explained.

"Okay, we'll work out the details when you get here."

"Tell Sam hi," Jeremy said in conclusion.

"I will. Get a good night's rest."

Sam came out of the bathroom wearing his flannel PJs and thick warm black socks. "Was that Dad on the phone?"

"Yes, he said to say hi." I pocketed my phone.

"Is he coming to Gram's funeral service tomorrow?"

"Yes, and we wondered if you'd mind staying here at the motel with Benny and Jamie for a couple of hours."

"Is that what you want, Mom?"

"Sam, if you want to go with us, I'll hire a sitter."

"No, I'm good staying here."

Fourteen going on nineteen, I realized. *Been there and done that.*

"I'm going to sleep now," Sam said. "At least nobody here will bother me." He crawled between the crisp clean sheets.

He means where the ghosts can't get to him.

How did Jeremy and I get in this fix? We couldn't just up and sell our house and leave the church without giving a reason. We were expected to serve our congregation for a minimum of one year. Four is standard unless we're booted out.

Troubled in my spirit, I wandered into the bathroom and turned the nozzle to the tub. The spewing water was barely warm.

Still I bathed and dressed for bed. The mattress was firm and the pillows soft. Prayerfully, I closed my eyes and tried to sleep.

10

WITH WEATHER-IMPROVED roads on Saturday, Jeremy drove to Henderson with our two younger boys and met me at the Caldwell Funeral Home where Becca and I were greeting people.

I planted a kiss on Jamie's plump cheek, hugged Jeremy then said, "I'm sorry Allison was unable to keep Jamie."

I spied weariness in my husband's expression and wondered what he saw in mine. We had both been traumatized for months.

"We made it fine, Brooke."

"I know. Thanks for coming."

"I'll be around," he said. "Do what you need to do."

A thousand things occupying my mind, I scurried Benny down a flight of stairs to the basement kitchen for a snack. My third-grader was sleepy-eyed and his clothes rumpled from the four-hour journey. "How was the trip?" I asked him.

"Boring," Benny scowled. "Do I have to see Gram dead?" He tore into a Dunkin Donut like it was his enemy then smeared chocolate icing across the front of his red sweater with a hand.

"Now look what you've done!" I pulled my naughty nine-year-old to the side, aware that accusing eyes were watching.

He snarled and tried to pull away. "Now you listen here, son, nobody wants to see your grandmother put in the grave." I jerked a breath to reclaim my composure. "After your father views the, uh, Gram, he's taking you and Jamie back to the motel. Sam will stay with you till we're finish here. Please, try to behave yourself."

With tears blurring his vision, Benny nodded. "I love Gram."

"I know you do, son." I hugged him tightly. "We all do. It's really a sad time." He nodded, swiping his mouth with a napkin.

"Can I have juice now?" he asked.

"Sure." I snagged a bottle from the table and uncapped it.

"Brooke?"

I turned around and faced Becca.

"They're closing the casket in a few minutes," she informed me. "The family's going to privately view Mom for the last time."

I observed the sadness imbedded in her expression.

"Tell Jeremy Benny and I will be right there. Oh, will you find Sam and let him know we'll be leaving shortly for the motel?"

Becca nodded and dutifully tramped back up the stairs.

Benny guzzled the last of his drink and dumped the plastic container in the trashcan. "Can we watch a movie at the motel?" he asked as I trailed him up the stairs to the viewing room.

"Sam's in charge, whatever he says."

"There you are!" Jeremy exclaimed, nudging me gently toward the casket as the curtain closed around our family like a black shroud. Suddenly, I felt weak and claustrophobic.

Sam took Jamie from Jeremy's arms and told Benny to follow him. "Where are they going?" I asked my husband.

"I arranged for the boys to be driven to the motel."

"By whom . . .?"

"The funeral director's sister; she's on the payroll."

My eyes collapsed upon my mother's lifeless form covered in earthly frill. Would I ever be able to put this image of her out of my mind? As if reading my thoughts, Jeremy cuddled me closer, the heat from his body comforting. Becca whimpered then turned away from the coffin. Her outburst prompted me to cry, too.

Mom's immediate family consisted of her three daughters. The youngest, Beverly, was conspicuously not present. I didn't know whether to be angry, or grateful she didn't endure all this.

I heard an organ playing in the auditorium across the hall where Mom's funeral service would be held. The music sounded almost angelic. But no soothing sounds or kind words could eradicate my guilt over not visiting my mother before she died.

How insensitive of me to trust human existence would last for as long as I wanted! Then the idea of a continual death, like the people who lived in our house, frightened me even more.

* * *

We were on our way home by late Saturday. Sam and Jamie rode with me in our four-door blue Malibu while Benny went with Jeremy in the Chevy SUV. Jamie was exhausted from being shuffled around all day and cried himself to sleep en route.

Pensively, Sam stared out the window as I drove toward home, his thoughts secretive and contemplative. I couldn't help but wonder what attracted his attention. We made the trip in record time, no stops to eat or potty. Just get there soon.

"Are you all right, Brooke?" Jeremy removed our sleepy Jamie from his car seat and carried him indoors.

"I guess." It was not a definitive answer.

"Hopefully, a good night's sleep will help us all cope better." The good shepherd of our family concluded.

Sam switched off the alarm system then began traipsing through our house turning on lights. Before he was finished you'd think our house was a vintage picture of a Christmas shop. Our fully decorated trees were still up in anticipation of a celebration.

I tromped back to the SUV, woke up Benny and guided him to the house. He groggily stumbled up the stairs to his bedroom.

Within the hour our boys were bedded down and Jeremy stood in front of our master bedroom closet hanging up his suit.

"All in all, your mother had a nice funeral—if anyone could describe it that way. The minister did a great job, evidently knowing your grandparents well." He closed the sliding doors.

"Funerals are powerful reminders of our past." I removed my makeup with a tissue. "Strange how your mind recalls snippets of history long forgotten during the burial process."

"The mind is a complicated computer," Jeremy quipped.

"I kept thinking of things Dad said to me, the ways Mom acted at times—good and bad moments." I noticed a few more gray hairs gathering at my temple. "Death comes to all."

"On that sour note, I'm going to bed." Jeremy smiled at me through the mirror. "I'll need my strength for another day."

After a visit to the potty, I donned my pajamas then pattered into the bedroom where I crawled into bed beside Jeremy. "Oh, I forgot to ask you about Barry Clayton's funeral."

"Sad, I left the church right after my part was over."

"I'm sure you did a great job," I said.

"A ton of teens were there, so I made sure they heard God's message of grace and His call to holy living." Jeremy yawned.

"What do you think is going on with Sam?" I asked.

"He's just sad about losing his grandparents."

"That, too, but I don't think he's ever gotten over the covers being pulled from his bed, or the unseen hand touching him."

"Does he know about the little girl crying out to daddy?"

"No, I meant to tell him."

"I was thinking . . ." he paused. "How would you feel about having our house blessed?"

"I'm all for it, who do you have in mind?"

"Someone I trust, possibly a member of the Methodist General Assembly. We need help kicking out these spirits."

"Are you referring to an exorcism?"

"I don't know about that," he said, "but we need to find a way to force this evil out of our lives permanently."

"Do you have anyone specific in mind?"

"I know Don Sedgwick pretty well," Jeremy replied.

"It's worth a try," I said as Jeremy yawned and turned over, his back facing me. "Is that a signal for me to shut up?"

"Go to sleep, Brooke. Let your mind rest, we'll be just fine."

Fine? I was far from fine. Not with mom's death or our ghosts. The last thing I recalled before falling through layers of sleep was praying that *they* would leave all of us alone tonight.

11

THE SECOND FRIDAY in January, there was a scheduled workday for teachers. Arriving early at school, I had finished my semester's lesson plans long before three p.m. We were excused once we were done, so gratefully I had the rest of the afternoon to myself.

When Jeremy was finished at the church, he was picking up Jamie at the daycare center and Benny from his extended-school program, so I headed off to the courthouse archives to find answers to the supernatural activity occurring within the four walls of our two-story historic farmhouse. Sam came with me to assist.

I spoke to an astute elderly couple employed by the county and soon realized they regarded the historic records as their own personal property. After signing my life away, Sam and I began combing the dim, dank domain reeking of aging paper, dust mites and stale tobacco residue. Boxes on shelves were stacked high.

"Oh, brother. . ." Sam took one look at the vast amount of information then meandered through the narrow aisles in the antiquated basement. Would I find anything here written about our house? I smiled at the thought: *Beware residents, Ghosts live here?*

"The boxes are pretty well marked by date." I encouraged Sam. "And we know our house was built in 1916 with our same address. We'll find the original owners, trust me."

An hour later I found my boxed answer.

The house was originally built on a five-hundred acre plot. Its first owner, referred to as Gibby in side notes, owned the property with his wife. Two workman houses originally stood on the acreage. One burnt down while Gibby was still alive.

Eventually, the property was subdivided into three parcels. The 3,964 square-feet house we lived in was situated on three and one-half acres. The second parcel with a natural spring was directly behind our house. The third parcel was across the road.

An elderly state senator owned the property to our left.

The facts on Gibby's property were straightforward. He lived in the house with his wife until the early 1940s. Prior to their deaths, his mother expired in the house. Gibby's wife passed next. Absent of heirs, when he died the property was sold off.

It was at that moment the idea of Gibby's ghost in the house became more real to me. "What's wrong, Mom?"

"Nothing," I replied. Sam had been surfing for sports events on his phone while I read Gibby's file.

"Did you find what you're looking for?"

"Yes, and I'm ready to leave now."

I took off walking and he trailed me. "Good, 'cause I'm supposed to hang out with some friends later today."

"What friends?" I asked as we exited the courthouse.

"Buddy, from church," Sam replied, inhaling in a cold blast of January air. "You know, his mom is Ginger Bacon. She works with church youth," he explained. "Buddy's a good guy."

"If you say so . . ." I tried to visualize Ginger as I popped the locks to the Malibu. It was getting darker with snow clouds gathering on the western horizon. Winter in all its beauty was bent on making its presence known in Middle Tennessee.

"Buckle up, Sam," I said when we were in the car.

Forty-five minutes later, we pulled into our driveway.

Jeremy opened the front door.

"Did you find what you were looking for?"

"Let's talk about it later." Jamie toddled across the foyer with open arms, whining for mama.

"He's not feeling well." Jeremy hung my coat on the hall tree as Sam scampered down the hall into the kitchen to grab a snack.

"Is that pizza I smell cooking?" I picked up Jamie.

"One deluxe and one extra cheese," he replied. "I think we can bend the rules and let the kids have colas tonight?"

We walked down the hall and into the kitchen.

"Are you asking or telling?" I rummaged through the fridge for salad mixings as I heard the washing machine swishing.

"Did you start the wash?" I inquired.

"No, maybe Sam did."

"Not me!" Sam uncapped a can of Pepsi as he collapsed in a chair at the kitchen table. "That's mama's territory."

"Well, your time is coming, son!" I retaliated. "When you go to college, you'll be responsible for your own clothes."

"When do we eat?" Sam peered at his dad.

"Ten more minutes till the pizzas are done."

Sam started playing a game on his iPad.

Jeremy curiously gazed at me. "Did you and Sam have a profitable afternoon at the county archives?"

"Somewhat. . ." I gestured with my hand as the coffeemaker dribbled strong Columbian. "Hold that thought." I scampered down the hall to the laundry room to see what was washing.

Oddly, the machine was pumping warm water into an empty basket. I switched the dial to "drain" and returned to the kitchen.

"Did you solve the washing-machine mystery?" Sam teased.

"No mystery, Sam." I locked eyes with Jeremy. "I found a folder with information on the original owners of our house."

"Who were they?" Jer asked.

Biting my lip I stopped short of telling him that Gibby's deceased family were our resident ghosts.

"You're bleeding, honey." Quick-on-his-feet Jeremy grabbed some paper towels and swiped the blood off my mouth. "Like you said, we can talk about the house later."

Thank you, I mouthed.

Using a pair of padded muffs, he carefully removed the two pizzas from the oven racks as Sam tossed me a knowing look.

My smart son can't be fooled, I thought to myself.

"I'll get the boys." Jeremy stepped down the hall.

"Benny, we're ready to eat," he called upstairs.

Half a minute later, I heard footfalls on the stairs and running shoes slapping the hall's wooden floors as Benny skidded into the kitchen. "I smell pizza!" He sized up the sizzling pans.

"Mom! Who poked you in the mouth?" Benny asked.

"Dumb me." I shrugged. "Bit my lip." My gaze skittered to Sam. Quiet as a church mouse, he had the good judgment to keep his comments to himself regarding the house's mysteries.

"Did you turn on the washing machine?" I asked Benny.

"No, Mom."

I sat Jamie down at the table and gave him a cracker. When I opened the back door to the porch, Boomer leaped inside. The shepherd skidded toward his bowl of Healthy Choice Dog Food as I filled his big water bowl. "Boomer stinks, he needs a bath."

"I'll give him one," Sam volunteered.

Jeremy prayed over our meal and we all ate like it was filet mignon. Cleanup was fast and the boys quickly retreated to their rooms upstairs to play their gizmos. I yawned, a bit tired.

"Sam's going out with a friend tonight," I informed Jeremy.

"What friend?"

I smiled, having asked him the same question.

"Ginger Bacon's son, Buddy. A good guy, according to Sam," I added. We walked down the hall to the living room.

Jeremy switched on the television and surfed for a PG movie that didn't involve spooky subjects. None of interest, he cut off the tube. Placing dry logs in the fireplace, he ignited a fire.

"This is nice." He sat down beside me on the sofa.

"What?" I eyed my handsome husband.

"Just sitting here on a quiet evening with nothing major to accomplish . . ." he sighed, leaning his head against the soft cushioned back. "As a kid, I never appreciated rest."

I chuckled. "Yeah, I'll take quiet over confusion anytime."

"About the house . . ." Jeremy was ready to listen now.

I relayed what I'd learned about Gibby and his family. They had built this house in 1916 and lived their entire married lives in it until death parted them. Gibby's mother was the first to die in the house, likely buried somewhere in a family cemetery.

"Well, I guess that's that," Jeremy said with finality. "Maybe if we leave them alone, they'll forget about us."

I smiled. *My husband, always the optimist!*

12

NEAR THE END of January a fascinating fact about our house came to light. Like mice carting cheese, Sam came home after a weekend visit with his politically connected father with a tidbit of information. "Mom, a little girl drowned in a well out back."

What? "In our backyard . . .? How do you know that?"

"Dad told me!" Sam exclaimed. "And Senator Lawson told Dad. He said Mr. Lawson's son used to live in our house."

Lawson was our next door neighbor and worked at the State Legislature building in Nashville where Sam's biological father worked. The idea of a child accidentally dying in our backyard reminded me of the little girl's voice we heard crying out to daddy during the night. This new information rattled me.

"Sam, are you sure about this?"

"Dad said. Cross my heart and hope to die."

"The well must have been capped off and covered at some point," I suggested to him. "Wish I knew where it was."

"We could look for it." Sam's eyes brightened with interest.

"Oh, I don't know . . ." We'd never be able to locate the well without hiring a professional guru with a divining stick. I wasn't about to confront Jeremy about spending more money for that.

But, as fate would have it, a spring article in *The Farmer's Magazine* featured our house as one of the first homes built in Tennessee with indoor plumbing. The laundry room used to have a hand-held pump with pipes going down into the cellar where I currently stored my jellies and jams. The indoor access to the well had long been sealed off. All good information, but with decades having passed since the well was operable there was no way to prove that a little girl actually drowned in that well. It was hearsay, but I mentally stowed that information for future reference.

In addition to the article there was a reprinted newspaper clipping reporting the death of Gibby, naming the cemetery where he, his wife, and mother were buried. Turns out Ancestry.com, reported the family cemetery was located on the parcel of land behind our property. With yet another lead, my interest piqued.

Finally, curiosity got the best of me. So one Sunday in late January, Sam rode with me to look for the old cemetery. We maneuvered down narrow dusty roads through hilly country encroached by new pine trees and greenery. Just like the article reported, the abandoned cemetery was located a few miles behind our house near a vacant church next to a natural flowing spring.

It was late afternoon when Sam and I exited the Malibu and started walking the site. "What are we looking for?" Sam queried.

"Gibby's headstone," I replied, feeling like one of those unsavory marauders looking for the Lost Ark.

Inhaling deeply, Sam gazed over the huge cemetery covered in a dense mist as dusk descended and turned the air colder.

"It sure is getting dark fast," he commented.

"Maybe we should come back another time," I suggested.

He shivered, briskly rubbing his arms.

"Are you cold or just spooked?" I kidded.

Grabbing Sam by the arm, I wasn't about to tread through the graves without holding on to someone human. "Just teasing—no ghosts here. Let's look around a bit," I added.

Sam frowned as his tennis shoes sank into a slushy patch of tall grass. "Great." He trailed me through rows of headstones.

Moss had nearly conquered the dozens of stone markers, making the carved script difficult to read. Thirty minutes later, I was about to give up and go home when Sam called out to me.

"Here it is, Mom. Gibby's name is on this headstone."

"Samuel, you're the best!" I threaded my way through the tangle of overgrowth toward him, measured triumph conquering any fear tugging at my psyche as it grew darker fast.

Sunsets in middle Tennessee are usually beautiful, but there's nothing more isolated than a country road by a vacant church near an abandoned cemetery. Only a sliver of mauve color was left on the western horizon as the sun prepared to take a final dip.

A cool breeze kicked up suddenly and brushed over my face like cobwebs. With a deep breath, I swept away my apprehension.

"There!" Sam pointed to the stone covered in a pall of moss.

"So, it is." I leaned over to read the inscription.

By this time it was twilight and I had no flashlight with me. We stood like dunces staring at the gravestone for a few minutes until I said, "Okay, it's getting too dark to see, let's go home."

"Can we come back another time?" Sam asked.

"Sure." I wanted to read the inscriptions on the other stones. "Time to go, Sam." I started walking back to the car.

"In a minute . . ." Sam's eyes were glued to the markers.

"Okay, but hurry, it's getting colder."

As I opened the car door, I heard Sam screaming, "Stop, Mom! Wait for me." Turning around, I spied my son twenty yards away; racing toward me like a snake was after him.

"Run, get in the car! Hurry, don't look back!"

He picked up his pace and arrived out of breath.

"Sam . . .?" I was flabbergasted at his behavior.

"Mom, get in the car, lock the doors!" He hopped in the passenger seat as I quickly joined him in the car. Seconds later, the locks were secure. "Mom, did you see it?" Sam asked.

"See what, Sam?" I started the engine.

"That *thing*," he said, terror clawing at his face.

"Sam, calm down. Your imagination is running away with you." I drove away from the cemetery, putting some space between us and those dead residents. "What spooked you?"

Sam struggled to get his breath, close to hyperventilating. He'd experienced something awful, too terrifying to talk about.

"Tell me what happened, son."

"Something green. . ." his eyes were engaged in remembering.

73

"A lot of things are green," I said. "Whatever you thought you saw . . ." I trailed off. "Relax, Sam, we're perfectly safe."

He jerked his head to look back, as if he feared we were being followed. "Sam," I touched his hand, "trust me, we're fine."

Honestly, I needed to hear exactly what Sam had experienced. But not now, not until he had calmed down and thought about what he'd seen. And certainly not until we were safely home.

I parked the car in the driveway, locked up, and we went into the house. Jeremy faced me when I opened the door.

"Why are you so late getting home?" he asked.

Sam swept past me and bounded up the stairs.

"What's his problem?" Jeremy asked me.

"We found the cemetery."

"What cemetery?" Jeremy shut the door and locked it.

"We found the original owner's gravesite."

"Really . . ?"

"But something spooked Sam, big time."

"A cemetery after dark would spook most people."

"Oh, Jamie fell asleep in the truck coming home. Should I wake him up for supper?" We walked to our bedroom.

"Want me to fetch him?" Jer asked.

"If you don't mind . . ." I was stumped about the "green thing" my teen thought he saw. I tossed my purse on a chair and told Jeremy, "Supper can wait. I need to speak to Sam first."

"Guess I could phone Subway and order sandwiches."

"Jer, quit obsessing over food, okay?"

"Wow. What's set you off, honey?"

"Sam. I just need to talk to him. Where's Benny?"

"Out back in the shed, building a model airplane I believe."

"Okay." I did my best to settle my nerves. "Subway sounds good if you don't mind making a run. I'll tend to Jamie."

"Are you going to tell me what happened at the cemetery?"

"Later, after I speak to Sam." I started up the stairs.

"Wait, what kind?" Jeremy called out.

"Huh?" I turned around. "Oh, sandwiches—you choose."

I found my teen crouched in one corner of his bedroom, hands clasped to both knees as he gently rocked himself. He'd been terrorized by something. "Sam . . .?" I quietly said.

Pleading eyes glanced up at me.

"I really did see it, Mom."

"I believe you saw something." I moved to the corner and sat down by my usually brave thirteen-year-old. With my hand placed over his cold one, I said, "Tell me what happened."

"It was round and green and really scary."

Sam's eyes were saucers. He was shivering, and for once, I didn't know what to say. But he did.

"It came out of the grave and chased me." His gaze was far away with recall. "For a second, I thought it was going to crash into me then it just sped past my arm like a shooting star."

I let his statement, his explanation, settle in my mind.

"You do believe me, Mom, don't you?"

I nodded, near tears. "I do, Sam." I squeezed his hand then told him about all the ways Jeremy and I had been haunted.

"But, do me a favor, Sam," I said in conclusion.

"What?" His hazel eyes engaged the dim lighting of night.

"Don't tell Benny or talk about it around Jamie, it might spook them." I almost giggled at the absurdity. Of course, it would scare the sox off them. Panties, too, and I was a grownup.

* * *

The following Saturday afternoon Don Sedgwick with the Methodist General Assembly knocked on our front door. Once a preacher of the Good News, he was a few years older than Jeremy but had not aged well. My gaze was drawn to the wiry tufts of hair ringing his baldpate and the wrinkles gathering under his eyes.

Jeremy had invited Don for supper but he'd declined due to an unavoidable meeting in Chattanooga. So this was business.

"Thank you for coming, Brother Don." Jeremy shook his friend's hand. "This is my wife, Brooke."

Don's peppery eyes made contact with mine. "Nice meeting you, Brooke." He glanced around our house. "You've done a beautiful job of decorating. My wife would love this place."

I don't think so. I reciprocated Don's firm handshake.

"Thank you so much for coming," I told Don. "My three boys are upstairs and I guarantee they won't interrupt us."

Don bellowed out a laugh. "I have boys of my own—almost grown, but like all teens, they lack wisdom." He heaved a breath. "So, tell me, folks, are you enjoying your new location?"

I looked to Jeremy for help in answering.

"Living in this house has been quite a challenge," Jeremy told Brother Sedgwick. "The job is fine. We love our church."

I suppressed a chuckle. *Tell me about it.*

The two friends talked about a few incidents in the past then Don turned his attention to me. "Brooke, you're mighty quiet for the woman of the house." He chuckled. "If you were my wife, you'd be talking nonstop about the house and its renovations."

I glanced over at Jeremy to bail me out. Once I'd started expounding on our haunting there would be no stopping place. Neither of us wanted to lie to Brother Don, so avoidance was clearly the best option. "We just want our house blessed," I said.

"Okay, let's get down to business."

From a brown leather satchel Don removed his Bible, a gold cross, and a small vial of holy oil from Jerusalem. When he'd finished anointing our house and praying a blessing over our family, he stayed for a cup of coffee then went his own way.

Jeremy and I stood on the front porch and waved at Don as he drove away in a bright red Volvo. "Do you think they heard?"

"Are you referring to *them*?" I actually grinned.

"Yeah, I am. Did he discourage them any?"

"Only time will tell." I shrugged.

The Second Year in the House

13

JEREMY'S INCOME WAS generous, plus I was teaching school. Over the years we had saved a chunk of change. So before school turned out for the summer, he asked me to call a contractor and get quotes on installing a new roof, energy-efficient windows, extra insulation in the walls, and exterior vinyl siding.

I reminded Jeremy that the three fireplaces were losing heat during the winter and should be fitted with new gas grills. In addition, we decided an electrician needed to rewire the overhead light fixtures for safety reasons. So the work began in early June.

Near summer's end, the updating of the house was completed and I felt good about the repairs. With the added insulation, this winter's energy bills would be lower. My hope was our uninvited guests would disapprove of our renewal efforts and move out.

At least, they'd given us a rest since Brother Sedgwick blessed our house. Based on past experiences, it appeared that most of the ghostly activity had occurred around the holidays: Halloween, Thanksgiving and Christmas. So I was surprised when Gibby's family started picking on ten-year-old Benny near the end of July. We loved our son and had protected him from harm the best we could. But how could I exempt him from the haunting?

The fact was . . . I couldn't.

But before Benny was spooked, our whole family was shaken by another incident. While seated around the kitchen table eating fried chicken, smashed potatoes, green peas and hot biscuits for supper, we all heard a loud crash coming from the hallway.

"What in the world was that?" I voiced.

"Keep your seats, I'll go check." Jeremy tossed his paper napkin and took off down the hall toward the front of the house.

"What is it, Mama?" Benny whispered. "Ghosts . . .?"

"I doubt that." My darting gaze dared Sam to comment.

"Woo . . . woo . . ." Benny mimicked a flying Casper.

"That's enough, Benny!" I snapped.

Jeremy came back into the room. "It was this thing." He held up the large, round metal fire detector in his right hand.

"It fell on the floor?" We'd attached it firmly in January.

"No, it was on the floor in the living room," he said.

"How is that even possible?" Sam asked. "It just came off the hall wall, rolled to the front of the house, then made a right turn and went into the living room? Give me a break."

Jeremy's chocolate eyes skittered to Jamie. "Look at you, little boy. You're falling asleep in your green peas."

Heads turned toward three-year-old Jamie. Licking his thumb, eyes half closed, he anointed his head with smashed potatoes.

We all laughed at the sight.

I nabbed Jamie's two hands and removed him from his highchair. "Big boy needs to bath and a bed."

"What about the fire detector?" Sam asked.

"It just fell, son. End of story," Jeremy said.

"Jer, would you mind seeing that Benny gets his bath and pajamas on while I take care of Jamie."

"What about dessert?" Benny asked.

"I'll make an executive decision and let you know."

Jeremy began clearing the table. "Sam, help me out here."

Crossing the hall, I took Jamie with me into our master bathroom and drew a warm tub of sudsy water. After stripping off his dirty clothes, I plopped him in the tub with a pile of rubber toys and went into the bedroom to collect my wits. I was more rattled about the fire detector than willing to admit.

While Jamie played in the tub, I read my Bible and prayed for wisdom. I never believed that Catholic priests had the power to cast out evil spirits, but if I could protect my family, maybe it was time I investigated exorcism. I began to plan a time for me and *them* to have a serious discussion. But I would need help.

* * *

School resumed the second week in August and we were all so busy we didn't know which way was up. Using my laptop, I privately downloaded as much information as I could find regarding methods of performing exorcism on both people and properties. But it seemed there was never a good time for me to be alone in the house to address our residents.

September blew by. Then October had rolled around.

Mid-October a cold front barreled down out of Canada and assaulted Middle Tennessee's warmer air. Violent storms resulted.

One storm in particular put down a score of tornadoes racing across the countryside. The lights at our high school went out.

"Jer? It's Brooke. We lost electricity at school."

"We're out here at the church, too. Just heard that a tornado hit a community not far from here," he informed me.

"Any fatalities reported?"

"Far as I know, none yet," Jeremy replied. "I was about to leave for home and check on our house. I probably won't be back at the church but don't drive home until you've heard from me."

"You think our house received wind damage?"

Seconds later the lights at school blinked back on.

"We've got power," I told him. "Check on the house and call me immediately. I'm going to see if my students are calm enough to continue class." I walked down the hall to Room 106.

"You guys okay?" I spied my French students hovering outside the door. "Go inside the room, I'll be there in a minute."

"Anything else I need to do, Brooke?" I realized Jeremy was still on the phone. "Call the daycare center and see if they have power. I have a feeling our principal is going to cut the day short and send students home on buses." We ended the call.

Forty-five minutes later, my cell phone vibrated. The bell had sounded for my fifth class when I answered.

"Hi, how's the house?" I asked Jeremy.

"I need for you to come home right now."

"I still have another hour before I can leave."

"Get someone to cover, just come home. Please."

"Okay." I ended the call and walked down to the office to alert Dr. Rose that I had an emergency at home. It was my planning hour, so no flack was offered as I signed out.

"Oh . . ." Gladys called out, "did you get tornado damage?"

I turned around and faced the school secretary. "I don't know. Tell Sam to wait in the office, I'll be back to get him."

While driving home, I called Ginger Bacon who had a son in Benny's class and asked if she minded bringing him home for me. Buddy's mother didn't since she lived a few miles from us.

The windy storm had let loose its fury on our property. Our yard was cluttered with fallen limbs and wind-dragged debris. We'd need to hire a tree surgeon to put everything back in order.

I dreaded seeing the damage our pear trees had sustained out back. Jeremy heard me drive up and opened the front door. I waved as I exited the car, noting his dire expression.

"What's wrong?" I asked as I stepped on the porch.

The wind was still churning, but much cooler as the storms vented then succumbed to a more peaceful atmosphere.

"You'll see. Upstairs," he said. "Take a gander."

I walked straight through the foyer, down the hall and up seventeen steps to the top landing then stopped dead in my tracks.

"Jer? What's happened here?"

The heavy antique lace curtains covering four elongated windows overlooking the backyard lay crumpled on the floor. It appeared an angry hand had torn them from their large gold rods and haphazardly tossed them aside on the landing.

Jeremy pointed down the hall. I turned around, stunned.

The curio cabinet situated against the wall opposite the stair rail was overturned and its contents scattered down the hall in both directions. The large Rubbermaid box, weighing some fifty pounds, was overturned and the boys' books strewn in all directions. The illuminated fake pumpkin sitting on the top the box had been thrown fifteen feet toward the front windows.

"Who did this, Jeremy?" I turned to my husband.

"You tell me." He took a hefty breath and moved close enough for me to inhale his shaving cologne, brown eyes penetrating me like knives. I'd never seen my husband so rattled.

Tongue-tied and bewildered, I wanted to embrace Jeremy and say that everything would be okay but I couldn't know that. We were dealing with forces outside the scope of reality.

"When, uh, I came in the house an hour ago, I turned off the security system," he explained, eyes wide and glassy.

Ideas materialized but words were stuck in my throat.

"Then I headed upstairs to see if there were any leaks in the roof." He stalled a moment. "And I found this big mess."

"Did someone break in?" I asked the obvious.

"No. I checked every window in the house, Brooke" he said in a shaky voice. "They were all locked down tight."

We stood there, gazing at one another. Since no alarm had triggered a break-in, I was confident no one had illegally entered our house. Realizing Jeremy was through talking, I said to him, "So you believe this is an inside job. . ." I almost laughed.

"You might say that." Wrinkles gathered in his brow.

I nodded with understanding. He asked me to help him right the curio cabinet. We worked for thirty minutes getting books picked up and put back in the Rubbermaid box. No way we could repair the bent rods and hang the curtains before Benny arrived home. In silence, we hurriedly worked to set things in order.

"I don't want the boys to know about this," Jeremy said when we'd finished. "If we can't understand it, they won't either."

"It's our secret!" I gathered the strewn curtains in my arms. "I'll put these away in the storage closet while you detach the bent curtain rods. They're no good so throw them in the garbage."

I knew for certain Sam would notice the drapes were missing and ask me why I took them down. What could I say that made sense? *I don't want them to know* . . . Jeremy's voice crept over me.

Fifteen minutes later, I was on my way to the high school to pick up Sam. With a mug of hot coffee in one hand, a prayer lingering on my lips, and my foot on the accelerator, more than ever I needed to get cracking on an exorcism.

These people were downright mean-spirited and needed a good talking to. How could I allow them to terrorize our family?

14

THE FALL BASH at our church was a huge success. I refused to let our children wear anything remotely resembling ghosts. But they had a big time regardless. Unfortunately, the night we held the festival in the parking lot it was blustery and spitting rain. I caught a nasty cold and had to call in sick on Monday.

Alone with the tools required for an exorcism, it was now or never. I thought of Elvis Presley's song and how life had not ended well for him. Still, I couldn't wait for *them* to attack again.

I stood in my foyer glaring up the stairs as if Gibby himself was watching back. With my Bible shakily clutched in one hand, I crossed my heart with the other like religious Catholics do.

Jesus, help me do this, I uttered in my spirit.

After placing my Bible on the side table at the front door, I opened a bottle of holy oil and anointed the top of the door transom. Luckily, I was tall enough to reach it. Next, I took care of the living room and kids' playroom, feeling somewhat empowered. Trekking down the hall to my master bedroom, I finished up in there then anointed the top of our backdoor.

The kitchen, dining, and office windows received a similar treatment. Each time I anointed a door or window in the house I splashed on holy water from Israel and said, "In the name of Jesus, bless this house. I command any evil spirits to leave now!"

If Jeremy had been watching, he would have said I was overdoing it a bit. Finished downstairs, I repeated my exorcism upstairs. Having gone full circle to exorcise evil, I stood again in the hall of our historic house with only one thing left to do.

"Gibby," I said, "this is *my* home now and not yours. If you want to live here peacefully, okay. But no destructive behavior will be permitted. If that's not satisfactory, you'll have to leave."

Feeling emotionally spent, I sat down on the last step of the staircase, clasping a string of rosary beads as I repeated the Lord's Prayer. *Protect us from evil,* especially that part. Then I was done.

My head full of infection and mucus, I spent the afternoon on the living room sofa nursing a huge box of tissues. The TV was on but I wasn't paying it much attention. I had a cup of broth for lunch and drank all the water I could hold. So the day passed.

Jeremy came home late afternoon with the three boys. By that time I had bathed, dressed casually, and made a pot of beef vegetable stew for supper. Uncertain if my actions had cast out the presence of evil in our house, I was proud that I had made the effort. One thing I knew for certain, Jeremy would never let these beings drive us out of our home until we were ready to leave.

We both were dedicated to Christian ministry. Our allegiance was to Jesus Christ and His church. Nothing would deter that. When Jeremy received a new charge, we'd leave then.

Not one second before! I hoped Gibby had read my mind.

* * *

The remainder of our second year in our house passed peacefully without supernatural intrusion, unless you count my baby sister's unannounced visit just before Christmas.

Beverly Ann Kane, twenty-eight and single, speaks Spanish, French, and understands a few African dialects. After graduating from Vanderbilt University she joined a world mission tour that never ended. Athletically fit and pencil thin from running marathons, she's a health nut who thrives on fresh vegetables, fruits and nuts, and seldom eats meats and fish. Her flamboyant personality is more like our mother's than either Becca or me.

And she's chockfull of intriguing missionary stories. I get most of my information off her FACEBOOK page.

Fortunately, Becca had phoned me from the International Airport while waiting for our baby sister to arrive on an international flight. "Why didn't Bev call me?" I fussed.

"Why does our sister do anything she does?"

Good point, I considered how she liked surprises.

"Do me a favor, Brooke. Don't insult Beverly by offering her meat while she's staying at your house," she cautioned. "Have plenty of Greek yogurt and raw veggies to munch on. . .

"Oh," Becca remarked, "She doesn't drink regular milk. Soy, unflavored, is all she tolerates. I know she's a pain."

I couldn't disagree with that statement. "You're preaching to the choir," I said, "I know how to handle my sister."

With kid gloves, I thought to myself.

"Not this time," Becca countered, "Beverly's in love."

"Don't tell me she's bringing a boyfriend."

"A fiancé," Becca informed me. "She emailed me a picture of the huge diamond ring she's wearing on her left fourth finger."

"Well, haven't we prayed she'd settle down and marry some nice guy?" I didn't understand why Becca was uptight about it.

"He's a sheik," Becca blurted out, nervously giggling.

"An oil guru, Iranian, barbarian . . . .?" I let my mind wander through a list when Becca said, "An educated prince from Egypt."

"Really . . ?" That title shocked me.

"His name is Terah Amr Houssam," Becca said.

That conversation took place around lunch yesterday.

While reviewing the contents of my pantry, I heard the doorbell to our front door chime and pattered to the foyer.

Peeking through the beveled glass, I spied Beverly dressed in one of those full-length embroidered-cotton Egyptian kaftans. Wearing a pair of leather ornamental sandals on her petite feet, I hoped she had the good judgment to have on warm garments under her costume since the temperature approached freezing.

Beside Beverly stood a tall, lean man I assumed was the soon-to-be husband. When I opened the door, I nearly fainted. Becca's beau was drop-dead gorgeous. With huge midnight eyes hooded by thick eyelashes, he might have borrowed his thick black shoulder-length hair from the movie star of *Pirates of the Caribbean.*

"Welcome," I eked a salutation and hugged my sister, my gaze glued on the handsome sheik. Did I say *rich* sheik?

All bubbles and wrap, tongue-tied with surprise, my giddy excitement was embarrassingly evident.

"I'm glad to see you, too." Beverly swept past me like she owned the place and stood in the foyer. "Wow. You did pretty good, big sis." She tore off through the study and I lost sight her.

"That's what I love most about your sister most," *Rich* said.

The sheik grasped my right hand and planted a wet kiss on my knuckles. I actually blushed, but said, "Different strokes for different folks." Seriously, what was wrong with me?

"Terah," he said with a big smile. "My name, in case you ask." His spacious grin reflected he knew I was impressed.

I reclaimed my hand. "I'm Brooke, as you've probably guessed then turned around. "Where did my—"

"Behind you, Sis," Beverly said as we nearly collided.

"Come, Terah! I'm sure Brooke has a cup of hot tea and her latest favorite dessert recipe waiting for us in the kitchen." Beverly walked backwards, tugging Terah down the hall like she was enticing him to join her on the floor for her first coed dance.

I almost laughed at my baby sister's ridiculous antics. But that was Beverly—always the optimist. Playful and never *ever* dull!

"Love, you know I am fasting," he offered with lovesick eyes.

"Oh, I forget," Beverly piped. "Well, the tea is allowable."

Pinch me so I can wake up.

15

WHILE TRAILING THE two love birds down the hall into the kitchen, I contemplated how I should react to Beverly's bossiness. For a nanosecond I questioned who the guest was, her or me. Then my social training kicked in as I removed a foil-covered blueberry pie from the oven and put on a kettle of water to boil.

As I opened a box of gourmet teabags, I noticed how Terah and Beverly were so into each other. I don't think they realized I was even in the kitchen. How could I ask the questions going through my mind without intruding on their privacy? I wouldn't.

"Love . . ?" Beverly actually batted her eyelashes. "While the water for the tea heats up, why don't you bring in our suitcases?"

Sleeping arrangement? I hadn't thought of that yet.

Are they sleeping together?

Obedient to Beverly's request, Terah took off down the hall to the front of the house. "He's so adorable," she quipped.

"He seems like a decent guy" was all I could muster.

"I assume you have rooms for us. It's just a couple of nights and we'll be out of your way." Bev made eye contact with me.

"No, I mean yes, we love having both of you here."

"I'm sorry I didn't call first, but I assume Becca warned you."

I nodded, somewhat frustrated and inept at coping with the unique situation of a wealthy sheik sleeping under our roof.

"Does that mean we're welcome and I'm forgiven?"

The question lingered in the atmosphere until I had the good judgment to say, "Sure. What is there to forgive?"

I removed three ceramic cups from the cabinet and set them on the kitchen counter. The sugar bowl, jar of honey, and other accruements were on the table. I turned, eyes misting, "Beverly?"

"Yes?" Her blue gaze bloomed.

"We've all missed you. Are you through circling the globe?"

Beverly came over and hugged me. "I haven't been a good sister." She held me at arm's length. "But you know me."

Yes, we all know you, I didn't say.

"Mom's funeral was elegant and our family met many relatives. She was a good woman," I added.

"I can't stand to be around death," Beverly said.

Then don't stay at our house, I thought to myself then asked, "How did you meet Terah?" I scored the pie with my knife.

"At a gala event in Africa," she replied.

"You came a long way to introduce me to Terah, why are you really here?" Beverly wasn't family-oriented. She hadn't visited me in five years. To be honest, I'd written her off. But seeing bleary eyes, I felt terrible for what I'd said.

"I miss Mama." Tears cascaded off Bev's pink cheeks.

"Oh, honey, we all do." I melted like hot wax.

"When we leave here, Terah is taking me to Henderson to visit Mom's grave," she said. "Daddy's, too," she added.

I nodded, feeling that old knot of guilt kicking me in the gut for not visiting my mother when I'd learned her cancer was terminal. "I'm sure you would have come if you hadn't been half way around the world. Your missionary work is important."

Beverly snagged a tissue from its box and blew her nose. "Thank you." We both heard gurgling water boiling on high.

"Where shall I put these?" Terah asked from the doorway.

The rattling tea kettle whistle went off, startling me.

"Oh, just sit them down at the foot of the stairs and we'll put them away after we refresh ourselves," Beverly told him.

"Where's Jeremy?" Beverly asked me.

"At the movie theater with Sam and Benny," I replied. "How do you take your tea?" I asked Terah.

"Honey and plenty strong," he replied.

"I'll fix mine." Beverly busied herself at the counter.

At twenty-eight Beverly was gorgeous, exhibiting hereditary genes passed down through generations of beautiful women. Our great grandmother from Italy had been a petite woman with feminine assets in all the right places. Unhappy my sister was no team player I still loved her and knew she would never change.

"Will you have a slice of pie?" I asked Bev.

"No, I'll pass for now." She added honey to her tea.

"Okay." I would wait, too.

We had just settled down at the breakfast table with our beverages when I heard a door slam outside. "That must be Jeremy back with the boys." I excused myself from the table.

"Your sister's nice," I overhead Terah whisper to Beverly as I scurried away from the kitchen. "Beautiful, too, like you."

"Should I be jealous?" Bev coyly remarked.

"No, my love, I am hopelessly enamored with you." There was a pause. "If I didn't know you were an American Christian, I'd accuse you to being a witch." I heard them kiss.

I should have been embarrassed to eavesdrop but what can I say? The compliment empowered me to be a better hostess.

I greeted Jeremy at the front door and sent the boys upstairs to their bedrooms to clean up. "Sam, will you wake up Jamie and watch him for me while I talk to our guests?"

"Who's here?" Sam asked.

"My sister Beverly Ann and her fiancé," I replied.

"Can I meet them?"

"Later, I want the adults to talk first."

Sam argued that he wasn't a kid anymore. By the time I arrived in the kitchen, Jeremy was shaking Terah's hand. "Welcome to Tennessee." His gaze captured my sister.

"We're having hot tea, Jer, would you like some?" I asked.

"Any coffee left over?"

I shook my head no as Beverly embraced my property rather improperly. With all the grace of royalty, the sheik laid his napkin aside and came to his feet, all in one swift movement. I'd never seen a man with a more perfect physique and impeccable skin texture. Truly, he and Beverly made a stunning couple.

"Is that blueberry pie I smell?" Jeremy asked.

"Yes, just out of the oven." I noticed Sam and Benny exit through the backdoor, probably headed out to the shed to finish building that model plane they'd been working on for a month.

"Would you like a slice now?" I asked Jeremy.

"A small one with a cup of coffee," he replied then set the coffeemaker into motion. "What time is supper?"

"What time do you want to dine?" I asked Beverly.

"We just ate not long ago," she replied.

I shrugged at Jeremy, making eye contact with the sheik. "So, Terah, how long has your family lived in Egypt?"

"Centuries." He delicately sipped from his cup. "Except for a few unsavory stragglers who made their way into Europe, our family has owned the same property." Dark eyes apprized me.

How're mom and dad? I wanted to ask. *How do they feel about your engagement to my sister Beverly? Is she going to live in a castle?*

"You must be famous, a sheik and all . . ." I said instead.

"Ah . . ." Terah chuckled. "Being a sheik in my country is relatively insignificant," he explained. "The title also applies to Muslims, a reference to men from various Islamic sciences."

I wasn't exactly following Terah's train of thought.

"In our culture, 'sheik" applies to elderly men, the ones with financial and political means and influence." He perused his audience for interest. "My father was political and died young."

"So, you what, inherited the title?" Jeremy inquired.

"Yes, but I'm not as committed to politics like my father."

"How so . . .?" I knew Egypt was America's ally and received millions of dollars from us every year to earn their support in the Middle East. I also knew the Egyptian culture was diversified, a rich environment of many ideologies that created political conflict.

"My father was a good person and partnered with political leaders in order to protect our oil investments," Terah explained. "Our family has profited greatly from land rich in black gold."

I glanced at Jeremy, no comment to top that.

"Egypt is a semi-presidential republic," Terah reported. "But due to influential Muslim organizations, a powerful movement is underway to transform our country into an Islamic Republic."

"If that occurs, what will happen to Christians?" I asked.

He gave the slash-of-the-neck sign. "Off with their heads, my lady." He quoted the Queen from *Alice in Wonderland,*

The Islamic movement to establish a Caliphate in the Middle East and Africa had troubled the civilized world for decades. In the past few years, ISIS had mobilized with a jihad goal to punish nations that didn't embrace Islam. Beverly's beau was no intellectual slouch, and I laughed with the others at his cruel joke.

"That's enough about me," Terah said.

We talked a few more minutes about his family then I cleared the table. Jeremy suggested we retire to the living room where we would be more comfortable. On our way to the front of the house, I stopped off in our bathroom to freshen up.

Jeremy followed and eyed me through the mirror.

"Is Terah for real?" he whispered in my ear.

"Not my call," I replied. "Beverly's smart enough to figure out if he's a fake. Who am I to judge their relationship?"

"You're right. Bev knows her way around."

"Please give Terah the benefit of the doubt, Jeremy."

He laughed. "I may not be a sheik but I'm no dummy."

Jeremy headed to the living room to entertain our guests while I went outdoors to check on the boys. By the time I joined them, Terah was deep into a discussion regarding the persecution of Christians around the world. I paused in the doorway.

"Sorry I took so long." I peered at Jeremy. "Jamie fell in the mud and I had to change his clothes. What did I miss?"

"I learned from Terah how he received his name."

Jeremy waved me over to a chair. "It's biblical," he explained. "It was his great grandfather's name."

"So you're not a Muslim," I concluded.

"Not everyone from the Middle East embraces Islam," Terah reported, prompting me to recall how Father Abraham's homeland was in Egypt, formerly identified as Mesopotamia in Old Testament. Abraham's father was also named Terah.

"My immediate family is dedicated to the work of our church," he said. "Our Christian faith is a great heritage."

As if waking up to the moment, Beverly suddenly became animated and interjected, "Terah is a Coptic Christian."

"Excuse me?" I thought she'd said *cocky* for a second.

"Most of the churches in the Middle East are Coptic." Terah began to elaborate. "Our faith embodies a form of Roman Catholicism that stretches back more than nineteen centuries."

With limited knowledge on the subject, I kept quiet.

"You can see why I'm so interested in traveling abroad." Beverly began to highlight a few of her mission trips overseas.

Terah intently listened, not interrupting, clearly in love with the American who had stolen his heart out of Egypt.

I heard Jamie crying. "Jer? Do you mind showing Terah and Beverly where they will sleep tonight while I see about Jamie?"

Without waiting for an answer, I padded down the hall toward the rear door. This was my house, so the sleeping arrangements were my decision. The sheik could have Sam's bedroom since he was spending the night with Buddy, and Beverly could have Benny's. He'd be sleeping on a blow-up mattress.

So that was that, like it or not.

16

TERAH DID NOT come to the dining room table for the supper meal Saturday evening, already retired in his designated bedroom.

"Will he eat something later?" I asked Beverly.

"No, he brought special food with him." Beverly crunched on a carrot stick. "He's disciplined when it comes to eating."

Jeremy looked up and shook his head. *Let it go, babe.*

It's uncanny how we communicate. Taking his cue, I said, "Actually, we all should be as vigilant." I patted my stomach.

The adults had leftover vegetable casserole while Sam and Benny scarped down Mac and Cheese. Jeremy quietly nibbled on the broccoli salad, certainly not his favorite. I started to offer to make him Mac and Cheese when Beverly interrupted.

"We've had to compromise on some issues."

"Are we talking about food or something else?" I asked.

"Our religious preferences differ somewhat."

Jeremy perked up at Beverly's comment.

"Are you going to become a Coptic Christian?" he pried.

I cringed at where Bev's answer would lead, certain that Jeremy was troubled by the sheik rambling around upstairs alone. What if he fell on a misplaced toy, or took a tumble in the bathroom, what kind of compensation would be expected?

"We love each other enough to work it out," she replied.

Nosy us, I was embarrassed. But to be honest, my sister handled herself well. She'd probably been through the same scrutiny with Becca at the airport. Her husband Gary, a successful architect, likely quizzed her about the castle Terah's family owned.

Bottom line, we all cared about Beverly Ann and wanted the best for her. And it was my understanding that Egyptian divorces were not so easy to acquire under any circumstance.

"Work it out? What does that mean?"

Contemplating Jeremy's question, Beverly opted for the middle ground. "We're still in the debating stage."

Ah . . . the threads of an argument about to unravel?

"What church do you belong to now?" Sam asked.

"I'm independent, though I've often worked with the evangelical mission churches," Beverly replied.

"How is church in other countries different?" Sam asked.

"Christian culture around the world differs in many ways, Sam. Belief in Jesus Christ as God's only Son is primary to Christianity. Copts are among the most devoted worshippers."

Beverly explained that early on in history Copts and Muslims lived peacefully together until a more radical element of Islam wanted to control society through government guidelines.

Of course, Copts rebelled when they came under persecution but never fought back with weapons. They took very seriously the idea of forgiveness and offering one's cloak to their enemies.

We soon learned that Copts fasted two-hundred ten days out of the year. During the time of denial, no animal products were allowed. Plus, no food or drink whatsoever was taken between sunrise and sunset. "Is he fasting now?" I thought to ask.

"He's made an exception," Beverly said. "He adopts a special healthy diet for the Advent season. The Fast of Nativity celebrates the birth of Christ. It's a very holy holiday for Copts."

"Will you live in Egypt?" Sam asked Beverly.

Benny was at the table listening, but had no comment.

"Terah's family has a home there," my sister replied. "They also own a castle near Alexandria. However, I plan to keep my apartment in London. I'm a free spirit and need my space."

I hiked an eyebrow at my husband. This would be no ordinary marriage. Then maybe before I-do was said they would both come to their senses. Oil and water don't mix.

When we finished our meager meal Beverly helped me with the dishes. "I can see how much Terah adores you," I told her. "But are you sure he's the right person for you?"

"He's the kindest, most decent person I've ever met."

If that wasn't a facet of love, I didn't know what was.

I carried a cup of decaf coffee with me into the living room. Beverly sipped on her herbal tea sweetened with honey. It was a rare moment to be alone with my intellectual sister who had traveled to many other countries and experienced diverse cultures.

"Where was Terah educated?" I queried.

"At Berkley, in California," Beverly replied.

"Really?" I was shocked. "What motivated him to go there?"

"He has relatives living in Los Angeles and wanted to get a feel for America." Beverly sighed. "He loves to travel."

"So he's a free spirit, too. But I wouldn't say Berkeley is the best place for a devout Copt to obtain a higher education."

Beverly frowned but failed to comment. There again, I was judging him. "Sorry, I just meant the college is so liberal."

"He had a full scholarship, and a Coptic Church was nearby."

"Really . . .?" I seemed to be stuck on one word.

"Copts are all over the world. They pray for the reunion of all Christian churches. Especially for Egypt: the Nile, its crops, its president, its army, its government, and above all the people. They pray for world peace and for the well being of all humanity."

"It sounds like to me Terah is a very special man," I said.

"He is and I love him dearly."

"Then you go girl!"

* * *

"Did you get a chance to talk in depth with Terah?" I asked Jeremy as we prepared for bed. "Did he say anything significant?"

My husband looked at me funny. "Significant?"

"Jer . . . aren't you the least bit curious about what common bond drew those two odd ducks to the relationship?" I crawled in bed with him. "I just can't picture them with children."

"It's not for us to judge, I'm sure he loves children."

"I can sure pray for them," I said.

"From listening to Terah, he appears pretty intense about most subjects. When I asked him if he embraced the Holy Spirit, he reminded me that Saint Mark brought Christianity to Egypt during the second century. A descendent of devout believers, he's looking forward to Christ's second coming. Is that significant?"

"Well, yeah. What does Terah mean by that?"

"That Isaiah 19:23 has special meaning for Copts." Jeremy ferociously yawned. "He even quoted the scripture to me."

"Will you repeat it for me?" I slid under the warm covers.

"In that day there will be an altar to the Lord in the midst of the land of Egypt, and a pillar to the LORD at its border."

I pushed up on an elbow. "Where is that found in the Bible?"

"Look it up tomorrow, it's your assignment." He stretched out in the bed. When I hit him hard on the forearm, he grunted.

"I don't think Terah approves of wife abuse," Jeremy teased.

I sighed and collapsed on my back.

"Okay, for your education, Copts believe that scripture reference pertains to Jesus Christ's earthly reign," he explained.

"So they believe in the Millennium reign of Christ?"

"Apparently. . . " Jer switched off the table lamp. "Pretty significant, don't you think? Good night, love. Sleep tight."

"And don't let the bedbugs bite," I added, silently praying no bumps in the night would disturb our happy couple upstairs.

17

MORNING STUNNED MIDDLE Tennessee with brilliant sunlight and warmer weather. It was the second Sunday in December. Our houseguests from overseas had made themselves at home, assuming their rigid normal routines—as opposed to our loose ones? I chuckled at my comparison. I dragged from the bed.

Terah had slipped out the back door an hour before sunrise, I presumed to walk the wooded trails behind our house. The sun was cresting the hillside when he came into the kitchen, greeted me warmly then went upstairs to take a quick shower.

Around 7:15, Beverly sleepily wobbled into the kitchen and fixed her own breakfast: plain yogurt with whole grains and dried Egyptian fruits. I almost felt guilty for serving my family syrupy pancakes before we took off to church. Still I ate my portion.

Our guests were dressed and ready to leave for church long before we were. Terah and Sam rode with Jeremy in the SUV while the younger boys and Beverly piled in the Malibu with me.

Our Methodist congregation graciously welcomed them.

Jeremy did a great job with the sermon and we hung around the sanctuary until the last person left. Then we returned home to have lunch. Our family changed clothes, they didn't.

I served turkey sandwiches to my family with a large tossed salad for our picky eaters. For dessert, I'd prepared a large bowl of sliced fresh fruit. Then we all rested or napped while the boys watched videos in Sam's bedroom. When I woke around 2:45, I found Bev in the living room perusing a spring bridal magazine.

"I have something I want to show you," I told her.

Bev trailed me to my bedroom where I presented her with six designer silk scarves that once belonged to our mother.

"Becca asked me to hold these for you," I explained.

"They're beautiful." She appeared delighted.

"I thought you could use them overseas," I added.

From my jewelry box, I selected several beautiful antique pins, some adorned with rare stones or natural seed pearls.

"Please take any of these," I told Beverly. "These once belonged to our great grandmother on daddy's side."

She selected two glittering pins to go with her three colorful silk scarves then filled me in on their wedding plans as we sat on the edge of the bed. Terah's parents had insisted he marry in their Coptic Church where his ancestors had attended for generations.

"Old-world tradition is unbreakable," Bev pointed out. They would have an Egyptian-style wedding with an elaborate formal reception. "Do you think you and Jeremy can come?"

"To Egypt . . ?" Mental wheels turned. "What's the date?"

"June fifth, next year, if all goes well."

"What does that mean?" I frowned, sensing a problem.

"Well . . ." she paused, "Terah's mother is not completely on board with our engagement. She had another girl picked out."

Oil and water, I thought. "Maybe if you spent time with his parents it would make a difference how they feel about you."

"I doubt it. He's breaking tradition in marrying me."

And you aren't? I had no idea how marriages came about in the Egyptian culture, but I suspected most nuptials were pre-arranged according to class. Beverly had not come from royalty.

When our conversation concerning an Egyptian marriage ended, I inquired about Terah's profession and learned he was a licensed electrical engineer and worked for a company in Cairo.

A bright idea was emerging as I stared at my sister.

"What? Don't hold back, you never do."

I chuckled, then said, "I read somewhere that electrical engineers sometimes use the same equipment as ghost-hunters."

"That's an odd comment," she noted, no smile.

"Just saying. . ." I'd promised Jeremy not to disclose our secret guests to outsiders. But my fleshly sister is a smart cookie.

"Wait. Are there ghosts in this house?"

I shuddered at my transparency.

Gulping air, I admitted, "We've had some problems."

"What's happened, Brooke?"

I stood up and faced the window, badly needing to get an opinion from someone other than Jeremy concerning our haunted house. Plus, I trusted my sister to keep my confidentiality.

I turned around. "If I tell you, I'm breaking a pledge."

"Oh, pooh, Jeremy doesn't count."

"We don't want whatever is going on in this house to harm our Christian ministry. You can't talk to Terah about this."

Beverly gazed into my eyes. "Are you sure? He might shed some light on your problem. A haunting is not uncommon in some of those centuries-old buildings in the Middle East."

That was all it took for me to spill my guts on the subject.

Beverly took me seriously and listened attentively as I detailed some of the supernatural events our family had experienced.

"What do you think?" I asked in conclusion.

"That you have a huge problem with intruders." She huffed. "I also think Terah might be able to locate the hotspots in your house with the right electronic equipment."

"Like a real ghost-hunter?" I'd viewed a few TV shows.

"But of course, it's up to you. And Jeremy," she added.

Dilemma, dilemma . . .

"I understand you need his permission," she said.

"I'll consider it." I'd read about how ghostly appearances were often associated with faulty electrical wiring, although ours had been tested by a professional electrician and declared safe.

Was it possible Terah's sensitive instruments would identify "hot spots" the electrician missed? "Thanks for listening, Bev."

"My pleasure." She smiled. "Let me know, we'll be leaving soon. Terah will need to rent equipment for his investigation."

Another night passed with only the usual noises associated with old houses. *Bumps in the night,* we had labeled them. Footfalls in the hallway or on the stairs, creaky old floors . . .

But if walls could talk, what would they tell us?

* * *

A cold rain ushered in a bleak Monday scarred with dingy clouds. It was another work week for our family, so Sam and Benny were up early and already dressed for school by the time I came into the kitchen to prepare breakfast. First off, the coffee. . .

Terah trotted down the stairs shortly before seven with their suitcases and stowed them in the trunk of their rental car while Beverly enjoyed a last cup of hot tea in the kitchen with me.

Jeremy was helping Sam gather pillows and fold blankets in the living room to stow away. Dreading to see Bev go, I cleared away the breakfast dishes and packed lunches, denying tears.

"Is Jeremy going to allow Terah to test for hotspots?"

I dried my hands on a towel. "He seems reluctant."

"Doesn't Jeremy want to know?" She locked eyes with me. "There's still time for Terah to rent the equipment."

"He's left it up to me," I replied.

"Well, you'd better decide quickly."

"Decide what?" Terah asked from the foyer.

"Brooke has a ghost problem!" Beverly blurted out.

I shushed my sister, afraid that Benny might overhear our conversation. But seconds later, his boom box blasted loud music through the house. "What did you have in mind, Brooke?"

"She wants to test for hotspots," Bev answered for me.

Embarrassed, I uttered, "I shouldn't delay your plans." They were driving to Henderson to visit our parents' graves.

"Maybe someone else can take a look," Bev suggested.

"If the harassment continues, I'll consider it."

"Really, Brooke, it's no trouble for me to investigate," Terah said. "You've been a great hostess, and helping you is a pleasure."

"I think not right now," I decided.

We walked toward the front door and Jeremy joined us in the foyer. "You guys taking off already?" he queried Terah.

"I'm afraid so." Beverly hugged him. "We've had a great visit, but life must go forward." Didn't I know that was true?

My sister, the optimist, I thought to myself.

"Thanks for your gracious hospitality." Terah bowed slightly to Jeremy. "We hope you will attend our wedding in June."

"Brooke and I will discuss it," Jer replied.

"I love you so much." Beverly tightly hugged me.

"I love you more," I said, tears bubbling.

"I wish you could drive to Henderson with us today and visit Dad and Mom's graves," Beverly said. "Can't you miss school?"

"No, I've already used most of my sick days."

It was a reasonable excuse. I couldn't possibly stand over Mom's grave so soon after the ground consumed her.

We stood outdoors and waved them off before I made a mad dash to see if Jamie was ready to leave for his daycare. I heard Jeremy and Benny arguing across the hall. "Son, you can't miss school again. You're grades will suffer. You have to go."

"Come on Jamie, let's go." I led him down the stairs, donned my coat then grabbed my purse and lesson-plan book from the office. We stood waiting at the front door. Minutes passed.

"What's the hold up, Jer?" I called out.

"The boys want to stay home and play sick," Jeremy called down to me. "Won't happen!" The wise dad settled the matter.

"Okay, I'm taking Jamie to school. See you later."

18

THE NEW YEAR CAME. A year and a half had passed since we'd moved into our talking house. Our boys were growing like weeds. Sam would soon be fifteen. Jeremy and I were wiser concerning the occult activities, praying they'd eventually give up taunting us.

"We're not going anywhere!" Jeremy constantly reminded me. "It's our home and I won't be chased out of it."

I wasn't so sure Gibby and his family felt the same way.

Our ghosts in residence had taken a break from haunting me after my private exorcism last spring. However, they turned their maliciousness on Jeremy and our two older boys. The mama bear in me bristled at their audacity. It was unacceptable, plain mean.

How could I fight what I couldn't see?

One afternoon, Jeremy closed down the church early due to the threat of an ice storm. He returned home before school let out and was about to turn off the security system when he heard a noise in his office. He stepped to the door. Oddly a box of pencils had overturned on his desk and scattered across the floor.

Then he heard some bumps. He jaunted down the hall and stood at the foot of the staircase. A few marbles slowly tumbled down the steps, a bump at a time. He glanced up and realized they were dropping from the stairwell ceiling. In his wildest imagination, he considered if an unseen hand was releasing them.

As if trapped in the Twilight Zone, he leaned over to pick up a marble when a couple of pencils from the study floor suddenly zoomed past his head. How was that possible? He ducked.

Startled at the phenomenon, he hurriedly ran down the hall and closed the door to the study then came back and began gathering the marbles, his heart thundering with anxiety.

An hour later when I came home with the boys, I immediately recognized he was upset. "What's wrong, Jer?"

"I'm not sure." He weirdly gazed at me.

Jamie pulled loose from my hand and took off running down the hall. "Is something wrong at the church? Did someone die?"

"Get the boys settled upstairs and meet me in our bedroom." He took off walking, all business and no hug for me.

Five minutes later, we were seated on the edge of our four-poster, him holding my hand. "Are we losing our minds, Brooke?"

My heart leaped. "What do you mean, Jer?"

"Is what happening in our house our imaginations?"

"What happened to make you ask me that question?"

Beginning from the time he'd opened the front door to when the pencils flew past his head, moment by traumatized moment, he detailed the bizarre incident, his voice trembling all the while.

"They're at it again!" I told him about my exorcism.

"Do you think you made them madder?"

"That wasn't my intention," I replied. "I guess they consider this house more theirs than ours. Something terrible must have occurred here. Is it possibly someone died violently?" I knew Gibby had a wife and mother. They all died in the house.

"What about that little girl we heard crying for her daddy?" Jer recalled. "She was drowned in a well in our backyard."

"We have no proof," I said. "*They* make our lives miserable. Underneath our smiles, we walk around this house with dread."

He nodded in agreement. "I don't know what to do."

"I know you don't want to move out."

He glared at me, his will to fight waning.

"Jer! Living like this is unacceptable!" I shuddered to think how our boys would view life, impacted by ghostly apparitions.

"I always thought scary movies about haunted houses were pure fiction," he uttered. "But now I know firsthand *something* sinister exists in this house. And they aren't going anywhere."

We were silent to a fault, grieving over our situation.

"Maybe these malicious beings are demons taking on the physical appearances of people who once lived in this house." A chilling thought. "If we die here, we will become part of it."

He looked at me strangely. "Now you are really scaring me," he croaked. "Who will stop *them* if God doesn't?"

"You think I haven't prayed? And waved the cross in their faces?" I said. "There's so much we don't understand about the afterlife, Jer. I don't think we are qualified to figure it out."

"I don't either," he said.

"Maybe there's a cemetery underneath our house."

"Do you know how paranoid that sounds, Brooke?"

"Paranoia is when you think something's happening and it isn't!" I countered. "You and I both know there's something sinister going on in this house. We're not all crazy."

"Point well taken. . ." he sighed.

Silence ruled the moment. We had no solution.

"I'm going to check on the boys," he said and walked out.

"I need to start supper."

I ventured across the hall and into the kitchen. We never discussed the pencil or marble episode again. However, the spirits were not finished with their tormenting. In April, the old grandma began picking on Benny. Sometimes she would hover over him at night as he lay in bed before falling asleep.

Once he got so scared he ran into his bedroom closet, shut the door and switched on the light. It didn't help. Doors didn't matter: Grandma appeared in his closet beside him. Too terrified to move a muscle, when the light in the closet blinked out, Benny screamed to the top of his lungs and came running downstairs.

"What does she look like?" I tried to quiet him.

"She's old, Mom, tall and thin . . ." Benny envisioned the apparition. "She had on an old hat and a dark suit." His gaze wandered. "She's really scary, Mom. Make her go away."

I doubted my prayer skills could pull that off. Still, I told Benny the old woman couldn't hurt him, but I wasn't absolutely sure I was right. When I told Jeremy what happened, he offered no solution to the problem. I was ready to pull out my hair.

The last week of May arrived and public schools closed for the summer. Our family had ten full weeks to relax and enjoy our vacation, including swimming and sports. With Beverly's wedding a week away, Jeremy surprised me by purchasing my airline ticket.

He even arranged for Becca to meet me at New York's JFK terminal so we could fly to Cairo, Egypt together. It was a trip overseas I had always dreamed of taking. So I packed enough clothes for a week, suffering guilt at leaving my family behind.

Jeremy would be responsible for watching the boys. Sam was old enough to help out and we had good friend support.

"Don't worry about anything," he reassured me. "I've asked a few women at the church to help out with our younger boys. Folks will bring casseroles to the church for me to bring home for meals. Boomer will even get fed." He grinned. "We'll all be just fine while you're away. So go, love, and enjoy the wedding."

* * *

The day arrived for me to catch a flight out of Nashville. I stood in the hallway, a little sad. "Oh, I'm going to miss all of you terribly." I planted kisses on the cheeks of my three boys. "I wish we were all going to Beverly's wedding." I clung to Jeremy.

"You can tell us all about your trip later," he said.

"It won't be the same as being there," I countered. "Viewing Egypt's landmarks in full techno color will be fabulous."

"Send me pictures on your iPhone, Brooke. Don't feel guilty for taking some time off. Our family can go another time."

"Do you know how much I appreciate you?"

"Yes, and ditto, plus add a measure of love."

Staring at my husband, I stood there about to cancel my trip.

"Don't even think about not going." Jer was ready to shove me out the door. "You deserve a break, honey. You'll have so much fun you'll forget to come home," he lovingly teased.

But the boys knew their mama well enough to laugh at that comment. However, I knew what Jeremy meant. A responsible mother takes care of her husband, her job, and the family. Plus she runs the household, shops and cooks and cleans. Add a few ghosts to the mix and she needs a break. Besides, when Becca and I arrived in Egypt we'd be busy preparing for the ceremony.

"Okay, I'm going now." I noticed my friend Alice Jacobs had pulled in the driveway to fetch me. "Love and kisses!"

"Wait." Jeremy kissed me lightly. "Get out of here, girl!"

Alice had the AC going in her Cadillac. She greeted me enthusiastically and on our way to Nashville we talked about vacation opportunities during the summer months. Alice had taken off work to keep a doctor's appointment. After learning I needed a ride to the airport, she had volunteered to take me.

I shared with Alice some information about Coptic weddings that I had downloaded on the Internet. Their ceremonies were more involved than our American nuptials.

Alice pointed out that marrying into an Egyptian family and accepting its culture was a huge commitment on Beverly's part.

I agreed, but said they were hopelessly in love.

More disturbing, I informed Alice, were the recent reports that Muslim terrorists were looting Christian churches in the area.

We failed to solve the world's problems in the hour and fifteen minutes it took us to get to the airport. Alice let me off in front of the Nashville International and wished me well.

Standing at the entrance to the terminal, I took a huge breath of the warm June air, humid with the promise of rain. As I rolled my bag behind me, I wondered how hard it would be to adjust to Egypt's dry climate with intense daytime heat. Hopefully prepared to step into a foreign culture, I'd packed a wide-brim straw hat and lightweight summer dresses. If I needed anything else my handy American Express Card worked quite efficiently.

I became more excited as I stepped inside the terminal and approached the ticket counter. *Maybe I'll get a ride on a camel.* My wild imagination took flight as I checked in at the front desk then ventured through the checkpoint, realizing how blessed I was.

My family would be fine without me. Sam was staying a few days with his friend Buddy, and Benny was going to a water park on Saturday morning with his baseball team. I knew there would be plenty of mothers willing to watch Jamie. Our friends at church would make sure there were adequate meals at the house.

So here I was. My flight was at five p.m.

19

THE NASHVILLE FLIGHT took off as scheduled. Two-and-a-half hours later I deplaned at JFK International Airport and faced nightmarish congestion maneuvering from one end of the B Concourse to the other end of the A where I knew Becca was waiting for me at the United Airline's Gate 5.

"Hey, you almost didn't make it." She briefly hugged me then hustled me toward the Jetway where both children and adults were already boarding the huge double-decker plane.

"It took me awhile to negotiate the crowd," I explained to Becca above the din of noise. "Did you eat lunch yet?" My stomach was grumbling from not having eaten in seven hours.

"I had a Big Mac." We took our place in line to board.

"Do you think they'll feed us in flight?" I queried.

"It's a ten-hour flight, Brooke. They'll have to or we'll pass out." Becca smiled as the line inched forward. "Good to see you again, Sis. And I'm elated that it's just you and me going to Beverly's wedding. We three need some serious sister time."

"You got that right." I knew I'd miss my family. "Gary didn't put up a fuss?" We were both submissive wives by choice.

"No, he would've come, too, but he had a convention conflict. He'll be in Canada for a week while I'm gone."

"That's convenient." I handed the flight attendant my boarding pass. "Let's hope Beverly has made the right choice."

"Well, it's a little late for her to back out now that we have our plane tickets to Cairo!" Becca exclaimed.

We both laughed, as if that mattered to Beverly. She usually did whatever she wanted regardless of the consequences. But that was what made her a unique individual. And I expect that was what Terah saw in our little sister, a free spirit willing to take risks.

When it was our turn, we boarded the Boeing and found our second-class seats. Twenty minutes later, after the pillows and small blankets had been distributed to passengers, the plane jetted off the tarmac in a brisk wind. Once the huge plane was in the air and leveled off, my stomach settled down from the bumps.

I read a magazine until I could no longer hold my eyes open.

Hours passed. We flew at what seemed like warp speed toward the sun while rapidly losing time. It was soon dark, stars glittering against a backdrop of black outside my small window.

After a healthy snack with a beverage was served, passengers nestled down to sleep in their seats. From personal experience, I knew the time change would disrupt normal sleep-wake patterns. We all wanted to avoid a sluggish first day on another continent.

The flight across the Atlantic Ocean was relatively smooth, no scary storms to maneuver around. I came to my senses when the attendant announced we were about to land in Cairo.

I nudged Becca, who was actually snoring in a REM sleep.

"What?" Eyes popped opened. "Are we there yet?"

I chuckled. "I wish I had a penny for every time Benny or Sam asked me that question." I smelled fresh coffee brewing.

"I expect we drove our parents nutty often enough." Becca roused and glanced around the plane. "Well, that wasn't as uncomfortable a ride as I'd expected." She reached for her purse.

"We're almost there." The arid Egyptian landscape passed below us and zoomed closer as we neared the airport.

Touchdown was effortless. We deplaned with the other passengers and were hustled through the custom checkpoint with no problems. Before my current teaching assignment, I'd traveled to France twice with my senior students so I knew the routine.

Becca and Gary were gold-star world travelers, having visited many countries including Africa, Russia, Japan, and China.

The second we stepped outdoors, the bright light and windy heat infused with sand slammed us. "Welcome to Egypt."

Becca fanned herself with a straw hat. "We'll adjust." She glanced around the airport. "Beverly said she'd be here."

Shading my squinting eyes with a hand, I perused our surroundings through dark sunglasses. "You know if she doesn't show as promised, we don't have a clue what to do next."

"We can always take a taxi to a swanky hotel in downtown," Becca countered. "You have a credit card, right?"

"Right. Funny girl."

"There she is!" Becca exclaimed as a limousine pulled up to the curb. "Are we riding in style or not?"

I rolled my suitcase toward the sleek black monster puffing carbon fumes. "I guess Egyptians haven't heard about global warming and CO2 emissions." Becca trailed a pace behind me.

Beverly pushed open the far rear door and rolled out, squealing like a teenager. "You're here!" She ran over and hugged us both. "Get in, Saad will stow your luggage."

With the limousine door still open, we climbed inside as the Muslim driver placed our suitcases in the trunk and returned to his role as driver. A dark, middle-aged man, with shadowy coal eyes, he wore traditional Egyptian attire including a headdress.

A button on the dashboard closed a window between the front and back seats, giving us complete privacy. Momentarily, soft music sifted through the speakers. *This is fine.*

"How far is it to Alexandria?" Becca asked. "And why isn't Terah with you?" I curiously asked Beverly.

"Not far, it's a pleasant ride," Bev replied. "Terah and I are not seeing or talking to one another until after the wedding."

"I guess the rituals associated with Egyptian Coptic marriages are plentiful," I interjected, having no idea what to expect.

During the hour drive through the countryside over to the castle, Becca and I got an earful of what to expect prior and during the wedding ceremony. As Beverly talked, I envisioned the pastor coaching the couple through each stage of the process.

Beverly was set to wear a traditional floor-length white gown and an elaborate headdress with a lacy veil attached. The groom would break with tradition and wear a black silk tuxedo with a red bowtie, black shoes, and no headdress. His parents wanted to incorporate an American tradition into the wedding to accommodate Beverly's family and guests. Go figure.

"Since the wedding is not until Friday . . ." Beverly took charge of our schedules, "we have three days to sightsee. After you've settled in at the castle I want to take you to Quitbay Fort."

"Is it a historic landmark?" Becca inquired, enjoying the soft eastern style music alongside the comfort of flowing AC. "All I know about Alexandria is that it's on the Mediterranean Sea."

"Well, I hope to increase your knowledge of the city."

Once outside the ancient city, and away from the vegetation lining the Nile River, the terrain grew flat and sandy. I'd read that some one-hundred pyramids were located in Egypt, and that the three most prominent ones were in Alexandria.

Beverly informed us that the Quitbay Fort was built on the ruins' site of *Pharos of Alexandria*, a famous lighthouse that guided ships into the Alexandria port during the fifteen century. Over time, earthquakes had eroded the *Pharos* and, with the threat of Ottoman Empire invasions, the fort was erected on the same site to protect the city. The overload of information made me dizzy.

By the time our baby sister finished her discourse on visitor hotspots in Alexandria, we had arrived at the castle. It was huge, constructed of stone, and most impressive. Surrounded by a mote with running water, we crossed the stone bridge and drove through a walled gate. I was overwhelmed by the idea that my sister would soon be a part of all this wealth and royalty.

Beverly was anything but traditional, scarcely recalling family birthdays and quick to change her schedule on a second's whelm. I couldn't imagine her functioning in Terah's family. But who knows, life is full of the unexpected, and we'd survived our ghosts.

We left the limousine and entered a castle fit for a king. Beverly took us to a spacious sitting room with a stone fireplace and asked a maid to bring us a tray of snacks. With a full servant staff at our disposal, I might never go home to slavery again.

20

"**HOW IS EGYPT?**" **JEREMY** inquired over the phone.

"Great! What about you and the boys?"

"Great!" he exclaimed and we both laughed.

"I miss you so much . . ." I rasped, sounding out a mushy kiss over my cell phone. "Hugs and kisses to the boys, too."

"I bet you don't miss the house."

Alarm! Alarms, going off . . .

"What do you mean?" I asked.

"Just teasing," he said.

"No, Jer, that's not something you'd tease about."

"You know me so well." He profoundly sighed. "Something did happen but we'll talk about it when you get home."

"No, I need for you to tell me *now* what you meant or I'm on the next international flight home, Brother Mac."

"Just a few bumps in the night," he said.

"Did something happen with Benny again?" I questioned how exposure to ghostly apparitions would affect our three boys.

Would they ever view life normally?

"Benny's temporarily sleeping with me," Jeremy reported. "Got spooked last night when the old gal showed up again."

I blinked with comprehension, assuming he meant Gibby's deceased mother. She was like a bad grandma.

"If *they* don't stop harassing us, I'm hiring a ghost-buster."

"I know, I've thought about calling one of my seminary professors at Louisville Theological Seminary and discussing our predicament," Jeremy revealed. "What do you think?"

"I'm not sure." I worried if word got out we lived in a haunted house it might create a media frenzy.

"Who do you have in mind?" I asked.

"Dr. Jeffrey Mahoney. He knows me pretty well, Brooke. He doesn't make rash judgments and he'll hear me out."

"Then do what you think is best." Jeremy kept in touch with Jeff at Christmas and they occasionally talked over the phone.

But letting the cat out of the bag might start a firestorm.

"Jeff is not one to condone spiritual matters at either end of the spectrum," my husband recalled. "He isn't a proponent of right-wing conservative theology, more an academia in his approach to interpreting biblical principles. I can count on him to keep an open mind. Honestly, our unique situation is baffling."

"If word gets out," I hitched a breath, "our problem could possibly destroy your ministry." It was a harsh conclusion.

The silence between us said we both were aware of the impact of public scrutiny should our haunting become known.

"I can't handle much more without losing it," I said.

"I know, honey, I'll pray on the matter." He paused then redirected the conversation. "So, are you ready for the wedding?"

"I still have an hour before we leave for the church."

"Have you seen the sanctuary?" he inquired.

"Beverly took us there yesterday and walked us through the ceremony, where we would stand, etc." I replied. "We also talked to the bishop—he's really a down-to-earth guy."

"Did you learn anything new about Copts?"

"Yes, the wedding ceremony involves more ritual than I anticipated." I reflected on my conversation with the bishop . . .

"Mrs. McLaughlin, what a pleasure to finally meet you."

"Bishop Haymanot," I acknowledged the clergyman, "this is the most impressive church I've ever been inside."

"Saint Mark Coptic Cathedral has a incomparable historic elegance as one of the few institutions that's associated with The Coptic Orthodox Church of Alexandria," he explained. "I've served here a number of years."

"I read about Coptic religion during my flight over," I said. "Your church has existed since AD 42. Copts have survived many hardships."

"To serve Jesus, we consider trials are worth it."

I stared up at the sculptured ceiling tile, its dome stretching fifty feet above my head. Surprisingly, the three rows of wooden pews divided by long aisles resembled the setup in my own church in Tennessee. The cathedral's most profound feature was a full-life icon of the Lord's Supper protruding from a front wall. Gold and silver vessels were used in sacraments.

"I prefer the title of Papas to Bishop," he clued me in.

"Our father," I recalled the meaning. "Okay, Papas."

I stared into a pair of twin eyes as rich as java. The bishop's beard was salt-and-pepper like the thick tufts of hair drizzling from the edges of his skull cap. Beneath his white robe was an ample well-fed stomach. Papas wore shoes I'd never before seen. Surely, there were Greek words that would capture his ambience but I wasn't a scholar of the Coptic Church.

"Your cathedral is magnificent," was the best I could do.

"Your sister Beverly is a beautiful soul," Papas said. "I can see that she's devoted to Christ and truly loves Terah. She'll make a good wife."

"I hope so." I chuckled. "She's very independent."

"God didn't make us all alike."

"Have you known Terah long?" I pried a bit, hands tucked at my back while loosely standing at the front of the cathedral.

"Oh, yes!" Papas exclaimed. "Terah was christened as a baby right here where we stand. As a boy, he attended every activity available to children. We were saddened when his family moved out in the countryside."

"When they inherited the family castle, you mean," I clarified.

"The Houssams are good people and regularly attend a rural Coptic church near their property," Papas offered, his robe silkily swishing as he shifted his ample weight and glanced around the cathedral with concern.

"Now where did your sisters get off to?" Papas muttered.

"I'd better look for them," I said.

"Never mind, we're here," Beverly called out as she entered the cathedral. "I was just showing Becca around this impressive church."

"For a minute, I was afraid you two were lost," Papas said.

We stood around talking about the wedding for another few minutes. Before we took off, Papas assured us that he would queue us in when it was our time to participate. "It's been a real pleasure, Papas," I told him.

"If all goes as planned we'll see you tomorrow evening," Becca told him.

Since the ceremony was set for six o'clock Friday evening, we would need to arrive by four. A reception was hosted afterwards by Terah's relatives . . .

Recalling yesterday at the church, I wondered how much time had passed. Had Jeremy hung up on me, thinking our call failed?

"Honey, are you still there?" I asked.

"Sorry, Brooke, I had to put down the phone and check on our noisy boys," his deep voice heralded over the airways.

"It's okay, I was zoning out while you were away."

"Did you get to visit some of the historic Egyptian sites?"

"Bev wore us out." I chuckled. "We enjoyed every minute."

"Well, I guess I'd better go," my husband said. "Duty calls."

After our call ended I heard a knock at the door. I was on the third floor of the castle in a guest suite with access to a semi-modern bathroom. Becca had slept in the adjoining bedroom.

"Come in." The door opened as Beverly stepped inside.

"We're about to leave for the cathedral, are you ready?"

"As ready as I'm ever going to be."

* * *

When we arrived at the church, Becca and I went to the dressing room to put on our floor-length bridesmaid's gowns. We even wore mauve elbow-length gloves with dyed-to-match satin pumps. On our heads were glittering tiaras. Feeling like royalty, we would soon be part of an elaborate Coptic marriage ceremony.

From that point on, everything went like clockwork. Shortly before six o'clock, the brides' maids, the groom, and Terah's best man Reuben stood in a side hall at an entrance to the cathedral.

As was the custom of Copts, Bishop Haymanot entered the cathedral first and led the audience through a litany of matrimonial prayers and hymns prior to the wedding party's entrance. At the onset of the organ prelude, the groom and his best man entered the cathedral and stood before the Bishop.

Then it was our turn. Becca and I kept step with the music as we approached Bishop Haymanot. The organ music was regal and loud as *Papas* staunchly stood with his Bible in hand in anticipation of the bride's glorious entrance from the back.

My heart pounded as the wedding march pealed forth.

Every eye turned toward the back of the cathedral. The flower girl entered through the door and meandered unsteadily down the center aisle, inciting chuckles as she dropped pink rose petals. As my sister Beverly stepped into view, I recalled that she represented Christ's bride, the church on earth in its divine purity.

Representing Jesus, the groom's eyes were on his bride, anxious to be wedded. The marriage ritual was symbolic of the Coptic's faith in Christ as they anticipated His return to earth. Before Jesus ascended into Heaven in a cloud, He'd promised His twelve disciples He would return to earth in a similar manner and rule with grace and truth. Every knee would bow before the King.

I realized that Egyptian Copts were not so different from me. Though denominations and religious sects around the world differed in the way they worshipped, their one common thread was the Kingship of Jesus. Appreciative eyes rested on my baby sister as she moved down the cathedral's center aisle with grace.

Dressed in layers of flowing white chiffon speckled with glittering rhinestones, Bev's headdress was attached to cascading antique lace that trailed behind her on the floor as she walked.

At that moment, the bride also represented every Christian woman's dream of a blessed marriage. I was so proud and wished with all my heart that our mother could witness the ceremony.

21

AFTER BEING GONE a week, I found home like I'd left it, except for the clutter of toys and games in my disarranged kitchen. But I was very happy to be with my family and clean-up was fast.

For awhile, I lived in a fairyland of exotic memories. Having viewed the pyramids at sunset and explored the historic Fort Quitbay with my two sisters, who could forget about the marvelous shopping sprees Becca and I took with Beverly?

These events shadowed my reality that my two feet were on American soil and I was wife to a busy minister and mother to three rough-and-tumble boys. I came to my senses when Benny fell out of a pear tree and broke his left arm. "Oh, brother . . ."

Sam brought Benny inside the house screaming to the top of his lungs, which set our new puppy barking and Jamie to crying.

I got right on the phone and called Jeremy.

"What's going on—I hear a lot of hollering!"

I covered one ear and walked into our bedroom.

"From the looks of Benny's arm, he's broken it below the elbow. Can you meet us at the county hospital ER?"

"How soon?" he asked.

"I can make it in forty-five minutes," I replied. "Sam and Jamie will be with me, so please arrange for their care while we tend to Benny." Jamie was a bit rambunctious for Sam to handle.

"I'm on it." Jeremy ended the call.

I walked back to the kitchen and wrapped Benny's broken, bleeding arm in a clean towel. "Sam, help Benny to the car while I change Jamie into clean clothes for our trip to the ER."

Before we left, I set Jamie on the porch and went back inside to arm the security system. My youngest was whimpering over the confusion, clutching his fluffy bear like it would protect him.

"It's going to be okay, Jamie," I said, "Benny will be fine."

Jeremy beat us to the ER and had already alerted the head nurse that I was on the way with Benny. Janice Graves, our church secretary, was waiting for us in the ER when we arrived.

I thanked Janice for coming and handed over Jamie for her care. My bleary eyes were on Jeremy, who appeared concerned.

Sam collapsed in a padded chair and bowed his head. I knew he was praying for his brother and that gave me more confidence that Benny's arm would be completely restored in time.

Dr. Melrose Lazarus was the attending ER physician and set Benny's broken arm, quietly talking him through the process. We were pleased with how the hospital staff responded to his medical need, and with the help of pain meds, he calmed down a bit.

Two hours later, we were driving home in the Malibu.

"It was nice of Janice's husband to drive your Chevy back to church," I said, grateful that Jeremy was behind the wheel and not me. "Benny, are you doing okay?" I was a nervous wreck.

"He's fine," Sam said, "sleeping on my shoulder."

"Good." I threw up a prayer. "I don't know how he's going to respond to the doctor's orders," I told Jeremy. "He can't go swimming or climb trees until the cast comes off in six to eight weeks." By that time school would be in fall session again.

"I was thinking you might take a year off work."

"What? Why, Jeremy . . .? Don't we need the income?"

"I've noticed how nervous you seem lately," my observant husband said. "Because I love you and am concerned, I question if you've taken on too much responsibility at school and church."

Is it that noticeable? I was experiencing the onset signs of menopause—night sweats, sporadic mood swings—what would I do with myself if I had eight hours a day alone in this house?

As if reading my mind, Jeremy said, "You could earn some extra money teaching private piano and voice lessons at home."

"On my grandmother's defunct piano . . .?" I countered. "It badly needs tuning." The disharmony hurt to think about it.

"We'll purchase a new electric piano and make the monthly payments with what you earn from giving private lessons."

Jeremy had obviously given the idea some thought.

"I'm with that idea, but I can't quit my job yet," I said.

"Why not . . ?"

"I promised my French students if they took a second year of the language I'd take them to France next summer," I explained.

"Okay, that's one reason," he said. "What's the *real* reason?"

Jeremy knew me so well it was scary. I lowered my voice and said, "There's no way I'm spending any time alone in this house."

Silence indicated my husband received the message.

"Look, Jer, I'll think about taking off the following year."

"Mom's right, Dad," Sam chimed an opinion.

I cringed. Big ears had been listening.

"Did you hear everything we said?" Jeremy asked.

"Enough to agree with Mom," Sam uttered. "Gibby would come after her big time. Home alone is dangerous."

"Gibby?" Jeremy stared at me.

"That's what Mom calls our ghost."

Thank God, Benny was dozing in the backseat and Jamie was too young to understand our nutty conversation.

"Sam, I enjoy teaching. Besides, this trip to France with my students has the full support of all their parents."

Sam made a face. "I'm not stupid, Mom"

"Sam!" Jeremy cautioned. "That's enough."

After we rolled into the driveway and Jeremy shut off the motor, he helped Benny into the house and upstairs to bed while I went straight to the kitchen to fix Jamie a snack.

"Did Sam go up?" I asked Jeremy as he entered the kitchen.

"He's in his bedroom with the door shut."

"You think we hurt his feelings?"

Jeremy only shrugged and removed a bottle of water from the fridge. After Jamie had a carton of yogurt, I asked Jeremy to watch him so I could lie down and rest before time to fix supper.

It wasn't like Sam to snap at us. Today wasn't the first time I noticed his moodiness. He wasn't feeling well and didn't look healthy. I decided to set an appointment with our family physician, Dr. Simmons. Something was going on with Sam and Jamie needed his booster shots before school resumed in August.

The Third Year in the House

22

BY THE END of July, Benny quit complaining so much about his broken arm after we presented him with a new video game. And like a responsible mother, I took Sam and Jamie to see Dr. Simmons for checkups. School was approaching fast.

Sam's lab report indicated his white blood count was slightly elevated. To take care of a low-grade infection, Dr. Simmons prescribed a round of antibiotics. With nothing else of concern showing up, I purchased one-a-day vitamins for all of us to take.

School resumed in mid-August, along with our rigid schedules. The female hormone I took daily minimized my physical discomfort. And Sam seemed to feel some better.

Jeremy was in perfect health and loved ministry work. Every Wednesday morning and evening he taught a Bible study. He never complained about long hours of work and visiting the sick and I was relieved he succeeded in ignoring our unwanted guests.

Music was my joy so I was involved with the choir, already practicing our Christmas cantata on Wednesday evenings. I even snagged a solo part. The boys were settling into their fall schedules. Our athletically-inclined Benny was looking forward to playing basketball with his school team as soon as his arm cast came off. Jamie, approaching five, was big into T-ball. Sam, now sixteen, was on the first string of the school's soccer team.

As always during fall, our family spent most Saturday mornings at the boys' sporting events. Life seemed fairly normal at the moment. And I was immensely relieved. No, blessed.

Beverly had phoned a couple of times to report how happy she was married to Terah and was living like a queen in the family castle some twenty kilometers from Alexandria, Egypt. When I had inquired if the Muslims were a problem, she'd changed the subject. I presumed she did not want me to worry. But I did, anyhow. Meanwhile, the media continued to report that Copts were regularly beheaded by terrorists for their Christian beliefs.

Radical Islam was spreading throughout the Middle East and spilling into European nations, crumbling cultures that disagreed with their Islamic tenets. Kill the infidel if they didn't convert.

September came and gave Middle Tennesseans relief from the oppressive lingering heat of August. Cooler October weather was even more welcome. Again the foliage showed off brilliant colors as the days grew shorter. Holidays were just ahead.

Except for a few bumps in the night, like creaky stairs or footfalls down the hall, Gibby's family had been relatively quiet.

Benny's cast came off but Dr. Simmons recommended no sports activities until his left arm gained strength. He was disappointed so we took him to see his team's weekly games.

Jamie, a joyful little boy, was growing like a weed. I couldn't believe we had been living in our farmhouse going on four years.

Becca called to invite our family to celebrate Christ's birth at her house in Birmingham the weekend before Christmas.

"I know it's early, but I want a commitment," she told me.

"Our yearly open house date hasn't been set," I explained, unable to commit until the church calendar events were published.

"Okay, but you don't want to miss seeing Terah and Beverly, do you?" Becca dangled family in front of me.

"When was that decided?" I asked.

"Yesterday," she replied. "Please come."

"We'll try." I would make every effort to be there.

Nearing the end of October, the weather turned nasty a few days before Halloween, spawning sporadic storms. Plans for our fall fest at church were in place but I wasn't confident that the weather would be favorable. However, our congregation had never let hail or high water hinder us before. If the day turned blustery, we would move the event indoors to the Fellowship Hall.

A few days before All Hallows Eve, following our evening meal, Jeremy was with Benny upstairs in his bedroom playing his newest video game. Benny gazed past his dad strangely.

"Dad . . .? Do you know that man standing behind you?"

"What man?" Jeremy jerked his head to the left and felt a hand touch his shoulder. He was suddenly thrown backwards on the floor. Stunned, he sat up and looked at his frightened son.

"There he is!" Benny pointed at the doorway.

"Where . . .?" Jeremy was freaked. Then he heard a phantom door slam. No one was there. "What did you see, Benny?"

"The man's gone now."

"What man?" Jeremy locked eyes with Benny.

"Didn't you see that scary old man?" His cryptic gaze reflected the memory. "He went out the door and disappeared."

Jeremy blinked, concern eroding him. He pulled Benny to his feet. No wonder he didn't like sleeping in his bedroom.

"Let's go downstairs, son." He nudged Benny toward the door. "I'm in the mood for some hot chocolate, how 'bout you?"

Trying to stay calm, Jeremy debated over whether to tell me about the incident since I was already a nervous wreck. But, a couple days later, he decided it was a secret he couldn't keep.

A week later, Benny came bounding down the stairs and into our living room just after the ten o'clock news went off.

"Mom, Dad!" He heaved to catch his breath.

"What's wrong, Benny?" Jeremy approached him.

"She just tried to choke me."

What? I spied the fright in Benny eyes.

"Who tried to choke you?" Jeremy asked.

"That same old woman," he replied. "I can't sleep in my room anymore!" he cried. "Please don't make me, Mom!"

As good parents, we tried our best to convince Benny that there was nowhere anyone could hide in his room. We read Bible scripture to him, like, "He that is within us and stronger than he that is in the world." Jesus would protect him, we promised.

But Benny would have nothing to do with it.

In the following days, we'd tuck Benny into bed at night and say a prayer of protection over him. Then, in the wee hours of the morning, I'd wake up and find him asleep on the floor beside our bed. Jeremy would place him between us in our bed for the remainder of the night. But I couldn't sleep soundly, praying constantly that God would intervene and release us from the terror they perpetrated on us. As parents, we needed to solve Benny's problem. How do you fight what you don't understand?

Benny finally agreed to sleep on a floor pallet in Sam's room.

The first evening I was alone in our bedroom with my husband, I said: "We can't continue like this, Jeremy. Benny will never feel safe again, and we'll all be sick from lack of sleep."

"I hear you, Brooke."

"Well, hear this. We have to change something."

"I know, but I just don't know how."

In preparation for bed, I stood at the sink brushing my teeth as Jeremy walked by. Then I heard the commode flush.

It was the beginning of another horror.

From that night forward when Jeremy passed our two bathrooms, the commodes promptly flushed. A plumber came out and checked both then assured me that automatic flushing without human stimulation was physically impossible. He insisted our rapid-flush commodes required pressing the button on top.

Still, it kept happening. Finally, Jeremy ignored the flushing and went about his business. Eventually, it stopped.

Benny became irrational as the weeks passed. His fear of the old woman escalated. Jeremy agreed that Benny should talk to a professional counselor about mounting fears. We wanted to hire someone outside our community to provide a fresh perspective.

We decided on a psychologist in Nashville, away from anyone who might recognize our family, concerned our congregation would find out and Jeremy's ministry would suffer the consequences. Regardless of how anyone felt, we could not allow Gibby and his family to destroy Benny or chase us out of ministry.

We were fighting back. It was our only recourse.

Dr. Phyllis B. Carter was Benny's child psychologist. She had worked at several hospitals in the northeast before moving to Nashville. To look at her, one would never guess her occupation.

Appearing younger than her forty-five years, Dr. Carter had an athletic build—thanks to regular gym workouts, I'm sure—and a no-nonsense bobbed hairdo. Gazing at me through hazel eyes brimming with intelligence, she immediately had my confidence.

On each visit to the Nashville clinic, we left Benny alone with Dr. Carter for an hour then returned to get him. After several sessions with our boy, she requested a private meeting with us.

The Saturday we drove over to Nashville to meet with Dr. Carter, we'd arranged for a sitter to keep Jamie at the house. Sam had other plans, and we did not want to tell him what we were doing. Although I despised secrets, I didn't want Sam to worry.

I was apprehensive about what Dr. Carter would tell us. Actually, I was as nervous as the proverbial cat on a hot tin roof. I feared what we would learn. But then not knowing would be even worse. Would it be necessary to hospitalize Benny for treatment? As fear mounted, I grasped Jeremy's hand as we checked in with the office manager and took our seats to wait.

"Reverend and Mrs. McLaughlin . . ?"

Dr. Carter received us graciously. "Thank you for coming."

Her smile was genuine and set me at ease. She filled a seat behind a polished desk cluttered with file folders.

"You have a very interesting son, Reverend McLaughlin."

"Is that a good report?" Jeremy locked eyes on me.

"Yes, I've thoroughly enjoying my sessions with Benny." She gazed at us through the lens of her horn-rimmed spectacles.

"He certainly has a vivid imagination." Jeremy cleared his throat, nervously chuckling. I was too frightened to comment.

"That's what I wanted to talk to you folks about . . ."

"Do you think Benny is mentally ill?" Jeremy inquired.

"On the contrary, I believe he's telling the truth."

You do? I thought but didn't say.

"Every time that I asked Benny to repeat an experience he detailed what happened in exactly the same way."

"Okay," I jumped in, "what does that mean?"

"I believe your son is a *sensitive*," Dr. Carter reported. "He's spiritually open to what people normally don't experience."

I nodded to Jeremy that I agreed.

"Benny's not insane, rather a scared little boy," she added. "Have either of you experienced supernatural encounters?"

"Just the normal bumps that haunt an old house," I said, not the whole truth. Jeremy had felt something in Benny's room.

"Well, I recommend we treat Benny for anxiety."

"Meds," Jeremy said. "He's only eleven."

"Your son needs to calm down. He's traumatized over his visions. You've probably noticed he's lost focus—his grades aren't as good as they were. His eating habits may have changed."

"What did Benny's report card show?" Jeremy asked me.

"He's dropped from A's to C's in several subjects."

"Why didn't you tell me that, honey?"

"I just figured school was getting harder," I replied.

"I didn't mean to start World War III," B. Carter interrupted. "Let me give you a prescription. Fill it, put Benny on the tablets then report back to me in thirty days if you notice a difference."

"What about therapy sessions?" I asked.

"Let's suspend them for now, shall we?"

"That's it?" I said.

"You can settle your bill with Gail at the front desk."

Jeremy wrote a check so we wouldn't have to file insurance on Benny. We needed to keep our unique situation private.

I considered if anything worse happened to Benny if he would mentally survive. As a mom, what *could* I do against these sadistic spirits? Except for Jesus, I was totally helpless.

23

WE WERE SET to spend the weekend before Christmas with Gary and Becca in Birmingham. It had taken some arranging but we'd pulled off a few free days. I was excited about seeing both my sisters. But at the last minute, Beverly phoned Becca and begged off due to an influenza bug she was sharing with Terah.

I was annoyed that Beverly hadn't called me, too. But our baby sister had always looked up to Becca, the eldest in our family. I'd have to live with that, though sometimes it hurt my feelings.

Honestly, I never expected the newlyweds to return to the states so soon. On a positive note, Bev had mentioned to Becca she hoped to be pregnant soon. Married to Egyptian royalty, producing an heir was expected. A male preferably, but I knew if Beverly gave birth to a female she would be delighted.

We arrived at Becca's late Thursday and settled into one of their three guest bedrooms in their impressive two-story colonial house. Jamie slept in Sam's room while Benny had his own space.

Becca and I spent Friday downtown, doing some last minute shopping and enjoying a lunch out while the guys took our boys to the public park to view the elaborate Christmas decorations.

The day passed entirely too quickly. By the time we finished supper, the sun had set hours ago. Becca and I were enjoying a cup of decaf coffee in the living room in front of a roaring fire.

"I forgot to ask how your open house went." Becca peered at me as our guys retreated to Gary's office. My boys were in the game room, playing a video on the big-screen TV.

"Open House went great!" I replied. "We had over two hundred souls pass through our portals." *Not counting ghosts.*

"It must be a relief to have that challenge behind you."

"I'll be even more relieved when Christmas is over."

"It's a reminder of Mom's death." Becca nodded.

"We didn't celebrate last Christmas on Christ's birthday," I revealed. "Did you?" So much we had not spoken about. . .

"No, we were en route to Henderson on Wednesday." Becca peered at me. "When did your family open Christmas gifts?"

"On Sunday, the day after Mom was buried. The boys had already sneaked a look at a few of their gifts, but celebrating late didn't have the same excitement." I fell silent with recall.

"We need to stay positive about Christ's birthday," Becca reminded me. "It's not about us, Brooke. It's about faith."

"I know." I sniffled a bit. "This year I want our children to forget about their problems and just enjoy Christmas."

"That's an odd comment, what's going on?"

"Nothing I care to discuss right now—by the way, the cheesy baked lasagna we had for supper was the best!"

Becca respected my privacy then said, "It's our Aunt Lily's recipe. Didn't you get her latest cookbook?"

"I have it somewhere . . ." my mind hadn't exactly been on cooking since Jeremy and I had thought of nothing but Benny's mental health and how to help him resolve his fear.

"I guess I should clear away the dishes," Becca said.

"Can I help?" I stood and stretched my stiff body.

"Sure, bring everything from the dining room."

Master of her own kitchen, Becca scurried circles around me while she loaded the dishwasher. Meanwhile, I hand-washed and dried the pots and pans, stowing them in their proper cabinets.

"I'm so glad you came, Brooke. I couldn't bear going through another holiday season without seeing my family in the flesh."

We both knew our every holiday wish hadn't been fulfilled. Beverly's absence from our gathering further created a hole in our hearts. To fill the void, Becca and I planned to view a movie of Mom and Dad's funeral services prepared by the funeral home.

"Beverly's happy, I guess that's what really counts," I said.

"I just wish they were here." Becca rested wet hands on the edge of the sink. "Do you think the influenza was an excuse?"

"I've never known our sister to lie," I pointed out.

"I suppose she's blissfully happy," Becca noted. "I've heard nothing negative out of her mouth regarding the marriage."

"Maybe I was wrong about them."

"How so?" Becca asked.

"Oil and water do not mix." I laughed.

"You said that to her?" Becca reacted.

"Goodness, no, food for thought for Jeremy's ears only!" I laughed. "Who wouldn't be happy—a honeymoon in Greece then a tour across the Aegean Sea? Back home to a sheik's castle?"

"Hey, you know it takes more than a great trip or a castle to keep a marriage intact!" Becca huffed. "But, Bev seems happy."

I looked at my sister and wondered if there was a fly in her marriage batter. She seldom spoke of her relationship with Gary, more often complaining about their busy work schedules.

"Well, that's that! Dishes are done for another day."

"I'm about to pop." I patted my stomach.

Becca agreed we'd all eaten too many calories.

"I hate to see you leave tomorrow," she said.

"All good things must come to an end," I stoically stated.

We'd be gone from home since Thursday and would travel home tomorrow afternoon to be present in church on Sunday.

"Wonder if the football game's over?" Becca mused.

Our guys were still up in the office watching a playoff between Atlanta and Tennessee. "I'm going to check."

"Hey, Mom!" Sam stuck his head into the kitchen. "Benny's acting up and Jamie's screaming. Can you help?"

"Go, do the mom thing," Becca told me.

"Where is Benny?" I asked Sam as we walked down the hall.

"He's up in his bedroom, acting nuts—looking in closets and under the bed," Sam reported. "He swears he heard something, uh, *funny* while he was in the bathroom. You know . . ."

I did know. His imagination was in full bloom.

I found Benny seated in the middle of the bed, his knotted fists pressed into his eye sockets, tears streaming down his cheeks.

"Tell me what happened." I cautiously approached him.

Shaking his head, he unfolded his body like an accordion and stood up on the bed. "They followed me here!" he belted out. "I can't see them but I know they're here somewhere. I hate them!"

"Sit down, Benny, before you fall off the bed."

"Mom! It's that same old woman that lives in our house!" He leaped off the bed and paced the bedroom like a caged tiger.

"Benny, that can't be true." I reasoned with him. "We're safe here. Did you take the meds I gave you last night?"

"Make them go away, Mom!" he screamed.

"What in the world?" Jeremy bolted into the room and spied Benny's tirade. "Son, what is wrong with you? Why are you so upset?" he mouthed to me, "*Did you give him his meds?*"

I opened the palm of my hand, holding another dose. "He isn't due to take them until ten." It was nine thirty.

"Well, give them to him now!" Jeremy sat down on the bed and pulled Benny into his lap. "Son, I need for you to calm down. Nobody's after you. Aunt Becca's house is perfectly safe."

Is it really? I wondered. *Or can they attach to us and follow?*

When Benny settled down, I went into the bathroom, retrieved a paper cup of water and brought it into the bedroom. Jeremy handed Benny the pills and told him to swallow them.

"I'll take it from here," Jeremy said to me.

Sam stood in the hall watching the whole episode. When I came out of the bedroom he closed the door behind me.

"Do you think Benny will be okay?"

"I don't know, Sam. He's pretty messed up."

I went downstairs to the den where Becca was rocking little Jamie to sleep as she viewed an old silent western flick. Gary was kicked back in the recliner and snoring gourds. I removed Jamie from her arms and quietly thanked her. "I'll put him to bed."

"Are we going to watch the funeral video?" she asked.

"Not tonight." I nodded at Gary. "Maybe you should put your husband to bed, too." Jamie was a heavy chunk in my arms.

"Naw, this is a preparatory nap," Becca piped. "He'll wake up—never misses the 10:00 o'clock news and weather forecast."

"See you in the morning." I trudged up the stairs and laid Jamie in Sam's bed then raised the safety bar I'd brought with us. He was still small enough to roll off the bed during the night.

Seconds later, I heard water running and knew Sam was in the hall bathroom prepping for bed. As soon as Jamie was asleep, I tiptoed out of the room and walked a few steps down the hall.

"Thanks, Sam," I called out through the partially open bathroom door. "You did great tonight, I'm proud of you."

"What did I do?" he asked with a mouthful of foaming toothpaste as he nudged the door open with a bare foot.

"You alerted me to Benny's tirade—poor kid is terrified of shadows." I shook my head, clueless how to help him.

"Mom, we're all terrified, or don't you get it?"

Huh? I did a double take.

"The last thing I want to do tomorrow is go home to that house and those awful people!" He swiped saliva from his mouth with a small towel. "Aren't you scared, too?"

I was but instead said, "They're not real people, Sam, just images of what once was. They can't do anything serious to us."

"Except torment us, you mean." Sam shoved past me.

I didn't believe anything I said would make one iota of difference. Trembling with tears poised to flow, I prayed for a full minute that God would allow us leave our haunted residence. I no longer had the will to fight them. As parents, we were failing to protect our children. There was something evil that had taken root in that house. Our boys were too innocent to survive.

24

COUNTING STOPS, IT took four hours to drive home on Saturday. While Jeremy went inside the house to turn off the alarm system and the two younger boys napped, I turned in my seat to face Sam. After Benny's outburst last night at Becca's, and the fact he'd been chased by Gibby's green orb the day we visited the old cemetery, I thought it was time I shared Jeremy's and my supernatural experiences in our house. "Sam, are you okay?"

"I guess." He shrugged. "Not so much," he added.

"Sam, I know the way Benny's been acting bothers you."

"Well, yeah . . ." he made a face.

"I think you should know your dad and I have had problems with Gibby's family, too." Admitting we had ghosts was hard. I told him about the ringing doorbell with no batteries, and the sliding covers off my body and the little girl's cries in the night.

"I knew it Mom!" He slapped his leg. "We got ghosts!"

"Sam, do you recall that day it stormed just before Halloween? We had all that wind damage in our yard."

Sam did, so I told him about the day his dad came home early to make sure a tornado hadn't struck our house.

"He found those heavy lace curtains on the windows at the top of the staircase torn from the rods and lying on the landing."

"Was a window broken?" Sam asked. "Was it the wind?"

"No broken windowpanes and the security system had been operating during the entire storm," I revealed.

"Mom, that's crazy."

"Plus, the curio cabinet and storage bin against the wall were overturned and their contents spilled twenty feet across the floor."

"No way!!" Sam slapped his leg again. "That freaks me."

"Me, too," I confessed. Sam was old enough to realize God *is* our protector, our Life-giver, and our Savior. If Jeremy and I never teach our children another lesson, it has to be faith in God.

I spied Jeremy at the door, waving me to come inside.

"Stay with the boys," I told Sam.

"Okay, but keep the motor running. It's freezing."

I hopped out of the SUV and hurried inside. Our sacks of groceries sat on the floor by the door. On our way through town we'd stopped at McDonald's and bought sandwiches, although there were frozen containers of soups and leftovers in our freezer.

I hurried down the hall to find Jeremy then realized he must be upstairs checking on our intruders. I walked through the kitchen into the dining room, the study, and came out in the foyer.

He was waiting for me there. "Any sign of trouble?"

"All's quiet on the home front, let's bring in the boys."

"Wait. You should know I told Sam about the curtains."

"Brooke? Okay, how did he take it?"

"He knows something bad is going on in our house."

Jeremy nodded, no other comment needed.

* * *

Sunday morning came in cold with overcast skies. Frost speckled our windowpanes. Contrasting last winter's holiday season, no snow was forecast for the next seven days. With Christmas falling on Thursday, today would be the last Sunday service before we celebrated Jesus' birthday. However, Jeremy would hold the community Advent Service on Christmas Eve.

We followed protocol on Sunday, including afternoon naps and seasonal movies served with popcorn after supper. No supernatural events occurred over the weekend, thank God.

Monday arrived and the boys slept in late. Gratefully, school would not resume until the first full week in January. After the boys had cereal for breakfast, I sent them outside to the shed to work on their airplane projects with Sam's supervision.

Jeremy had gone to the county hospital to visit sick church members. My job was to hold down the fort and entertain the boys. While they were occupied outdoors, I cleaned house and wrapped a few last-minute presents I'd purchased in Birmingham.

Later in the morning, I stirred up a big bowl of sugar cookie dough, and the two younger boys helped me cut out Christmas shapes to bake. Sam didn't feel well and went to bed for a nap.

When the cookies had cooled, I helped Benny and Jamie decorate them with various colored icing. Jeremy was home by mid-afternoon and we chilled out by the fire, each with a book in our hand. Monday schmoozed by with little effort.

Tuesday, I drove the boys into town to rent movies for the week. We lunched at the Pizza Parlor and I took them bowling afterwards. So went the first three days of Christmas week.

Wednesday, the boys and I met Jeremy at the church for our Christmas Eve service. The women's organization had beautifully decorated the sanctuary with fresh pine greenery and red poinsettias. Burning candles crouched on every window ledge.

At the front was a half-sized manger scene perched on a long table in front of the pulpit. Jeremy and the choir director stepped on the stage, signaling for the organist to play her prelude.

Two youngsters wearing white robes welcomed the Holy Spirit as they ignited the candelabras at the front of the church.

At the choir director's prompting, the choir stood and we all sang *Away in a Manger*. Then the congregation celebrated Advent with the partaking of the Lord's Supper as directed by Jeremy.

Jamie was in the nursery. Sam and Benny were seated further back, distancing themselves from parents. Seated on the third row pew, I sensed something amiss when Jeremy lost focus on what he was saying, licked his lips often, and seemed confused.

I turned around in my seat to see what had grabbed his attention. Even more alarming, Benny shot up out of seat near the back and was walking down the outer aisle toward the front of the church. My heart quickened as he sat down on the first pew.

What was going on? Whatever it was had upset Jeremy, too. I prayed for both of them. Hurrying to conclude the service, Jeremy regained enough composure to finish his remarks.

As people came forward to kneel at the front of the church, and pray for the arrival of a new year, I moved to the side of the organ. Then I sang *O Holy Night* followed by the congregation hymn, *Silent Night*. Jeremy said a closing prayer and lit a candle.

From the single flame, the light was passed through the congregation until the dark auditorium sparkled with tiny lights. As our congregation left the sanctuary in silence, flames were snuffed out. Afterwards, families picked up dozens of cookies to be delivered to those working on Christmas Eve—to businesses like Dollar General, gas stations, and other mom-and-pop local businesses. Meanwhile, I made my way to the front of the church.

Jeremy and Benny were involved in an intense conversation. "What's wrong, son? Did something bad happen?" I asked.

"Mom!" Benny was trembling. "That man, back there. . . ."

"What man?" I spun around to see who he was talking about.

"He's gone now—he's evil, Mom!"

Benny's speech was clipped. He was terribly upset.

"You should've seen him, Mom. He was tearing pages out of a song book and then he started ripping up a Bible."

"Benny, stop a second," Jeremy interrupted. "Are you sure?"

"Yeah, Dad, come back with me and I'll show you."

Jeremy's dreaded expression locked on me as the three of us walked toward the back of the sanctuary. "Here?" I pointed.

"No," Benny answered, glancing at the rows of seats.

"Where was this man sitting?" Jeremy inquired.

Benny gazed down every empty pew as he walked from the back of the auditorium toward the front. "Here, Dad. He was right behind me." Benny pointed to the pew where he was seated.

I slid into the pew and began checking in the backseat pockets of the pew in front of me, looking for torn song sheets and saw none. "Benny, there's nothing here," I told him.

Jeremy sidled up to our son and hugged him. "Did you fall asleep, was I that boring?" He minimized the incident.

"No, Dad! I saw that man! He was right there!"

"Brother Mac . . ."

Jeremy turned and faced our custodian. "Yes, Jim."

"Folks are gone. Do you want me to close up and set the alarm?" Jim asked. "Or do you wanna do it when you leave?"

"We're leaving now, Jim. Check the classrooms and make sure no one stays behind then set the alarm on your way out."

We found Sam in the foyer talking to some friends. Betty who worked with children's ministries was standing by the door, holding Jamie's hand. "Thanks." I took charge of him.

"No problem. George is waiting in the car for me."

Betty went out the side door.

"Sam? Are you ready to go?" I asked. "Jim's locking up."

Jeremy ushered Benny out the back door as he grumbled, "Dad, I really did see that man. Why don't you believe me?"

"Get in the Chevy, son, you're riding with me."

"Why don't you believe me, Dad?"

"I believe you saw something, Benny." Jeremy waved me off. "We'll talk more when we're alone. Okay?"

I was home with Sam and Jamie before Jeremy arrived with Benny. I assumed they were having a father-son chat. Sam went straight to his bedroom to get ready for bed. I gave Jamie a bath and put him to bed. Then I went downstairs to the kitchen.

Jeremy arrived fifteen minutes later with little to say while Benny snagged a Sprite from the fridge and bounded the stairs to his bedroom. Christmas Eve was supposed to be a serene event.

I was settled down in the living room with a cup of hot cocoa when Jeremy joined me. "I wish I could say I did a good job with the sermon," he offered as he collapsed on the sofa next to me.

"The service—beautiful but you seemed, uh, distracted." He stole my cup of cocoa and swallowed some sips.

"I don't recall ever forgetting a sermon, Brooke."

"I admit it's not like you." I reclaimed my hot chocolate.

"I drew a blank a couple times and lost track of where I was," Jeremy recalled. "That's why I ended the service so quickly."

"People probably didn't notice." I tried to be kind. "Do you think your distraction had anything to do with the man Benny thought he saw?" Evil, our son said—tearing pages out of a Bible.

"I don't know." He seemed to wilt in front of me.

I nodded with nothing constructive to offer.

"I've been very happy at this church, how 'bout you?"

"The people here are the best," I replied.

"We've been here three, going on four years and—"

I sat up, startled. "Wait, Jeremy, have you been assigned to a new congregation? Is that where you're going with this?"

"No, no," he said. "But I'm rethinking selling this house."

"It's not a healthy environment to raise our boys."

Jeremy's mouth set in a downward curve like he needed for me to decide. "Maybe we just need a vacation," I suggested.

"But we just got home from Becca's," he countered.

"I know, but you have the rest of the week off."

He nodded, twisting his lips in consideration of the idea.

"Joe Norwood said we could use his cabin in the Smoky Mountains anytime we wanted." I'd seen pictures of Joe and Mary Ellen's beautiful chalet overlooking Gatlinburg, Tennessee.

"We could leave late tomorrow morning after we've opened our presents," I embellished my proposal. "Please, Jeremy."

"What about Christmas dinner?"

Jeremy was old school when it came to tradition.

"We'll eat before we go and take some turkey sandwiches with us." I became more excited. "I hear there's a fresh layer of snow on the ground and Benny will love it—Sam and Jamie, too!"

"Is this about distracting Benny?"

"It gets us out of this house for a few more days," I replied. "I saw no evidence of torn pages from a song book or Bible to support Benny's claim, did you? Do you think he had a vision?"

"Of evil intent, you mean?" Jeremy calculated the possibility. "Maybe, Benny's always been tuned into spiritual matters."

I nodded. "Good and evil, like Dr. Carter said."

"Okay, I'll check my email messages in the morning, and if no emergency arises at church, we'll drive to the Smokies."

"Great!" I exclaimed. "We'll have so much fun the boys will forget about spooks." I noticed he was frowning. "What?"

"Why do I feel like we're running away from Gibby?"

I laughed. Gibby sounded funny coming from his mouth.

As the hour approached midnight, I called our two older boys downstairs to the living room for our traditional family Christmas Eve service. Jeremy read the story of Christ's birth from Luke then prayed for our family. Before I sent the boys to bed, we all pigged out on hot chocolates and decorated Christmas cookies.

After tidying the kitchen and making a list of food and clothing items to take with us to the mountains, I slipped into bed beside Jeremy, already fast asleep with visions of sugarplums dancing in his head. I prayed no ghosts tonight, please!

Remarkably, I instantly slept.

25

CHRISTMAS MORNING FEATURED gloomy overcast skies as a snowy front rode in on the heels of a humid barometric low barreling out of the Gulf of Mexico. I was up and switching on the tree lights in the living room while Jeremy ventured upstairs to wake the boys. It wasn't long before I heard a stampede of feet.

"Merry Christmas!" the boys exclaimed and gave me hugs.

While Sam separated the gifts in five piles, I fixed five mugs of hot cocoa and topped them off with mushy marshmallows. Jeremy helped me carry the drinks into the living room. "Careful, boys," I teasingly warned, "no spills or Santa Claus might notice."

Jamie typically drank from a "Big Boy" cup." It was cute watching how carefully he handled the grownup mug too large for his small hands, as if it were my best china and might break.

"Big Boys don't spill," I reminded Jamie.

Once everyone had clicked mugs to toast Christ's birth, we downed our beverages. It was time to open our gifts.

Benny received a set of remote-controlled race cars and a new video game. Jamie squealed over his little-boy bike with training wheels and rode it up and down the long hallway like James Bond.

Sam rejoiced when he tore into his package and spied the most updated iPad. In addition, we presented our two younger boys with the electric motor required to fly their two model airplanes constructed over many months. Other gifts included table games and new clothes that our growing boys needed.

Seeing the joy on their faces made me happy.

Jeremy gave me a diamond pendant on a gold chain and a new velvet robe the shade of a ruby. He loved his new iPhone with more capabilities than NASA had in the 1980s. We were all content with our gifts and sat around in the living room talking and laughing for an hour until Benny complained of being hungry.

After a country ham and pancake breakfast, I called for cleanup help in the living room, cautioning Jeremy and the boys to save the reusable paper, boxes, and ribbons for next Christmas.

Afterwards, we gathered in the living room for a powwow.

"Am I in trouble?" Benny piped. "What did I do?"

I laughed, "No, Benny, Dad has something he wants to discuss with our family." I looked over at him. *Your turn . . .*

Jeremy cleared his throat. "Mom and wondered if you boys wanted to take a trip with us to the Smokey Mountains?"

"What can we do up there?" Benny asked.

"Well, you can have fun," Jeremy replied. "Mr. Joe from our church has a chalet overlooking Gatlinburg, Tennessee, and said we could borrow it anytime we wanted." He glanced at Brooke.

"Gatlinburg has a sky lift and walking trails."

"Your mom talked to Joe and he said 'Go for it!'"

"Whut does 'go-fer-it' mean?" Five-year-old Jamie asked.

"It means we can spend the night at Mr. Joe's cabin if we want to," Sam told his little brother. "You'll have fun."

"After our Christmas lunch, we'll pack up and go," I said. "There's fresh snow on the mountains so some of us can ski."

"Can we take our sleds, too?" Benny shot up his hand.

"Sure," I said. "What about you, Sam?"

"I think I'll stay home, if that's okay."

Jeremy blinked with surprise. "Is there a reason you don't want to go with us on a short trip, Sam?"

"No, it's not that . . ." he bit his lower lip.

"Then what is it, Sam?" I probed.

He shrugged. "I guess I'm just not up to the long ride."

I gazed at Jeremy then Sam. "Well, if you want to stay home, I see no reason why you can't. You're sixteen and know how to take care of yourself as well as I do." But I was disappointed.

"Is it okay with you, Dad . . .? If I stay home alone . . .?" Sam asked. "I have some reading I need to do for school."

"No problem," he agreed. "You can phone if you need us."

"Can I take my remote cars?" Benny was pumped.

"No, you'll be too busy doing other things," Jeremy said. "But take your Game-Boy for the ride." He tossed Jamie over one shoulder. "Meanwhile, I'll get this little guy ready to go."

As Jeremy headed up the stairs with Benny scampering in front of him, I put together a shorter version of Christmas dinner.

By eleven thirty we were gathered at the dining room table. Jeremy's favorite recipe was Aunt Lily's cornbread dressing served with baked turkey. My sides were sweet potato casserole, stir-fried green beans, fruit salad, rolls and sweet tea. The boys wanted to wrap up all the desserts and take them with us on our trip.

I left Sam a slice of pecan pie and a container of Christmas cookies to munch on. There were plenty of leftovers in the fridge if he got hungry. He'd be fine, I told myself, a bit concerned.

We left the house at one o'clock in the Suburban. Benny and Jamie settled in the backseat, playing with their electronic gizmos.

As Jeremy drove I-40 toward Gatlinburg, the swishing windshield wipers shoved the melting snowflakes out of the way. He was quiet and after a big meal, probably wished he had a nap.

Meanwhile, I considered Sam's reason for not coming. Lately, his complexion was pale and he ate very little. He was losing weight. I feared something dreadful was wrong with him.

I needed to know, so I resolved then and there to set another doctor's appointment for him. God is our healer, ultimately.

* * *

We had a great time in Gatlinburg. Back home by nine Saturday evening, we discovered Sam was already in bed asleep.

Wired from too much Christmas candy, Jamie had difficulty falling asleep so I read him two Christmas stories instead of one.

Benny refused to sleep in his own bed again, so we let him watch television in our bedroom until we grew sleepy.

"Benny, it's time for you to go upstairs," Jeremy told him.

"Do I have to?" He snuggled between us under the covers.

"Benny, I need room to sleep, too," I teased.

"Son, no one's going to hurt you in your room," Jeremy said.

He was referring to the old woman who repeatedly appeared in Benny's bedroom. "Your dad's right, she can't hurt you."

"She chokes me sometimes," Benny said.

I looked at Jeremy for an opinion. He said, "Okay, Benny, I'll make you a pallet on the floor beside Sam's bed."

"No, I want to sleep here." Benny hugged the covers.

We were getting nowhere with him. "Okay, I'll go up and sleep in Benny's bed," I offered a solution.

"No, Benny and I will work this out." Jeremy picked up Benny and carried him down the hall and up the stairs.

I heard Benny loud protests and cringed, hoping he would not wake up Jamie. But that's exactly what happened. Our youngest started screaming to the top of his lungs. Oh, brother.

I scampered up the stairs to help out. By this time Sam was fully awake, standing outside Jamie's room, curious about what was going on. It took a while to settle everyone down. It was after midnight before Jeremy and I crawled in our own bed.

* * *

Sunday morning, my phone alarm went off at 6:30 a.m., sending me straight to my feet. I shut it off with a limp hand.

Grabbing my new ruby-red robe, I tugged it on and walked barefoot across the hall into the kitchen to switch on the coffeemaker. Seconds later, I heard Jeremy in the bathroom.

After perusing the fridge contents, I hauled out a gallon of milk to the counter and profoundly yawned. A bowl of cereal would have to suffice in order to get to church in time for the first service at 8:15. Pouring myself a cup of Joe, I yawned again.

Sam came dragging down the stairs last, sniffling with a head cold. After pouring himself a glass of orange juice, he turned to me and said, "Mom, I feel too bad to go to church today."

"Do you have a fever?" I felt Sam's forehead. "You're warm and clammy." I got the thermometer from my bathroom cabinet and came back into the kitchen to check his temp. He had 101 F.

"Guess I have the flu," Sam said, bedraggled and sleepy-eyed.

"You had your influenza shot in October." I reminded him. "I'm going to get you an appointment with Dr. Simpson. Meanwhile, take these two Tylenol capsules and go back to bed."

Sam gulped the meds down with OJ and bypassed breakfast. I stood at the foot of the stairs as he went up to make sure he didn't stumble and fall. He was a pretty sick puppy.

"I have to leave now, Brooke," Jeremy called out.

"Okay, Sam's sick so I'll bring the two boys with me." I caught up with him in the foyer and kissed him on the cheek.

"You look nice and smell even better," I said.

"Amazing what a bar of soap and a shave can do for a guy."

"See you later, love." I returned to the kitchen.

"Can I stay home with Sam?" Benny asked. "I'm tired."

"I guess—if you promise not to disturb him. Sam's sick and needs his rest." I had no strength left in me to argue.

When I'd finished putting my kitchen back in order, I quickly dressed and called Jamie down from his bedroom. When we arrived at the church, the organist was already playing the prelude.

I left Jamie off at his class and entered the auditorium five minutes late. The choir was already in place and Alice Jacobs mouthed to me, "Why aren't you singing, Brooke?"

I waved my hand at her and looked for a seat. The greeter was reading off the names of the sick and hospitalized as I located a space near the back of the sanctuary. I noticed Jeremy staring at me, probably wondering where Benny was. I just shook my head.

Call me paranoid, but I looked around the church for a strange man that might fit Benny's description: the creep that tore out pages from the song book and Bible. He wasn't there.

Half paying attention to Jeremy's sermon, I barely managed to stay awake. As much as our family needed a trip to the mountains, it had taken its toll on us. I dozed off twice.

After the service, Alice came over to talk to me.

"Do you have laryngitis?" she queried.

"It's just some minor sinus problems," I replied.

"We missed your pretty voice in choir this morning."

"Sorry, we were struggling to get here after getting to bed so late last night." I looked a wreck and I was frowning.

"Yeah, I heard your family took a trip to the mountains."

"Good to know the church grapevine is functioning."

"Is something wrong, Brooke?" Alice asked as she walked me down the hall. "You seem distracted, not like yourself lately."

We were good enough friends for her to pry.

"I'm just really tired," I said. "Sam is sick and Benny was so tired from the trip he stayed home, too. We'll be fine," I added.

"Okay, no more prying." Alice forced a smile. "I'll be in town on Tuesday to shop for groceries, think you can meet me?"

"I'm not sure, the boys are home."

"Brooke, I need to talk to you."

"Oh. Okay. Are we talking about lunch?"

"Yes, let's meet at the Coffee Shack on Main."

"Fine, I'll see you there."

What is that about? I questioned as Alice walked away.

"What was that all about?"

I turned around and faced Jeremy. "Are you a mind-reader? I was just thinking that myself. Alice was pretty mysterious."

"Mysterious," he chuckled. "She did seem a bit intense," he noted with a twist of his lips. "I didn't see Willard here, did you?"

"She insisted I meet her in town on Tuesday."

"Did Alice say what was bothering her?"

"Not a clue." Our eyes were locked.

"What's even stranger, on our way home from the mountains while you were napping, Willard phoned me on my cell and set up an appointment for ten a.m. tomorrow. He wants to talk."

Humph . . . but before I had a chance to comment, Jamie burst from his classroom and nearly knocked me down.

"Slow down, son, you're going to hurt somebody."

"Mom, Mom, look at my drawing?" Jamie held up a sheet of white construction paper featuring a huge orange pumpkin.

"It's very nice, Jamie. But Halloween has already passed, so why didn't you draw a Christmas tree or a pretty angel?"

"Cause they're not as scary," he replied. "Oooo . . ." he mimicked a ghost with waving hands and twittering fingers.

"Enough, Jamie . . .!" I placed my hand over his mouth. "We'll talk about your picture when we get home."

"Where's Benny?" Jeremy asked me.

"He stayed home with Sam," I replied.

Jeremy gave me that 'You shouldn't have' look.

"Benny said he was tired, so I let him."

"I guess you're not staying for the late service." Jeremy grabbed Jamie's hand and walked us down the hall to his office. After closing the door, he asked Jamie: "Why a pumpkin, son?"

He stuck a thump in his mouth and clammed up.

"Jamie told me it was scary," I informed Jeremy.

"Did something scare you, Jamie?" Jeremy asked.

"Can I have a lollipop now?"

Jeremy gave me a look and shook his head.

"Sure," I said. "Take some home for your brothers."

"I guess I'll see you at home around 12:30?" Jeremy looked at me. "Should I bring lunch home?" Jeremy asked.

"No, there are plenty of leftovers in the fridge."

I slipped into my long woolen coat and began helping Jamie with his. It was time to go home and wait for another shoe to fall.

26

AFTER CHURCH I found Sam asleep in his bed and Benny seated on a beanbag in his bedroom playing his new video game.

I glanced into his room. "You okay, son?"

He continued playing as he said, "She didn't come."

"Excuse me?" I stepped into his bedroom.

He looked straight at me. "The old woman didn't come."

I knew exactly what Benny meant. "Okay." I didn't want to set off a bombshell. "I'll be downstairs working on lunch."

I purposely left Benny's door open then walked down the hall to see how Sam was doing. His forehead felt even warmer than earlier so I trekked downstairs for a glass of water and the Tylenol.

I waited for Sam to come out of the bathroom. He slumped past me, still wearing pajamas. "How do you feel, Sam?"

"Terrible." He climbed in bed and pulled up the covers.

"I want you to take two more Tylenol."

"Okay." He set up and swallowed them. "I'm freezing."

"It isn't cold in the house, Sam. You still have fever."

I removed the thermometer from its tube as Sam opened his mouth to cup it under his tongue. After a full minute I read the results: 103 F. He needed to see a doctor today.

"Okay, we're taking a trip to the walk-in clinic this afternoon as soon as you feel like getting up," I said.

He moaned and rolled over in the bed.

"I'll get you some extra cover."

"Thanks, Mom." He uncontrollably shivered.

"Try to sleep, son." I quietly closed the door behind me.

Jeremy arrived home shortly after one o'clock and shed his coat. "Is Sam feeling any better?" he inquired.

"He had a 103 temp when I last checked," I replied. "After we have lunch, I'm going to drive Sam to the walk-in clinic and let a doctor examine him. He might need an antibiotic."

"That's a good idea," Jer agreed. "What about Benny?"

"In his room playing his new video game," I replied. "Oh, he said the old woman didn't come." Jeremy failed to comment.

"I'll get him." He walked down the hall and called up the stairs. "Benny! Come on down, it's time for lunch."

Jamie was playing with a toy truck on the kitchen table while I warmed up lunch. I handed him some Saltines to munch on.

Missing Sam, our family gathered at the table and Jeremy blessed our food. I was hungry and ate my fair portion of leftover turkey and dressing with sweet-potato casserole.

"Second service go okay?" I looked at Jer.

"Yep, my mind worked perfectly." He chuckled.

"I expected no less." I recalled his loss of focus when Benny shot out of his seat at the back of the church, thinking he saw a man tearing up a songbook and Bible. "No, no, Jamie."

Our youngest had crumbled his roll on the floor. I glanced at Benny, quiet as a church mouse. "Can I go now?"

"You didn't finish eating," I told him.

"I'm done." Benny shot out of his chair and left the kitchen.

"Don't do that, Jamie!" I snatched his toy truck away from him. "The wheels will scar the tabletop." I was fit to be tied.

"I know you're worried about Sam." Jeremy reached for my hand. "Chill out, Mama. I'll take care of the cleanup."

"Thanks. I'll fetch him and head on over to the clinic."

* * *

Sam leaned back in the Malibu's passenger seat, half-sleeping as I turned on Fourth Street, hoping I wouldn't be ticketed for an illegal left turn. I parked the car and we hurried inside the clinic.

The nurse on call recognized Sam's condition and ushered him through a door to see the doctor as I presented Sam's medical credentials to the receptionist, thinking I had never seen her before. I read her name tag. "Are you new in town, Tessa?"

"Yes, I am. I moved here with my husband in November from Columbus, Ohio. He's working for a pharmaceutical company out of Nashville," she explained. "We love it here."

"We do, too," I said. "I'm Brooke McLaughlin and my husband is the Methodist minister in town. I'd like to personally invite your family to visit our church on Third Street."

"Oh, that's so nice of you—we used to attend a non-denomination church, but we're not fussy about where we go as long as Christ is preached," she confessed with a smile.

"You can always count on Brother Mac to preach the Bible," I vowed. "Our Sunday morning services are at 8:15 and 10:30 a.m., and we have a nursery for infants. Children under the age of five can attend classes organized by our children's director."

"I have a one-year-old," Tessa reported.

"What's your husband's name?" I inquired as I waited for her to copy Sam's insurance cards. Under thirty, Tessa was an attractive young woman with golden hair and sky-blue eyes.

"Claude Kiel," she said with a smile.

I offered to shake her hand then withdrew it. "Better not shake hands, germs you know." Tessa chuckled at my comment.

The walk-in clinic physician came through a door an hour later to discuss Sam's diagnosis with me. "Mrs. McLaughlin, I'm Dr. James Feller. If you're not in a hurry, I want to run a battery of blood tests on Sam before I prescribe any meds."

"Whatever Sam needs," I responded.

"It appears to be influenza but we can't be too careful."

Careful of what? My mind invented a dozen scenarios, none of them good. All toll, we were in the clinic for nearly two hours.

By then it was approaching 4:30 p.m. and the last threads of light were dissolving on the western horizon. The weather of late had been topsy-turvy, one day in the forties, two days later in the teens. Once in the car, I glanced over at Sam and patted his arm.

"Hang in there, kiddo, one more stop. Then we're headed home, I promise." I drove the car with purpose.

CVS had Sam's medication ready at the pick-up window when we got there. I paid with a credit card and we headed home.

"I'm thirsty, Mom. Can I get a drink somewhere?"

"Sure." I whizzed into a Quick Stop, kept the motor running so Sam would be warm while I ran inside and purchased two Cokes, thinking a cola would sit better on his queasy stomach.

"Thanks, Mom." He uncapped the Coke and took a sip.

We arrived home an hour later and I guided Sam into the house then called out to Jeremy. "Sam needs your help."

Jeremy came into the foyer, his eye on me. "How is our boy?" He wrapped an arm around Sam. "You okay?"

"Help Sam to bed," I said, "he's weak." I noted my husband was limping. "What happened to your knee?" It was bandaged.

"Tripped on Boomer and took a fall in the kitchen." He pointed to a bluish lump on the side of his head. "What did the doctor say about Sam?" Deep circles rimmed his tired eyes.

"Influenza, possibly—Dr. Feller is running a battery of tests to investigate." I held up a bag with Sam's meds. "Right now, our boy needs rest and liquids. We'll get a report on Tuesday."

Relieved to be home, I ventured into the kitchen to make myself a cup of hot herbal tea. While the teapot worked up steam, I popped two vitamin C tabs in my mouth, hoping to fend off any viral germs floating about. The backdoor slammed.

I spun around as Benny bolted into the kitchen. "Hi, Mom, what's to eat?" He rummaged through the fridge.

"Where were you, Benjamin?" I gazed at my middle son.

"In the shed, playing with my model plane," he replied, scouring the crisper drawer and coming up with a bag of carrots.

"Is this all we got left to eat?" he fussed.

"I'll shop for groceries tomorrow. Why don't you nuke some leftover pizza or fix yourself a peanut butter sandwich?"

"Seriously . . .?"

"As serious as I can be at the moment." I threaded my fingers though his thick brown hair. "I'm not cooking tonight."

"That stinks," he yawed.

"Get over it."

Leaving the food choices to Benny, I crossed the hall and spied Jeremy lying on the bed. "Don't tell me you're getting sick, too?" I didn't have the makings of a patient nurse anymore.

"No, not sick, just worn to a frazzle," he replied. "If you don't mind, I'm going to take a quick nap before supper."

"No problem. I'm not cooking, anyhow."

"Since when . . .?" He raised his head from the pillow.

"Hey, bud! Are you conspiring with Benny against me?" I tossed an afghan over him and shut the bedroom door as I left.

With my mug of hot tea in hand, I headed for the living room to emotionally chill out. After igniting the gas flames in the hearth, I did my best to relax on the sofa, spying Jamie in the doorway. "Are you bored, honey? Want me to read to you?"

Always joyful, Jamie ran into the playroom and brought a book back with him. But before we began, Benny ran down the steps and looked over the railing. "Mom, Sam wants you."

I sighed, so much for relaxing.

After giving Sam two Tylenols I helped him to the bathroom. On our way back, I glanced into Benny's room and realized Jamie was seated next to Benny and perfectly content with viewing *Toy Story*. What I needed most was a little quiet time.

When Sam was back in bed, I ventured downstairs to the living room again, grabbed my devotional book from the shelf, and kicked back in the comfy recliner to enjoy the fireplace.

I was on the fourth chapter when Jeremy called out to me.

What now? I spotted my page with a bookmark, set it aside then headed down the hall toward the back of the house.

"Did you need me, Jer?"

"This!" He held up Benny's remote-controlled racecar.

"What about *this?*" I glared at him from the doorway.

"It was running around under my bed," he explained.

"What do you want me to do about it?" *Seriously.*

"If you don't mind, go upstairs and tell the boys to quit running these things around the house. I'm trying to rest."

"Okay."

I trotted down the hall, up the stairs, wishing I had a nickel for every time my foot hit a stair. The boys were driving us both crazy with those remote cars. Glancing into Benny's bedroom, I spied them glued to the TV. Turning around, I trotted down the stairs and down the hall to report my findings to Jeremy.

"Jer, it's not the boys."

"It's got to be them."

"Nope, they're watching *Toy Story.*"

He looked at me funny.

"It's not them," I said. "Besides, I removed the batteries to both racecars and set them on the floor in your office by Jamie's Scooby Doo Castle. You must have been dreaming."

"Brooke, I heard *this* car circling under my bed!" He held it up for me to see. I felt like we were in a shootout standoff.

"Like I said, you must've been dreaming, dearest. Toy cars can't run without batteries—which I'm certain I removed."

"This car . . ." he held it up in his hand, "*was* fully operating and racing under my bed!" He hopped out of bed and trotted past me, purposely prodding down the hall to prove his point.

I trailed after him, inept to deter him.

"I'll see if Benny's put the batteries back in the gizmo and is operating these cars from upstairs," he called back.

So much for a restful Sunday evening . . .

At the doorway to the office, I was met by a thudding noise. My heart quickened as I spied a toy racecar crashing into the Jamie's Scooby Doo Castle then backing up and taking a run at it again. *What in the world?* In disbelief, I froze in my tracks.

Jeremy grabbed the toy car off the floor and checked it for batteries. Holding a car in each hand, he plopped down at his desk and warily glared at me. "See if the remote is turned on."

I nodded and picked up the boxy control unit. "No," I said, blinking back fear. "Nothing runs without batteries."

We glared at one another as we processed the impossible scenario. I was terrified that we were actually awake. With a defeated expression clawing at Jeremy's face, his mouth opened but nothing came out. I just shrugged. No words mattered.

Then Jeremy uttered, "Uh . . . have we both lost all sense of reality, Brooke? You saw them hitting Scooby Doo, right?"

"I can't explain it, Jeremy. It's the house, I guess."

He nodded then placed both silenced cars on his desk. Terrified of what it meant, I heard Sam called out to me.

"Let's talk about this later, Jer."

I hurried upstairs and found Sam in bed sweating buckets, a positive sign the antibiotics were working. I removed a clean pair of underwear and pajamas from the dresser drawer and told him to change in the bathroom while I checked on his two brothers.

"Hi, boys, did you finish the movie?"

"Yeah, when's supper?" Benny asked.

"Didn't you eat a little while ago?"

"I'm still hungry."

"I'm hungry, too," Jamie said. "Can we have hotdogs?"

I glanced at my watch. It was nearly seven. "Let me check on Sam again then we'll go down to the kitchen and see what I can whip up for supper." Hotdogs were a real possibility, if I had any in the freezer. Were there buns? I was mentally on overload.

Downstairs, I ducked into the office and noticed both Jeremy and the racecars were gone. Jer wasn't in our bedroom either.

I later learned he'd boxed them, suspecting they were outside in trashcan never to be dealt with again. By the time I got to the kitchen, Benny and Jamie were already seated at the table.

"What's Dad so mad about?" Benny asked.

"He's just tired." I blew off the question as I snagged two cartons of noncarbonated fruity drinks and handed them out.

A few minutes later, Sam joined us at the table.

"Here, Sam, drink my Coke, it'll settle your stomach," I told my frail teenager whose face was as white as fresh snow.

"Why can't we have Coke, too?" Benny fussed.

"Are you hungry, Sam? How 'bout some soup?"

"No thanks, Mom." He sat down and leaned forward to support his sweaty head with his hands. "I can't eat right now."

"Are you sick at your stomach?" I asked.

"A little," Sam replied.

"You're weak and need nourishment, Sam." I opened a can of Chicken Noodle Soup to warm over the gas stove flame.

Jeremy came dragging into the kitchen and removed a carton of eggs from the fridge and a package of shredded sharp cheese.

"I think an omelet sounds like an easy choice for supper."

"Is that good for you, Benny?" I asked.

"As long as I can have ice cream after that," he negotiated, bringing chuckles from Jamie, who said "Me, too."

"You okay, Mama?" Jeremy eyed me as he tossed in half a cup of chopped onions and added a handful of bacon bits into his concoction. "Trust me, guys. This will be a to-die-for omelet."

"Fine as cat hair," I mused, adopting Aunt Lily's cliché.

"Ugh," Benny grunted and Jamie giggled.

A minute later, the iron skillet was sizzling with butter.

"Okay . . . do you need my help?" I asked Jeremy.

"We guys got it covered." He hoisted Jamie onto a footstool and helped him pour the egg concoction into the skillet. "If you want it hot, Mama, come back in five minutes."

I laughed at the subtle underlying pun.

A few minutes later I stood over our Jacuzzi tub as it filled with steamy water. After adding bubbly gel tabs, I stripped off and slid into my piece of heaven and switched on the jets. A spray of pulsing water slammed into my back muscles as I relaxed after witnessing Gibby's ability to manipulate energy with the racecars.

Sinking deeper into the water, I thanked God Sam was feeling better and mentally shoved aside the racecar incident.

27

THE MONDAY BEFORE New Year's Day on Thursday, Jeremy headed off to the hospital to visit members of our church who were recovering from surgeries and various illnesses. My day's routine kicked in when Benny and Jamie bounded into the kitchen in search of breakfast. Afterwards, they went out to the shed.

The shed was a relatively small free-standing log building with an open fireplace for heating. The owners before us had installed electricity and lights. The space was probably formerly utilized as a kitchen before indoor plumbing was installed in the house proper. It was a perfect playhouse for our boys. And they spent many hours out there constructing their model planes.

Still too weak, Sam didn't come downstairs for breakfast so I prepared a tray for him. Sliced toast, dry, with scrambled eggs, then took it up to his bedroom so we could visit for awhile.

"How are you today, son?" I felt his forehead.

"Better." He sat up and situated the tray on his lap.

"You don't have a temperature and that's encouraging."

Sam bit into the toast then said, "I heard you and Dad down in the office fussing yesterday. What was that about?"

"Oh, Sam, we weren't fussing. It's nothing for you to worry about." I threw open the curtains to invite the sunlight indoors.

"Why can't you tell me why Dad was screaming?"

Was he screaming? I tried to recall.

"He was just upset about Benny's remote cars."

"Did one break? Did Jamie break it?" Sam asked, guzzling orange juice before he lifted his hazel eyes for an answer.

"No, one of the cars was running around under our bed while Jeremy was trying to sleep," I explained. "We went into the office to see who was operating it." I stopped short of details.

A few seconds passed. "Was it Benny?" Sam asked.

"What?" I'd lost focus staring out the window at the frigid December day. I looked at my son. "What did you ask me?"

"Was Benny operating the remote car running under your bed?" Sam frowned. "Did something weird happen yesterday?"

His mouth was set firm, his eyes demanding an answer.

"Yes, Sam."

"Are you going to tell me?"

What choice did I have? I explained exactly what happened, and when I had finished, Sam drew his own conclusions.

"So . . . basically our ghosts can operate the equipment in our house." It was a profound statement that I could not refute.

"That's why the washing machine turns on and off by itself, and the commodes flush when Dad walks by," Sam concluded.

An explanation was beyond a mom's pay grade.

Sam was well enough on Tuesday to leave the younger boys with him while I drove into town to meet Alice Jacobs at the Coffee Shack for lunch. The outdoor temperature had risen twenty degrees since dawn but I still needed a warm wrap.

I was fitted for my excursion, wearing a thick sweater with a knitted skull cap and matching gloves to fend off the brisk wind as I exited the Malibu a block from the popular Coffee Shack.

Seeing Alice had not yet arrived, I sat down at a table and inhaled the delicious odors of European-style espressos and flavored coffees. Even though the Shack's menu was pricey for the average blue-collar Joe, our young people still found the funds to splurge for all kind of exotic drinks. Capitalism at its best. . .

Shortly, the Shack's owner hustled over to greet me.

"Hi, Brooke," Missy Pollard said. "Having lunch with us?"

"Yes, but I'm waiting for someone."

Missy had owned the Shack for five years and successfully turned it into a haunt for hungry lunch-goers. I immediately regretted using the terminology to describe such a restful place.

"How's your family doing?" Missy inquired.

"Oh, we're fine. Like most folks, we're just trying to stay warm till spring breaks. The kids are slaphappy indoors."

Missy chuckled. "I'm with you."

She handed me a copy of her newest laminated menu with expanded choices and hiked prices. A variety of new sandwiches and soup choices were listed. I thanked Missy and said I'd wait for Alice before ordering. "Alice Jacobs?" she inquired.

"Yes," I said. "Are you two friends?"

"Not exactly, she's a regular—heard she's getting a d-i-v-o-r-c-e." Missy spelled it out. "Don't tell her it came from me!"

So this is why Alice wants to talk to me, I surmised then said to Missy, "I don't know anything about that. Alice goes to my church and we're friends." *I'm done talking, Missy.*

"Oh." The owner hiked one eyebrow and hustled off.

Missy had it right, I wasn't about to gossip on a friend even if I knew the score. I heard the tingling door chimes and spied Alice limping through the door. She headed for my table, dropped her silver-studded bag on the floor next to the table, and collapsed in a chair. "Sorry I'm running late, Brooke. Did you order yet?"

"No—did you fall?" I noted a bruise under one eye.

"Tripped on the carpet in the den," Alice quipped.

"That's why you have a black eye?"

With a shrug of a shoulder, Alice piped, "Let's order first, Brooke, before we get into *all that* . . ." She plucked the menu from my hand and slowly perused it. "Everything looks tasty."

I blinked at how she dismissed her accident.

"Think I'll have a flavored latte with half a tuna sandwich," Alice muttered then looked up. "My treat, so order the works."

I couldn't hold the *works* even if I ordered it. Actually, I thought about excusing myself from lunch to check on Sam and the boys, but after hearing Missy mention d-i-v-o-r-c-e, I thought I'd better linger and hear Alice out. After all, she'd invited me.

Missy hustled over to our table, her floral apron flapping in the surge of heat coming from the ceiling unit. "What can I get you gals?" She blew a tangle of gray curls off her forehead.

"Bring me a large Irish Cream latte with half a tuna-salad sandwich." I went with Alice's suggestion.

"Same here," Alice said. "And bring two waters with ice."

Missy and Alice talked briefly about the weather, and thankfully Missy was gracious enough not to pry into Alice's marital affairs. As requested, Missy put our lunches on Alice's tab.

I assumed the account was hers, in light of *divorce*, but I wasn't sure. Should I mention what Missy told me?

As we waited for our orders to come out, I phoned Sam to see how he was feeling. When he didn't answer, I left a message I'd be home later, to call if he had a problem with his brothers.

Missy's daughter-in-law, Kara, delivered our sandwiches and coffees and asked if we would like anything else. I said no, but Alice asked Kara to wrap up two chocolate scones to go.

The sandwiches were delicious and we ate quietly.

I sensed Alice was heavy-hearted and wanted to talk to me, but every time our eyes met, her wet, lemony gaze emanated fear.

Finally, I could no longer contain my curiosity. "Alice, I know something's wrong. Do you want to talk about it?"

"Willard wants a divorce," she whispered across the table.

I sat back in my chair. So Missy had it right.

"How do you feel about that?" I asked.

By this time tears dripped on Alice's pink cheeks. I knew she was married before and had suffered through a nasty divorce. If possible, I was sure she wanted to make their relationship work.

"You can trust me," I said.

She nodded in agreement. "But not here."

"Let's go over to the church and talk about your situation with Willard," I suggested. "That way, we won't be disturbed."

Alice stopped by the cash register and thanked Missy for the wonderful lunch. We left the Coffee Shack together and walked a block to my four-door Malibu. Alice rode to the church with me. When we'd finished talking, I would bring her back for her car.

"It's really my fault!" Alice rasped when I'd closed the door to the classroom where our ladies held their weekly Bible studies. "He would not have hit me if I hadn't started in on him."

"Wait. Willard hit you?" I queried.

Glazed eyes the shade of lemons targeted me like daggers. I couldn't fathom the mild-mannered man I knew as Willard Jacobs, a faithful member of our congregation who had served on numerous committees, ever striking a woman, much less his own wife. I reached across the table and grasped Alice's cold hands.

"I fell and hurt my leg after he struck me," she explained.

Somehow I didn't believe her. "Mind if we pray over your situation?" I had no idea how to begin a discussion of this nature.

"Dear Lord . . ." I began, "we are in *Your* hands, as always. I ask you to guide Alice and Willard in this awkward situation. Help them to resolve their differences and move forward. Amen."

We held hands for awhile longer.

"Alice? Did you report the incident to the police?"

"God, no, Brooke, I don't want people knowing about this!" Fear ignited in her expression as she began to shake.

"I'm sorry, but it's a question I had to ask."

The silence in the compact classroom was palatable.

"It's only the third time he's ever struck me," Alice confessed. That answered my question. "I love Willard but he apparently doesn't love me anymore. He wants a divorce."

"Will he talk to a marriage counselor?" I queried.

"He won't," Alice replied. "He told me he's in love with another woman. He'd been in contact with her off and on since we married four years ago. He never stopped loving her."

"I'm so sorry, Alice." I was aware that Willard's marriage to Alice was his third. "Is there any way I can help you?"

"What would you do if Jeremy hit you?" she asked.

"Jeremy would never hit me."

"But if he did, and he hurt you real bad, what would you do?"

"I'd ask him to move out and think about whether he loved me enough to stop his abuse," I replied. "If another woman was in the picture, I'd ask him to quit seeing her and go with me to a marriage counselor. In some cases, divorce is unavoidable."

"And if he was determined to divorce you . . .?"

"I'd let him go," I replied. "I only want a man in my bed who is totally devoted to me. That's how I am, Alice. And I think that is what Jesus honors in a holy marriage relationship."

Alice nodded as her tears spilled on the table. Removing a tissue from her purse she dotted her cheeks. "You're right, of course, Mrs. McLaughlin. I'll talk to Willard tonight."

"Whatever you do or say, don't get into an argument with Willard," I advised. "He's already reacted violently, and you don't need to upset him more." I paused to assess her mood.

"You'll need to speak to a divorce attorney and decide how to best divide your assets," I continued. "Please don't walk away from Willard without compensation. You're the innocent party."

28

WHEN ALICE AND I finished talking, I drove her back to the Coffee Shack to get her car then called Jeremy on his cell phone.

"How's your day going?" I asked.

"Fine, how did your meeting with Alice go?"

"We'll discuss it later at home," I replied. "I'm curious—did you talk with Willard yesterday?"

"No, we're actually meeting in a few minutes," he replied.

I heard him honk at a driver.

"I'm on my way to the church office now," he said.

"I'm actually on my way home, did you get lunch?" I asked, denying tears as I grieved for Alice and Willard's marriage.

"I had Arby's roast beef and it was pretty good." He hitched a breath. "You sound funny, did anything happen with Alice?"

"I don't want to talk about it while I'm driving."

"Okay, we'll compare notes tonight."

"Okay, see you later."

I ended the call and keyed in Sam's cell number. It rang several times then went to voicemail. Not leaving a message, I ended the call with mounting concern. When I got home I found Sam stretched out on the sofa in the living room reading a book.

"You didn't answer your phone," I told him as I racked my coat on the hall tree. "I gather you're feeling better."

"My cell is in my bedroom, Mom. Sorry . . ."

"Where are the boys?" I noticed how quiet the house was.

"They went out to the shed to play with their race cars."

I presumed Jeremy gave them back with special instructions.

"All that running around on the floor was driving me nuts," Sam added, flipping a page to his book to continue reading.

"Is that a reading assignment for school?"

"Yeah, English," Sam replied. "The Life of Abraham Lincoln is pretty interesting, but falls way short of a political thriller."

"Did you take your mid-day meds?"

"Mom . . ."

"Okay, just asking." I realized I'd better check on Benny and Jamie in the shed. They were accidents waiting to happen. "Can I fix you anything to eat before I check on your brothers?"

"No, I just had a tall glass of Gatorade," Sam answered.

"Good. You need to stay hydrated." I paused a few seconds longer. "Okay, I'll leave you to your reading."

I plucked my coat from the rack and tugged it on while walking down the hall and out the back door. I found Jamie and Benny diligently working on repairing a broken airplane wing.

"You crashed already?" I teased them.

"Just a little glue and it'll be good again," Benny said.

"Did you have lunch?"

Both boys shook their heads no.

"Come inside and I'll fix you both a ham sandwich," I offered. "After that, Benny, I need to see your homework list." I helped Jamie put on his coat. "School resumes on Monday."

The boys beat me back to the house and were already seated at the kitchen table anticipating a late lunch.

"What's for dessert?" Benny asked.

"Sandwich first then we'll talk about it." I had frozen ice cream sandwiches and packaged cupcakes in the pantry.

While they ate their sandwiches, I traipsed into the pantry and snagged a box of Little Debbie Cakes. Individually wrapped, I selected two of the vanilla with chocolate icing. When I returned, I noted that Benny already had a carton of chocolate ice cream on the counter and was digging the contents out with a big spoon.

"Okay, Benny's dipping. So Jamie, you unwrap the cakes."

They had water with their treats. Afterwards, I sent Benny upstairs to get his homework assignments while I laid out a puzzle on the kitchen table for Jamie to work. Thirty minutes later, I heard Sam's footfalls on the stairs as he made his way back to bed.

I balanced the checkbook in the office, realizing it was getting dark in the house. The oven clock registered 4:30 p.m. It was time for Sam's meds again. I heard the TV blaring in Benny's room and presumed Jamie was with him. They were two peas in a pod, and I was relieved that Jamerson tagged after Benjamin.

"I'm so glad you're better, Sam." I handed him his meds with a small plastic cup of tap water. "Anything I can get you?"

"No, Mom," he said, "I hate being sick."

"Illness is something people all experience in life."

"The thing is, Mom, I'm really tired all the time."

"If your red blood count is low, it affects your energy level."

"I eat healthy and take my vitamins." Sam sadly glared at me for answers. "What's wrong with me, Mom?"

"You have a virus, son. You'll feel better soon."

Benny was seated at the kitchen table working math problems when I came into the kitchen. I switched on the lights to dispel the darkness. While I set the dining room table with my second-best china, I thought about my deceased mother. I had missed her more than I thought I ever would. Tears threatened to flow.

I placed a silver-plated candelabras with white candles in the center of my mom's blue-and-white checkered tablecloth. I felt better after lighting them, hopeful. Beside each of the five place settings, I put folded blue-cloth napkins and polished silverware.

Smiling, I thought Emily Post would be proud of me. I stood back to appreciate my efforts. "Beautiful, if I say so myself."

"Who's coming for dinner?" Benny asked from the doorway.

"Just us, we're celebrating our family!" I answered.

"Is it somebody's birthday I forgot?"

"No, Benny, these are your Grammy's gifts to us," I said. "Don't you think we should honor her by using them?"

"I guess . . ." he lingered, eyes on me. "I finished my math. Can I go up to my room now and play a video game?"

"Sure, but don't wake up Sam, he's napping."

Alone with my tasks in the kitchen, I removed four sirloin steaks from the freezer, thinking I'd split one with Jamie. Nuke a few potatoes, stir fry a package of green peas, thaw out the blackberry cobbler, and we'd have a feast tonight.

"What's wrong?" I asked Jeremy as soon as he came home around six o'clock. "Why are you an hour late?"

Except for the time the ghostly old man in Benny's bedroom gave Jeremy a shove, I'd never seen my husband so rattled.

"Willard Jacobs found Alice dead when he got home after our meeting," he explained, shaking his head at the incident.

Dead? I tried to internalize the meaning. "How . . .?"

"Suicide, it appears. Both wrists were sliced. She bled out in the garden tub. I left when the forensics team showed up."

"You went over there?"

"Yes." Jeremy was trembling.

"What's going to happen to Willard now?" I found it impossible to process that my friend Alice was dead. We'd just had lunch together at the Coffee Shack. "How is he coping?"

"Terrible. He's beside himself." Jeremy placed a hand on the kitchen counter to steady his shaky frame. "I'm afraid there will be a police investigation into her suspicious death."

"You think there was foul play?" I couldn't believe it.

"The spouse is always looked at first," he replied.

"Why would you say that?" I was weak in the knees.

"Alice's sister didn't help the matter."

"What do you mean, Jer?"

"Elise called the lead detective and told him Willard killed Alice," he informed me. "There's more to the story than meets the eye." He looked at me as if I had answers that made sense.

"Oh, my, that's not good." I recalled my last conversation with Alice, who seemed anxious to amicably resolve their conflict.

"You had lunch with her. Was she depressed?"

"No. Is there evidence to support a murder theory?"

"It's a crime scene now. The authorities will determine if there's enough evidence to pursue a case against Willard." Jeremy loosened his shirt collar and sat down at the kitchen table.

I nodded, sat down by him, my hands cold and clammy.

"What did Alice tell you when you had lunch with her?"

I blinked at the question. "Let's have supper first. The steaks are warming in the oven and the boys need to be fed."

He nodded. "Let's don't tell the boys yet."

"I agree."

Supper wasn't the celebration of my mother's gifts as I had hoped, but rather a doleful occasion of regretful memories. How could I have missed what was going on in Alice's marriage? Am I such a terrible friend that she never confided in me about her problem before today? And why would she kill herself after telling me she would give Willard a divorce if he was unwilling to give up the other woman in his life? It was incomprehensible.

Unfortunately, Jeremy and I were smack dab in the middle of the family tragedy. Obviously, the police would come calling soon. I wanted to protect Alice's reputation. Still, if Willard had struck her, or in any way, hastened her death, everything she said to me would need to come out. I prayed for divine guidance.

29

BY FRIDAY, JANUARY 2ⁿᵈ Sam had basically recovered from influenza symptoms. Celebrating a new year had effortlessly come and gone with no ghostly incidents. Relieved, I boxed all our Christmas decorations that morning and the boys helped me carry them to the storage closet. After I fed them lunch, I cleaned and mopped the wood floors throughout the first level.

The doorbell sounded and startled me. On my way to the foyer I chuckled, thinking at least no ghosts this time.

"Coming," I called out in a lilting voice.

Peeking through the beveled side window, I spied a middle-aged man in a rumpled blue uniform. My heart leaped as I opened the door and confronted the county sheriff.

"Can I help you, sir?" I stammered.

"Mrs. Brooke McLaughlin?"

"Yes." I read his nametag. "Sheriff Winfield, I'm Brooke."

I held to the door like it was a magical defender, intimated by his imposing bulk. No other reason for his visit except Alice Jacob's untimely death. What was I prepared to tell him?

"If it's not a big inconvenience, Mrs. McLaughlin, I'd like to speak with you about a legal matter." Twigs of wiry gray hair shot out the sides of his cap and curled over hairy-lined ears.

"About Alice Jacobs, I presume." I invited him inside.

"Yes, ma'am. . ." He removed his cap as he stepped over the threshold and into the hallway then glanced around.

Petrified to say anything negative about Alice, I waited.

"Nice place you have here, Mrs. McLaughlin." A ghost of a smile quivered on his bulbous lips below a starched moustache.

"Thank you, Sheriff. Fixing up this old relic has been a challenge." We uncomfortably locked eye to eye.

"Why don't we talk in there?" He nodded at the living room then followed me there. "Use that fireplace much?"

"Yes, often in the winter. I haven't turned the gas flames on this morning," I said. "Could I fix you something to drink?"

He waved a hand. "No, thanks, this won't take long."

I couldn't imagine how I could assist the county sheriff's department in solving a crime. As Winfield shifted his hefty bulk on the sofa and turned gravelly eyes on me, I inwardly cringed.

"It appears you were the last person to see Alice Jacobs on Tuesday . . ." he scrutinized me, "a few hours before her death."

I jerked a breath. "I can't say for sure, Sheriff Winfield. I let Alice off in front of the Coffee Shack around two p.m. She could've spoken to someone else before going home."

He nodded, clasped his big hands together then made eye contact. "I guess you read the article in yesterday's newspaper."

"Yes, it appears Alice's sister has accused Willard of murder."

"That's correct." Winfield glared at me. "Have you had any prior contact with Ms. Jackson?" He shifted in his chair.

"No, I only heard Alice speak of Elise," I replied.

"Alice's death is a murder investigation now that Ms. Jackson has filed a formal complaint with our office," he informed me.

"Mom . . .?" Benny lingered in the doorway, wearing only his PJ bottoms. "What's going on?" He warily looked at the sheriff.

"It's okay, son, Sheriff Winfield is just asking me a few questions about a friend of mine," I told him. "We won't be long, but If you're hungry go in the kitchen and fix yourself a snack."

"Handsome lad," Winfield commented, clearing his throat.

"I already know Willard Jacobs is a person of interest, Sheriff Winfield," I offered. "But why are you here at my house?"

"I need for you to arrange for childcare and come with me down to the station and give an official statement," he said.

"What kind of statement?" I reacted. "Am I a suspect?"

"No, no, nothing like that," he said. "Just want to hear what Alice told you in confidence when you met with her on Tuesday."

"What can I say that will make any difference?"

"Motive, Mrs. McLaughlin. It has everything to do with whether Alice committed suicide or someone made it appear so."

I shuttered at Winfield's remark as his piercing silver eyes penetrated me like twin knives. "May I have one phone call?"

"Sure. I'll wait right here," he answered.

When I stepped into the foyer, I spied Sam glued against the wall, probably eavesdropping on my conversation with the sheriff.

"Are you in trouble, Mom?" Sam whispered.

"I'll explain later." I noted his concern.

We walked down the hall together to my bedroom.

"Will you keep an eye on Benny and Jamie while I take a ride into town with Sheriff Winfield?" I checked my purse for needed items, making sure my billfold was in there with my driver's license and social security card. "I won't be gone too long."

"Mom, why is the sheriff talking to you?"

"Alice Jacobs was a member of our church, and a friend. The police want to hear my perspective on her last day of life."

"Oh." Sam's hazel eyes alighted with comprehension.

"I have to call your dad now and let him know."

"Okay." Sam stepped into the hallway.

I closed our bedroom door for privacy and used our landline to call the church office. Jeremy's secretary answered the phone.

"This is Brooke, Janice. I need to speak with Jeremy." No time for chitchat or speculation today. "Is he available?"

"I'll see." Janice put me on hold.

The wait seemed longer than two minutes.

"Brooke? Is everything at home okay?" Jeremy inquired.

"Sheriff Winfield is here and wants me to come down to the station to give a statement concerning Alice," I revealed. "I'm a little nervous about it, but I don't think I have a choice."

"Is Sam staying with the boys?"

"Yes, could you meet me at the station?"

"I'm in the middle of a finance meeting, honey," he said. "You have nothing to hide, you'll do fine. Just tell the truth."

But if I did, it would get Willard in more trouble.

"When you've finished at the station, come by the church and we'll talk about it," Jeremy said. "I know you're scared."

I glanced at my watch. *9:50 a.m.*

"Maybe we can grab a quick lunch," I suggested. "I'll tell you all about what it's like being interrogated by the law."

We both laughed at my statement.

"Don't be scared, Brooke, just tell the truth."

"Thanks, Jer. See you later."

Sam had been listening through the door and opened it as soon as I had ended the call. "What did Dad say, Mom?"

"Tell the truth, nothing but the truth, and I'll be fine."

Sam followed me as I walked into the kitchen and removed a package of frozen lunchmeat. "Do you feel like fixing Jamie a sandwich for lunch?" I asked him. "Benny can fend for himself."

"Sure, Mom, go be a good citizen."

We both smiled at his statement.

Sheriff Winfield was on his cell phone when I returned to the living room. We had Wi-Fi and internet service at our house while most country folks were still in the dark. I waited until he finished his conversation then said, "I'll drive my own car."

He nodded and stood, adjusting his blue jacket as he followed me outside and crossed the porch. I waited in my blue Malibu until his black SUV pulled out of our driveway then I followed.

En route to the station, I switched on the radio and found a gospel station. I needed God's grace to get through the morning. I loved Alice. She is—was—practically my best friend at church.

As a pastor's wife, I always knew Jeremy would be reassigned a new church. So I was guarded with my emotions in making new friends. They were mine for now, but not forever. Letting go was part of the ministry. In some ways, it was a grieving process.

A two-story brick building a block from the courthouse housed the police station and city jail for offenders awaiting arraignment. I pulled into a space marked GUEST and switched off the motor. "This is it, Lord," I uttered as I exited the vehicle.

Sheriff Winfield was waiting at the station's entrance and opened the door for me. I trailed him through two security checks, down a disinfected white-washed hallway and into an interrogation room set up with a scarred oak table and four metal chairs bolted to the floor. In these surroundings, I was out of my comfort zone as I noted the soundproof wall and ceiling tiles.

The sheriff motioned me to a chair and I followed orders like a good citizen, recalling Sam's encouragement and Jeremy's urging to tell the truth. Seconds later, an attractive young woman hustled into the room with her electronic equipment, including a mini-tape recorder. All this was new ground for me. Never before had anyone in any of our churches been murdered or committed suicide! Just the thought of it was disconcerting if not frightening.

"Mrs. McLaughlin, this is our court stenographer, Karen Taylor," Sheriff Winfield informed me. Before I could comment, an imposing man with starlit blue eyes barreled into the room.

"And this is Detective Clay Bennett," Winfield added. "He'll be asking you questions while Karen tapes your statement."

I said fine and glanced over at the detective—huge, not just tall, and a scary six four weighing some two-hundred fifty pounds. I soon learned he was a former Army Special Forces operative.

"Good to meet you, Mrs. McLaughlin," Bennett said.

"Just call me Brooke, please."

Wrinkles gathered at the corners of the detective's steely eyes indicating he had some years under his belt. Muscle-bound like a wrestler, his wide jaw was set like concrete. If Detective Bennett smiled it wouldn't actually hurt him. To say I was overwhelmed with his oppressive demeanor was a gross understatement.

Or not . . . I said to myself. Three to one, there was no escape. I tried hard to keep it together so I could get my story right.

"Will this take long?" I inquired.

"It shouldn't," Bennett said, taking charge. "Just tell us what happened Tuesday afternoon, December 30, when you met with Alice Jacobs. Don't exclude minor points of your conversations."

"If you'll excuse me, Mrs. McLaughlin, I have an appointment." Sheriff Winfield said from the doorway. "I'll check with you later, Clay." Then he was out the door, poof!

Two to one now! My odds were getting better.

"Mrs. McLaughlin?" Bennett cleared his throat. "Please state your full name for the record." His steely gaze fell on Karen and she promptly switched on the recorder.

I said my name then began my story at the moment Alice walked into the Coffee Shack and I noticed her black eye. I was shocked to learn that Willard had struck her the day before, and that it wasn't the first time. I apologized to Detective Bennett that if I was leaving anything important out it wasn't intentional. He encouraged me to do the best I could with remembering. I told him I'd never dreamed I'd need to recall every word we said.

Detective Bennett said he understood. Building a case was about putting together a lot of information then analyzing it.

Privately, I feared if I added my interpretation regarding my conversation with Alice at the Shack, it would shift us to some alternate universe. When I'd finished telling my story, Detective Bennett followed up with questions, which made me nervous.

"In your opinion, after speaking with Alice on Tuesday at lunch, and later at the church, did you think she was depressed?"

"No, upset over the idea of a divorce, but not depressed," I answered. "She seemed willing to talk to Willard and work out a financial solution to their problem," I added. "Alice is a Christian, Detective Bennett, and I know she considered suicide a sin."

"So you don't believe Alice was depressed enough to end her life," Bennett concluded, looking to me for further insight.

"Not when she left me," I said with confidence. "But I don't know what happened later when she talked to Willard—if she talked to him." My global blue eyes were wide with speculation.

When Bennett kept silent, I tossed out a question. "Did Willard say he talked to Alice after we met at the church?"

"He says he didn't," Bennett reported. "He's set for a lie-detector test this afternoon." Those probing eyes assaulted me.

"If you're going to arrest Willard, Jeremy should know."

"Who's Jeremy?"

"My husband and pastor of the First Methodist Church."

"Elise Jackson has accused Willard of murdering her sister Alice," Bennett reminded me. "If I find enough evidence to support her accusations he will certainly be arrested."

Bennett glanced at the stenographer. As if reading his mind, she turned off the recorder and left the room with her equipment.

"That will be all for today, Mrs. McLaughlin."

"I can go?"

"Yes, but don't plan any trips, we may need to speak again."

"I understand." I unsteadily found my feet and wobbled out of the interrogation room. What had I gotten myself into?

30

I WALKED OUT of the police station stunned. Alice was dead. Willard was a murder suspect. And Detective Bennett had me on his radar. Ghosts were haunting our house. God only knew what else might happen next. With the weight of the world resting on my shoulders, I met Jeremy for a late lunch at Olive Garden.

My husband asked a lot of questions I couldn't answer. Upset over my involvement, I barely touched my soup and salad as I described my scary encounter with Detective Clay Bennett.

By the time I arrived home around two o'clock I was wiped. Benny's race cars were running around the house in circles—with batteries, I presumed. Jamie was napping, and Sam was upstairs in his bed resting. Alone in the kitchen, I sat down and cried.

Then the phone rang.

"Hello." I hurriedly grabbed the receiver off the wall phone.

"It's me, Brooke."

"Becca, what's wrong?" I heard tears in her voice.

"It's Beverly, she's been captured by Muslim terrorists."

It took a few seconds to process my sister's statement.

"Are you sure?" I asked. "Who told you this?"

"Bishop Haymanot—the Coptic priest who performed Terah and Beverly's marriage ceremony. He emailed me. Terah and his family were killed when their church was demolished by a terrorist bomb this past Sunday! All the surviving young women at the church were captured and taken to an undisclosed location!"

"No, Becca, this can't be true!" I rasped.

"Worse, these women will become Muslim prostitutes."

How could this be happening on top of everything else?

"Is there proof Beverly is still alive?" I asked.

"Her body wasn't among the dead, so they must have her."

"In the email Bishop Haymanot said he'd received snapshots of the seven women the Muslims captured," Becca reported.

"Was Beverly in the picture?"

"He couldn't be certain, they wore veils."

"Do they want money from the families?"

"No, if four Islamic terrorist aren't released from a European prison, they will be executed." Becca was bordering hysteria.

"Is there anything we can do?" I cried.

"Pray," she said.

On top of everything else going wrong, I felt dizzy and weak in the knees. My sister: the Christian missionary. Captured by terrorists? How improbable! And all I could do was pray?

"Brooke? I've placed a call to the American Embassy in London to see if they can help us get Beverly back," Becca said.

"What can I do to help?"

"I'm thinking of flying over to assess the situation myself."

My rationale was all over the place.

"Will Gary go with you?"

"I was hoping you would."

"I can't, Becca." I explained my situation with the sheriff's department, how I had been instructed not to leave the county.

"I understand," Becca said. "Still, I'm going."

"Please don't go alone," I pleaded.

"I don't see that I have much choice."

"We all have choices." I thought of Alice. Did she make the wrong choice? Or did someone else make it for her?

"I'll phone when I know more." Becca ended the call.

Jeremy found me in bed crying when he came home from work around five thirty. "What's happened, Brooke?"

Without a word, I leaped out of bed and flung myself at him.

"It's just unthinkable!" I eked out a response.

"Calm down, honey. Why are you so upset?" Jeremy grasped my shoulders and looked into my eyes. "Is it the kids?"

"No, it's Beverly." I stared up at him. "She was kidnapped by Islamic terrorists. She could have her head chopped off!"

"What?" Jeremy's attention shot up ten notches.

"It's true, Jer! Becca called and told me."

"When did this happen?"

"Last Sunday," I replied. "They burned Terah's church to the ground. He's dead with all this family. They took the young Christian women for prostitutes, Becca said. She's going to London and talk to our ambassador about getting Beverly back."

"Slow down, Brooke, I can't process all this at once."

I gulped back hysteria. "I told Becca I couldn't go."

"Get a hold of yourself, you'll upset the boys."

"Sam knows but I haven't told Benny. Jamie wouldn't understand anyway." I dried my eyes on my shirt sleeve as Jeremy dropped his hands to his side. "What are we going to do?"

"I don't think we have the power to do anything but pray. The Egyptian authorities are obviously investigating the matter."

"We have to do something!" I nearly screamed.

"Okay, calm down," he urged. "Let me change clothes and we'll talk more after supper when the boys are not in earshot."

We ate a meager meal of gumbo and I sent Benny and Jamie upstairs to watch a Christian video. On our bedroom TV, Fox News reported snippets of the kidnapping. I was exhausted but couldn't possibly sleep. Maybe I should read my Bible and pray.

Then, as Jeremy passed through the bathroom, the commode flushed. "Oh, that's just fantastic!" I uttered in disgust.

Jeremy half smiled. "Forget it, love, they're just lonely."

I actually laughed hard, a belated emotional release after my nerves were knotted and my mind crashing against mental walls.

"You can't go abroad even if you want to, Brooke."

"Detective Bennett said not to leave the county." I recalled. "I'm a key witness if there's a trial. And if Willard is indicted for murder one by a Grand Jury, there'll be a media feast."

Jeremy nodded, "I'd rather you didn't go, Brooke. Gary and Becca can handle any legal matter required by the embassy."

"I loved Alice Jacobs, but I love my sister more."

"It's not that, Brooke, leaving now might look like you're running from something." His coffee brown eyes rested on me.

"So what . . .? Sheriff Winfield pulls a pistol on me?"

Then I thought more seriously about what Jeremy had said. "I'll go by the precinct after school on Monday and talk to him."

"First, we have to get through the weekend," Jeremy said. "By then, the matter might be resolved and Willard cleared."

* * *

Saturday night turned into a "Gibby" event. Benny woke us up screaming to the top of his lungs. Jeremy leaped from the bed, hopped in his pants and raced down the hall toward the stairs.

I was right behind him after grabbing Benny's meds from our medicine cabinet, my housecoat flapping like a bat out of hell.

Not again! I cried to the Lord. *Please, not again!*

By the time I reached the threshold of Benny's bedroom Jeremy had him in his arms. The child was hysterical, coughing and choking between sobs. I stood there, gulping back anger.

"It was just a bad dream, son!" My husband the minister tried to calm Benny. "You're okay, I have you. You're safe."

"Here, Benny, take these." I held a cup of water to his lips and fed him two anxiety tabs.   In all the turmoil of concern over my missing sister, I couldn't remember if I'd given him his meds at bedtime. As if reading my mind, Jeremy looked at me.

"Brooke, did Benny already take his meds?"

"I'm sorry, Jer, I just don't recall."

Jeremy faced Benny. "What was your dream about, son?"

"What's wrong with Benny?" Sam asked from the doorway.

"Go back to bed, son, we'll handle it," I said.

By that time I heard Jamie screaming for me.

"I'll walk you back to your bedroom," I told Sam then peeled off, heading for Jamie's bedroom. "I'm here, Jamie."

My five-year-old son's covers lay crumpled on the floor, which made me question if he'd kicked them off or had help from *them*. "I'm here, Jamie," I repeated. "Quit crying, we're all okay."

Were we? I wasn't. Alice wasn't. Willard wasn't. Beverly wasn't.

After settling Jamie down with a story, I went back into Benny's bedroom and spied Jeremy listening to his account of what had upset him twenty minutes before. "It was that old woman again. She was choking me! I couldn't breathe."

"Are you sure you weren't dreaming?" I asked Benny.

"No, Mom! I woke up because she was choking me. I have to use the bathroom." Benny shot out of bed and ran the short distance down the hall, slamming the bathroom door behind him.

I shook my head, clueless, feeling I'd failed my children.

"Benny should sleep in our bedroom tonight," Jeremy said.

I agreed. When Benny came back, I ushered him down the stairs and into bed with me while Jeremy slept in his bed upstairs.

I suppose my husband hoped the old hag would show up so he could show her who was boss. But nothing happened.

I woke up Sunday morning and heard Jeremy piddling around in the kitchen. Inhaling the strong coffee brought me to my senses. Like a magnet its delicious odor pulled me to the kitchen.

"Good morning." I approached the counter.

"Good morning, love." Jeremy embraced me.

"Anybody show up in Benny's room after we left?" I asked. Through the bay window, I spied a glorious sunrise submerged in clouds of deep purple and red hues. Heaven was at rest.

"Can't say I got the best rest I ever had." Jeremy yawned. "Did you sleep any with that bucking bronco beside you?"

"Not so great but Benny slept like a log." I heard the shower running upstairs and knew it was Sam getting ready for church.

"Do you think Sam's still contagious?" I poured myself a mug of coffee and added cream. "I don't want him to infect others."

"If he has no fever and feels like it, we should let him attend the service." Jeremy retrieved two boxes of cereal from the pantry while I removed a gallon of milk from the fridge. We both heard Jamie's footfalls as he raced down the hall toward the kitchen.

"I'm hungry!" Our five-year-old announced.

"How about I fix you some Cheerios," Jeremy suggested.

"How 'bout you fix me some pizza?" Jamie piped.

The laugh was unexpected. It just rolled up from somewhere deep in my throat and erupted in a rage of chuckles I couldn't control. Call it nervous laughter, call it whatever. But the release was cleansing. No wonder people who laugh live longer.

"Have a seat, Jamie, and I'll make you pancakes," I decided.

Our family attended both church services. Questions and comments regarding Alice Jacob's sudden death echoed in the hallways. Did Willard do it? Did Alice commit suicide?

Jeremy gave a general comment regarding Willard's situation from the pulpit: "The police are looking into Alice's death. Let's not be too quick to judge. Let law enforcement do their job."

31

MONDAY MORNING ARRIVED wrapped in clouds with a tinge of frost in the atmosphere. Our family had breakfast then headed out to engage in the first full week of the New Year. Jeremy went off to the church, me and the kids to our respective schools.

It was a relief to resume work now that I knew there was little more I could do to help Beverly that the UN Peacekeepers were not already doing. Just before my third English class of the morning, I received a text from Becca that she and Gary were at the Atlanta airport boarding a Delta flight to London.

I texted a God-speed prayer back, asking for favor and protection over them. Though, in the back of my mind, I wondered if our little sister would become the first family member martyred. Much in life seemed out of human control.

During my lunch break I went over to see Sheriff Winfield about leaving the country. He was out in the field on a case so Detective Bennett talked with me. Lacking the capacity for empathy, Bennett told me to wait until I had more information before I engaged in a possibly unproductive wild goose chase.

At hearing his response to my concern, I became livid.

"I don't suppose you have a brother or a sister!" I viciously attacked him. "If you want to arrest me after I get back from London, please feel free to do so." I stormed out of his office.

When Jeremy arrived home just before sundown, he told me he'd left a message for Willard to phone him. Rumors were flying like confetti in the wind among our parishioners, and Brother Mac wanted to get the lowdown from the horse's mouth, so to speak. Then I told him about my conversation with Detective Bennett.

"If Becca doesn't find Beverly, we'll make arrangements for the boys and I'll go with you to London myself," Jeremy said.

"Honey . . . that's so sweet."

"If Sheriff Winfield objects, he can put one of those tracker gizmos on us." Jeremy twittered his fingers. "But I agree with Bennett, we should wait a few days until we hear from Becca."

"Thank you, Jer. Now I have some advice for you."

He expressed surprise.

"Stop talking to Willard," I said.

"Why, Brooke? He's a member of our church."

I told Jeremy that if evidence was discovered that Willard was responsible for Alice's death, he could be called as a material witness in a trial. The children needed one of us at home.

"Brooke, I'm Willard's spiritual advisor," he argued.

"I know what Willard tells you is confidential, but if he's guilty, all bets are off the table." Let's be clear here.

He nodded in defeat. We both felt whipped over Willard's situation. And we grieved over losing Alice to such a horrific death. Privately, I wondered what kind of funeral service would be planned. Would the police lab perform an autopsy? Or would Alice be stored on a refrigerated slab until the sheriff's department deemed it acceptable to release her body to the family for burial?

I could not imagine how difficult this situation was for Alice's sister or her grown son. Imagine the double whammy Willard was experiencing, first losing a spouse then being accused of murdering her. The human psyche was vastly fragile.

For supper, I served the boys hamburgers while Jeremy and I shared leftover vegetable soup with crackers. Cleanup was easy.

When it came bedtime, Benny refused to sleep in his bed so we made a pallet on the floor beside Sam's bed and that seemed to satisfy him. Big Brother would chase away the old woman.

But who would chase away Big Brother's evil?

* * *

Tuesday afternoon, before school let out, I received a text from Becca asking me to call her as soon as I had the opportunity.

As soon as the kids and I were home, I set Benny down at the kitchen table to do his homework. Sam took Jamie upstairs with him while I went into my bedroom and phoned my sister.

"Did they find Beverly?" I hurried asked.

"Not yet," Becca replied. "But an eye witness to the church bombing told one of the peacekeepers that there was a woman that came out the back door of the church just before it exploded in flames." Becca took a breath. "It might have been Beverly."

"But the woman wasn't sure," I said.

"No, but one of the peacekeepers took a walk behind the church and found a scarf snagged on a bush," Becca reported.

"A scarf I gave her?" My heart skittered.

"It looks like one of mom's. I'll email you the photo."

"Praise God!!" I grabbed onto a thread of hope for the first time since we'd heard about the church bombing.

"Other than that, Gary and I are waiting to hear if any of the hospitals have admitted a woman fitting Beverly's description. Knowing our sister, she's a survivor. Just keep praying, Brooke."

"I will, Becca. And thanks for giving me an update. Oh, send me a picture of that scarf." I ended the call and said, "Yes!"

"I take it you have good news." Jeremy stood at the threshold of our bedroom. Was that Becca on the phone?"

"Yes, she's hopeful the UN Peacekeepers will find Beverly."

"What was that about a scarf?" He unbuttoned his shirt at the neck and sat down on the bed while I told him what I'd learned. "I'm concerned Beverly can't call us. A woman wandering around in the desert alone without credentials might be picked up and taken hostage by a band of criminals."

"Let's not assume the worst, Brooke."

I considered that Beverly might be so traumatized over the bombing incident she could be experiencing temporary amnesia.

"If she's alive, why hasn't she called?" I uttered.

"Let the peacekeepers do their thing," Jeremy advised.

"What if she gets lost in the desert?"

I told Jeremy about an article I'd read concerning the persecution of Copts by Egyptian Islamic radicals. After President Mohamed Morsi was removed from office in a military coup, Christian churches and Christian-owned businesses came under attack from Muslims. Islam is a religion that takes no prisoners.

Open Doors USA, ministering to persecuted Christians around the world, estimated that some seventy plus churches in Egypt had been attacked by jihadist Muslims in 2013. Thousands of Christians who refused to embrace Islam were tortured and many beheaded. My sister had been dropped off in a part of the world beyond our comprehension. Only Jesus could save her.

Jeremy didn't respond after hearing my comments. Only the conviction of the Holy Spirit could change the way these indoctrinated radical Muslims thought and acted out. The church had its work cut out for them. And prayer was the weapon.

32

WEDNESDAY EVENING I LEFT Sam home with the boys and went with Jeremy to church. Sam had homework and promised to see that Benny studied for his math test. I gave Jamie a bath and put him in his PJs. Bedtime for him was eight thirty.

Jeremy was starting a new Bible study tonight in the book of James. Not much in the mood to sing, I attended choir anyhow, deciding my life had to go on even if Alice's didn't.

We finished choir early and I went out to the Suburban to retrieve my cell phone and call the boys. As I opened the door, a dark figure stepped up to me. "Oh, you scared me, Willard."

"What did you tell the police, Brooke?"

"I told them the truth, Willard." I stepped into my vehicle and was about to close the door when he stopped me.

"What are you doing, Willard? Are you stalking me?"

He let go of the door and took a step back. "Did Alice tell you she was having an affair?" His expression begged empathy.

I huffed, "I heard it was the other way around."

"That's a lie, Brooke. I didn't put those bruises on Alice, she did that to herself." He looked like a lost puppy in the dark.

"What do you mean?" I started the car motor.

"Can I get in with you?" he asked. "I won't hurt you."

"I don't know if I'm supposed to talk to you, Willard."

Jeremy showed up and stood beside Willard, motioning for me to roll down the window. "What's going on, Brooke?"

"Nothing," I answered, "Willard and I were just talking."

"What about . . .?" Jeremy glanced through the rear window as if he expected something sinister to be there.

Not answering, Willard walked away and disappeared into the dark of the night. I was shaking without realizing it.

"He came up to me before I knew it," I told Jeremy.

"Did Willard threaten you?"

"No, but he scared me pretty bad."

"I think we should report this to Detective Bennett in the morning." I turned off the motor and got out of the car.

"Oh, I don't know, Jer. I don't want to cause the poor man any more grief. No telling how Detective Bennett will react."

"Willard may have murdered Alice," he pointed out.

"And he might be innocent." I told him what Willard had said, that Alice had self-inflicted wounds and was having an affair. "You showed up before he had a chance to explain."

"Still, Willard should not have approached you in the dead of the night. How did we get involved in a murder mystery?"

"I need to get home, you drive," I told my husband.

* * *

Jeremy decided to talk to Willard first before we involved the police. However, Willard failed to return Jeremy's call. We talked about what had taken place at the church when we arrived home.

I was afraid that Detective Bennett would accuse me of interfering with his investigation if he learned I'd spoken to Willard. Both Jeremy and I could get into trouble. But, as always, my husband believed it was his responsibility to help a member of our church, so Jeremy urged me to stay out of the matter and let him deal with Willard. Although I wanted to bow out, I could not restrain the worry imbedded upon my mind like indelible ink.

After school on Thursday, Sam complained again of not feeling well. I felt his forehead and he was running a temp.

"What is going on with you, Sam?" I considered if he had Mono, a streptococcus infection imbedded in his glands.

"I don't know, Mom."

"I want Dr. Simmons to examine you." He was our family physician. "He can request a copy of your last test results from the walk-in clinic and compare them with any new tests he runs."

"Mom!" Sam protested, "I just had a round of antibiotics. I'm probably just rundown. You never got me more vitamins."

"Okay, after we pick up Benny and Jamie, we'll swing by CVS and get you some super-deluxe one-a-days," I said. "But if you are still running a fever tomorrow, you're seeing a doctor."

With that decided, I asked Sam how school was coming along. "I have straight A's, is that good enough?" He grinned.

"Perfect! How could a mama ask for better?"

Benny and Jamie fussed with one another the whole way to the house. I promised them ice cream when they got home, but even that didn't stop the bickering. I finally pulled the car to the side of the road and turned around in my seat. Then they hushed.

"Benny, what's got into you?" I pointed my mama finger at him. "It's not like you to treat Jamie so poorly."

Benny shrugged, looked out the window. Since his tousle with the old woman he'd become morose and aggressive. His homeroom teacher reported he was picking fights with his classmates. Our friendly, happy-go-lucky son had turned into someone Jeremy and I barely recognized. As a mother, I just didn't know how to make it better for him. Actually, I was as spooked over what was happening in the house as he was.

Only, I was much better at hiding my feelings.

When we got home, I gave the boys ice cream anyhow. Sam went straight to his room to lie down. When Jeremy came home at suppertime I asked him to look in on Sam.

"Says he's not hungry and wants to sleep," Jeremy reported.

"I made spaghetti for supper, hope that suits you."

Sam's condition was worrisome. Something just didn't feel right, a mother's intuition I suppose. After retiring to our bedroom for the night, I read my Bible and prayed. Jeremy climbed into bed beside me. "Are you asleep?"

"Awake now." I rolled over to face him.

"Willard phoned me this afternoon at the church."

I sat up, fully alert. "What did he say?"

"He wants to meet me at the church tomorrow."

"And tell you his side of the story?"

"I presume so. But you should stay out of it, Brooke."

"I'm already in the middle, Jer!" I spewed

"Can you be at the church around eleven a.m.?"

"I don't know if I can miss class." I mentally reviewed my morning schedule. "I'll need someone to cover for me."

"Maybe you can take an early lunch break."

"I'll talk to my principal; see if I can work something out."

Friday morning, I explained to our principal Ann why I needed my eleven o'clock French class covered so I could take care of a legal matter. She personally offered to sit in on the class.

Jeremy was already in the church conference room when I arrived shortly after eleven. "Good morning, Willard," I said.

"Good morning, Brooke. I owe you an apology."

I threw a hand like it didn't matter. "What counts is getting to the truth." I took a seat at the conference table.

"That's what I've been telling Jeremy," Willard said. "Alice has been seeing someone. I think it started six months ago when she flew to Las Vegas for her company's yearly meeting."

Who was I to believe, Alice or Willard?

"You're saying that Alice met someone while working, had an affair, and has continued the relationship until a now?" I just wanted to be absolutely clear concerning his accusations.

"That's exactly what I'm saying." Willard visibly wilted.

I looked at Jeremy, inept to comment.

"I wanted us to talk to a marriage counselor before she started divorce proceedings," Willard continued. "I actually didn't know any of this until two weeks ago." He fell silent.

I realized Alice's accusations were exactly in reverse.

"Alice didn't know squat about this man—he could be a serial killer," Willard said. "They were FACEBOOK friends."

"I thought you said she met him in Las Vegas."

"She did, but only after they connected on FACEBOOK."

"So . . . was the mystery man employed by Alice's company?"

"Brooke, let Willard tell us what he knows before you ask questions," Jeremy intervened, a reminder to be discreet.

"One more question, Willard . . ." I wasn't finished. "If you didn't hit Alice, how did she get a black eye?" I boldly asked as Jeremy checked his vibrating iPhone for a message.

"Brooke!" Willard exclaimed. "That's what I was trying to tell you in the car Wednesday night at the church. Alice did it to herself because we both signed a prenuptial with one exclusive."

"What was in the doc?" Jeremy inquired as he shut off his phone, his gaze warning me to listen and not talk.

"Since Alice had been beaten by her husband in a previous marriage, she wanted a clause in the prenuptial stating that if I ever inflicted harm on her she could get an uncontested divorce and receive compensation for pain and suffering."

"Okay . . ." I let that idea settle then asked, "Do you know if Alice has changed her will to stipulate a new heir?"

"What do you mean?" Willard gazed at me.

"Who benefits financially from Alice's death?"

"I suppose her son, Anthony, does," Willard replied. "I guess the reading of Alice's will has been postponed due to the status of her death. I presume her sister Elise spoke to Alice's lawyer."

"Did you tell all this to Detective Bennett?" Jeremy inquired.

"Yes, but I don't think he believes me," Willard replied.

"Do you have any idea if Alice has enemies?" Jeremy asked.

"She didn't like talking about her past," Willard explained. "Before she became a Christian I think she was pretty wild. We met at a singles' seminar after both of us had accepted Christ."

"Willard, think hard," I said. "You need a defense."

"Okay, Alice could've set off almost anyone in light of her former naughty behavior—an old girlfriend, the wife of someone she was seeing, a mistress . . ." he threw out some suggestions.

I realized I didn't know Alice at all.

"If someone intended Alice harm, she must have let them in the house. There was no sign of illegal entry," I pointed out.

Willard appeared confused, these ideas new to him.

"Okay, let's review the day Alice died," I said. "She left me at two p.m. Tuesday afternoon, December 30, when I dropped her off at the Coffee Shack to get her car. What time did you find her dead in the tub?" I shot a glance at Jeremy, who was frowning.

"5:05 pm.," Willard replied. "Maybe a neighbor saw someone go inside the house. Surely, Detective Bennett checked."

"The husband is always the first suspect," I said.

"If I knew the exact time Alice died, my problem would go away." Willard's shoulders drooped. "I didn't kill her."

"The only thing I know about criminal investigations is what I've read in novels or seen of TV," I said. "CSI needs forensic evidence to conclusively tie you to Alice's death."

"Do you know if they found any?" Jeremy inquired.

"My DNA is all over the place, Brother Mac. I live there."

"What about the knife?" I asked.

"My switchblade was in the tub with Alice," Willard told us. "I never carried it out in public with me." His gaze widened.

I shook my head, made eye contact with my husband.

"So . . ." Jeremy took over, "is there a way we can help you?"

"I wish," Willard said. "I just wanted someone I trusted to know the truth. Honest to God, I never cheated on Alice. I loved her, still do. I want whoever did this to her to pay plenty."

"I believe you," I uttered.

"But proving what you say is another thing," Jeremy added.

* * *

I was back at school before lunch break ended, my mind spinning with possibilities regarding Alice's death. I hoped the CSI team had confiscated Alice's computer and was looking at her FACEBOOK contacts. Call me paranoid, but the news media had reported murders committed by so-called internet friends.

As much as I desired to solve this mystery, I was unqualified. All I could do to assist Willard was to believe him and pray for the truth to surface. Jeremy and I both wanted justice applied to the perpetrator. Then Willard would be exonerated.

33

SAM STAYED HOME in bed the following Tuesday. After school, when the boys and I got home, I took his temperature and noted it was slightly elevated. "How are you feeling, Sam?"

"I ache all over," he answered.

"Did you take Tylenol for your fever?"

"An hour ago—I also ate a can of Chicken Noodle Soup."

"Good boy. I taught you well." I smiled at him. "Just to be on the safe side, I'm setting an appointment with Dr. Simpson. We need to get to the bottom of your problem."

Sam nodded in agreement. "Thanks, Mom."

The doorbell sounded and I hurried downstairs to answer the caller. As always, I peeked through the beveled glass before opening the door. Convinced no one was there I started down the hall toward my bedroom when the doorbell sounded again.

Pranksters . . .? Kids from down the road?

"Okay, that's enough." I opened the door.

No one stood there. But to make sure it wasn't Benny or Jamie teasing me, I tromped out around the house to the shed. There they were, working on a new model airplane.

"Oh, hi, Mom," Benny said.

"Did either you or Jamie ring our front doorbell?"

"Nope, not us," Jamie said.

"Okay, just wondering . . ."

On my way back into the house, I questioned if the doorbell was starting up again, even with the new one installed. No explanation coming to mind, I dismissed the incident and worked on preparing our supper. An hour passed quickly.

When Jeremy arrived home at 5:30 I told him about the ringing doorbell and that no one was there. He shrugged, walked over to the coffeemaker and poured himself a cup of brew.

"You think it was *them*?" I asked the obvious.

"I don't want to think about them."

"Did something bad happen?" I inquired.

"Detective Bennett arrested Willard."

"Poor guy," I empathized with Willard's plight. "Do you think he's responsible for Alice's death?" I fixed myself a mug of coffee, added cream, and sat down with Jeremy at the table.

"It's not for us to decide, Brooke."

"Still, I'd like to think that both Willard and Alice were the people we believed they were. Good God-loving Christians."

"No one can really discern the heart and motives of man."

"Jeremy!" I exclaimed. "Would you quit sermonizing and just be straight with me?" I resisted his verbal platitudes. "Are we going to be able to help Willard or not?"

"Not," he said and took his mug out on the wooden deck we'd installed a few months before. Sorry for my outburst, I followed him outdoors. "All we can do is pray for Willard."

I nodded, but at the back of my mind, I was plotting more.

Sam was better by Thursday and went to school. We were into our third week of January but it felt like a month. During my lunch break I drove over to the police station to speak with Detective Bennett. Considering the frenetic activity, one would think a serial killer was in our midst. I signed in at the front desk and asked if I could speak briefly with Detective Bennett.

"What is it, Mrs. McLaughlin?" Bennett displayed his typical unwelcome scowl, obviously irritated at the interruption. His eyes were bloodshot which told me he was a light sleeper.

"I wanted to see how the investigation into Alice's death is going . . ." I let my statement linger for a response.

"Murder. . ." he fumbled through paperwork.

"Do you mind stopping that?" My patience wore thin.

He looked up at me like I'd slapped him.

"None of your business, Mrs. McLaughlin, you gave us your statement and that's all we need from you. Good afternoon."

I couldn't recall when anyone had been so rude.

"Excuse me, Detective! I might have some information that would enlighten you." I wasn't about to be dismissed so easily.

He closed the folder, slammed back in his swivel rocker, hands parked behind his head. With a snarl on his lips, Bennett said, "Okay, shoot!" Eyes like daggers accosted my face.

At least I had his attention. "Jeremy and I talked to Willard about his situation," I began. "He said Alice was having an affair with a guy she met on FACEBOOK. She eventually met up with him in Las Vegas during a work trip. Did you know that?"

"He told me that." Bennett planted his feet squarely on the floor. "Anything else . . .?" Impatience imbedded his expression.

"Yes. Willard said Alice's bruises were self-inflicted."

"You believe him because . . .?" he rolled a calloused hand.

"Because I've never known Willard to be dishonest in the three years he's been a member of our church. Both he and Alice are professing Christians," I said. "They're good people."

"And even good people make mistakes."

"Also . . . apparently Alice has been talking to a lot of people on FACEBOOK. Maybe an online predator murdered her."

Bennett cracked his knuckles. "Do you have proof?"

"No, you confiscated her laptop. You check," I said.

"It was wiped clean—not that it's any of your concern."

"Oh, and you think Willard did that? What's his motive?"

"Look, Mrs. McLaughlin . . ." Bennett walked to the door, "I'll think about what you said. Meanwhile, I've got a busy day."

"What about Alice's sister?" I stood my ground. "Did you check to see if she financially benefits from Alice's death?"

"Is that all, Ms. McLaughlin?"

"Please, do your job, Detective Bennett!"

He dropped his head to hide his smug smile.

Then looked me squarely in the eye. . .

"A word of warning, Mrs. McLaughlin . . ." he piped. "By watching too many detective shows you might falsely assume you understand how to investigate a murder." He opened the door.

I said nothing in return, realizing I was finished here.

"Will you excuse me now?" He nodded to the door.

"Certainly!" I grabbed my purse and left in an angry huff.

Too many scenarios of what happened to Alice cluttered my thoughts for me to effectively teach school that afternoon. To remedy the problem, I pulled out some sample tests and gave pop quizzes to my last three language classes. In all fairness, I read off the correct answers and openly discussed their wrong answers.

Jeremy picked up Jamie from kindergarten that afternoon and the two older boys rode home with me. "How did your day go, Sam?" I glanced over at my pale teenager riding shotgun.

"You didn't ask me!" Benny called out from the backseat.

"How was your day, Benny?"

"Great! I'm going to try out for the junior soccer team."

"When does that start up?" I inquired.

"Tryouts are Saturday," Benny reported. "Can I play?"

"Sure. If I can't take you to the school gym, your dad will."

I looked over at Sam. *Poor guy . . .*

Bored with the standard ride home, the boys resorted to their electronic gizmos. Enjoying a few minutes of silence, I used the time to appreciate the morphing landscape. Middle Tennessee's ample rainfall would eventually ignite spring and usher in colorful buds on trees and bushes. The silence screamed at me.

"Sam . . .? Did you enroll in any sports?"

When he didn't answer, I glanced over at the passenger seat and noticed he'd fallen asleep. *What is wrong with you, Sam?*

* * *

Jeremy took Benny to soccer tryouts Saturday morning while I cleaned house. Jamie helped me dust; still young enough to think performing a big people's job was fun. Sam lounged on the sofa in the living room watching television. His appointment with Dr. Simpson was this coming Tuesday following school. Whatever was wrong with our sixteen-year-old, we needed to know so he could receive treatment before the ailment became imbedded. I was worried he had something fatal but said nothing.

Not even to Jeremy.

Sam and Jamie rode with me in the Malibu into town to meet Jeremy and Benny for lunch. After pigging out at the Barbeque Pit, we went over to the bowling alley to roll a few pins. Sam played, but I could tell his heart wasn't in the game. Jamie preferred testing out the gym equipment cordoned off next to the food vendors. Benny actually bowled better than any of us.

Our middle son was smart, athletic, friendly, and sensitive to the spirit world around him, according to his psychologist.

Saturday night at the house proved paranormally eventful. Around midnight, the doorbell went off and Benny came screaming down the stairs to tell us the old woman was in his bedroom again. Somewhat brain dead from sleep, I reacted rather calmly and told Benny I'd fix him a pallet on the floor in Sam's room. I sat beside Jamie's bed and told him a Christian bedtime story about how the Good Shepherd went after lost sheep.

Actually, the story was more for me than Jamie. I needed to know that Jesus, my Lord, understood what was happening in our house even if I didn't. I wanted assurance that God Almighty would look after my children, protect us from evil, and release us one day from living in this house. According to Jeremy, I cried out in my sleep as I mumbled prayers over and over again.

34

BECCA PHONED SUNDAY afternoon. "Did you find Beverly?" I spurted, praying that her call was bringing good news.

"No, but I'm still hopeful." Becca explained what was being done to locate our baby sister. "Gary and I checked all the Egyptian hospitals and they show no record she was admitted."

"Someone said they saw a woman leave through the back door of the church," I recalled. "Bev would call us if she could."

"I pray she's in a safe place," Becca said.

"You think she's hiding out?"

"I don't know, Brooke. But Gary can't stay off work much longer, so we may be coming back to the states soon."

"Should I come to London in your place?" I asked.

"No, Brooke. Someone from the UN Peacekeepers will call us if they locate Beverly." Becca paused. "If a terrorist organization is holding her, God forbid, they will contact the authorities to negotiate the release of their jihadists' associates."

"I feel so helpless." *On many levels*, I thought.

"Is everyone in your family doing well?" Becca inquired.

"Sam's sick again with flu symptoms."

"Sounds like a standard case of Mono to me."

"Hopefully, the doctor will be able to diagnose his problem."

We ended our conversation with a prayer. As I closed my cell phone Jeremy walked through the bedroom into the bathroom. A couple minutes later I heard the commode flush.

"Oh, that's just great!" I muttered.

"No problem," he called back. "That was me flushing."

Jeremy conducted Sunday morning services with finesse, no problems other than the side discussions concerning Willard

Jacob's arrest and upcoming court trial. I privately took the fifth when asked what I thought, adding no content to standard gossip.

I knew our congregation was curious and meant Willard no harm, but all the conjectures flying about weren't helping him. We needed serious prayer power to discern the truth. Only with the help of the Holy Spirit was that possible. God help us.

The fourth Monday of January, our family resumed our usual work and school schedules. Benny was less than enthusiastic about school and Sam stayed home, opting to do his assignments online. Jamie was the only happy soul anxious to get to his kindergarten class and see his friends. *Me?* I maneuvered through my morning classes in a mental fog, concerned over Sam's periodic bouts with fever and Beverly's absence from our family.

Tuesday, after school, I took Sam to the clinic. Promptly ushered into a lab room near the back of the office, a nurse drew vials of his blood for a battery of tests. While waiting for the results in the receptionist area, I read a magazine and Sam dozed.

"Samuel McLaughlin," the nurse called out his name.

It was our time to see the doctor. "Wake up, Sam."

Sam's laboratory results were on Dr. Simpson's laptop and easily accessed. Technology had vastly improved the time it took to analyze blood samples. He shook Sam's hand then told him to take a seat on the examination table. I waited outside the room until they were finished. The door opened.

"You can come back in, Mrs. McLaughlin."

"Sam's neck glands are swollen," he reported.

"My neck actually hurts some," Sam remarked.

"He's taken a lot of Tylenol in the past week," I chimed in.

"You're running a low-grade fever, Sam." Dr. Simpson reported then asked, "On a scale of one to ten, with ten being good and one awful, how you say you feel most of the time?"

"About a three, I think. Sometimes better," he replied.

"Is Sam's condition serious?" I asked the obvious.

Dr. Simpson swung toward me on his swivel stool, his stethoscope dangling on a silver chain. "Before I arrive at a diagnosis, I'd like to get a second opinion from a specialist."

"What kind of specialist?" My heart leaped.

Dr. Simpson gazed at me then Sam. "Let's not leap to any conclusions without more extensive tests, young man."

Sam nodded then asked, "Can't you just tell me what you think is wrong?" He sighed. "Is is bad?"

Bad is when ghosts haunt you. Bad is when your mother dies and you never told her how much you love her. Sam's question and Dr. Simpson's failure to diagnose his mysterious illness frightened me even more. "Sam, you should have the tests."

Sam was obviously upset, feeling bad and near tears.

"You're probably fine, Sam." Dr. Simpson tried to dispel his fear of the unknown. "I'll call your mom about a time to see the specialist. Meanwhile, I'm going to prescribe antibiotics."

Sam and I walked out of the clinic with the script in hand and had the meds filled at the CVS around the corner.

When we got home Jeremy was there with our two younger boys. "What did the doctor say about Sam?" he asked.

"He did some blood work done." I held up the CVS sack.

Jeremy nodded.

"He's starting another round of antibiotics." I filled a glass with tap water, removed a tab, and gave it to Sam.

I began preparing supper. Neither Sam nor I felt like discussing his doctor's visit with Jeremy and he knew it.

* * *

Wednesday afternoon, Jeremy drove into Nashville to meet with Dr. Jeffrey Mahoney, a professor on staff at the Louisville Theological Seminary. His intent was to share the ghostly events taking shape in our house and seek an opinion. Afterwards, he would go directly to the church for the evening Bible study at six.

With Sam feeling so poorly, I decided to skip choir practice and keep the boys home with me. It was a little after nine o'clock when I heard Jeremy come in the front door. Anxious to hear what Jeff Mahoney had said regarding our haunting, I prayed that visions of sugarplums danced in our boys' heads while they were nestled in their beds. We all seriously needed a good night's rest.

Jeremy wearily tromped into our bedroom, removed his clothes in silence, and donned his pajamas. I was already in bed, sitting up with a pillow at my back with a book open in my lap.

"Well . . ." I couldn't wait any longer.

"Jeff surprised me." He crawled into bed beside me. "After I summarized Gibby's activities in our house, he said I'd be surprised to hear that other ministers had similar experiences."

"No way, how is it we've never read of such?"

"You know why, Brooke. Nobody wants to talk about ghosts, demons—whatever spiritual mysteries we Christians don't understand." He grasped my hand. "It'll upset the status quo."

"*They* won't let us ignore them," I grumbled.

"Jeff believed me but had no suggestions as to cleansing our house," Jeremy continued. "I told him that Don Sedgwick had blessed our house with holy oil and it didn't change a thing."

"I really believed Jeff would be helpful."

"Me, too," Jer said. "I also told him you'd performed an exorcism." He patted my arm. "You did real good, honey."

"How did he respond to that?" I asked.

"He seemed amused then asked if it had helped."

"What did you say?" I asked.

"I told him some, but our guests had somehow found ways to continue making their presence known." Jeremy widely yawned. "I think the only way to escape them is to move."

"We've almost been here four years, is that a possibility?"

"We should pray about where God wants us to go."

Even more troubling was Sam's mysterious illness. I could deal with ghosts, but losing my son, that was another matter.

35

WILLARD JACOBS WAS arraigned in county court the second Monday in February. After pleading not guilty to murdering his wife Alice, he was denied bail and hauled away in chains to the county prison wearing an orange jumpsuit. Judge Daniel Hartford set the trial date for the second Monday in April.

Out of a pool of potential jurors, twelve would be vetted by the prosecuting and defense attorneys. The jury would then select a foreman to preside over their discussions. Since the accused was charged with first-degree murder, once the trial began, no juror would be allowed to return home until a verdict was rendered.

Evidently, Detective Clay Bennett believed he had a solid murder-one case against Willard, otherwise the prosecuting attorney would have requested more time before the trial date.

As I sat in the courtroom listening to the judicial process unfold, I realized no case of this criminal magnitude had occurred in our county. This trial obviously pushed other cases aside.

This I derived from deduction, but the material facts of the case were printed on the first page of our local newspaper. The trial would soon become a topic of national interest.

"I don't think Willard's getting a fair shot," I told Jeremy on Tuesday morning over breakfast. "He deserves better."

"Why do you assume that?" he asked.

"It's a hunch," I admitted. "But I actually believe Willard is innocent." Go figure. "If I could only speak with Elise, perhaps I'd learn why she thinks Willard killed her sister."

"Don't even consider it, Brooke!" My good-hearted husband warned me. "You've been instructed to butt out."

"Not if I'm called to testify in court."

Butt out, huh? I frowned.

"What more can you say to help Willard?"

"Maybe Alice's sister knows more than she's saying."

"Honey . . ." he made firm eye contact.

"I know, butt out . . ." My testimony concerning Willard's abuse of Alice was on record, though it was hearsay. In light of the forensic evidence, it appeared Willard was a prime suspect.

Innocent until proven guilty . . . which made me question how many innocents had served time in America's penitentiary system? Now a member of our church was accused of murder.

Unthinkable! I focused on my husband. "What did you say?"

"Is this matter settled?" Jeremy repeated his question.

"I guess . . ." My mind was working overtime.

"That's not a definitive answer, Brooke."

"Well, it's the best I can do for now."

Jeremy had a few nursing home visits scheduled so I took the boys to their respective schools then reported to my homeroom.

My first class was at 8:20. During the middle of my third-period English class, my cell phone buzzed inside my sweater jacket. Since my students were involved in a required reading assignment, I removed my phone and glanced at the caller I.D.

It wasn't a name I recognized. Still, immensely curious, I accepted the call. "Yes?" I stepped out in the hallway.

With all the static background noises I couldn't hear a thing.

"Is anybody there?" I started to end the call.

"It's me, Brooke."

The weak familiar voice suffused through the jumble of background noises. "Beverly?" My heart thudded like the hoofs of a hundred horses racing on solid ground. "Where are you?"

"I need help, Brooke."

"Of course, you do," I said. "Where are you?"

"I don't know—a refugee camp somewhere, I think."

"Are you in Egypt?" I asked.

"I don't think so. After the church was bombed, I stumbled into a band of people near the Libyan border."

"What?" I struggled to hear over the background static as it increased and Beverly's voice dimmed. I tried to recall the world map and picture exactly where Libya was in relationship to Egypt.

"Whose phone are you using?" I asked.

"I don't know. I found it on the ground by my tent."

"Do you have enough food to eat?" I hurriedly asked.

"It's isn't so bad, lots of dried fruits and canned meats."

"Beverly, you have to give me something if I'm to help you."

"I'm doing the best I can, Brooke."

"I know you are, sweetie." Time was short to obtain the critical information necessary for a rescue team to find my sister.

"Is anyone watching you as we speak?" I inquired.

"No—is the cell number I'm using on your caller I.D.?"

"Yes, it is." I verified by quickly looking.

"Contact the American Embassy in Egypt and give them this number. Hopefully, they'll be able to find the owner."

"Wait . . ." The connection failed and I lost Beverly.

"Dear God," I uttered, fearing the phone's battery had crashed and I would receive no further contact from my sister.

I suddenly realized Beverly was a widow and probably hadn't been told. Witnessing the explosion, she must have realized the possibility. Suddenly, the phone rang again and I answered.

"It's me again," Beverly uttered. "Terah must be going crazy looking for me. Will you contact him for me?"

"Sure," I said. "Call me back in a few days, okay?"

"Tell Terah I love him."

The connection ended and I leaned against the wall and wept. I hadn't lied to Beverly, but I hadn't told the whole truth. I peeled off the wall as one of my students came out to check on me.

"Mrs. McLaughlin? Is everything okay?"

"Jennifer, I just heard from my baby sister and I'm thrilled."

"The one the terrorist captured?"

"She's in a camp of sorts." I dried my eyes on my blouse. "Let's go back in the room and finish class." I gently nudged her.

Most students had finished their reading assignment and were quietly engaged in conversation. I glanced at each of them.

"Thank you for your patience, class." One hand on my desk steadied my shaky frame. "My missing sister, Beverly, just called."

"She's alive!" One of the bulky football boys stood up and started a slow clap. In the next thirty seconds all thirty students were applauding. I raised a hand to silence them.

"That doesn't mean you don't have another eight minutes of class." My voice caught in my throat. "But I'll go easy on you."

Laughter and applause erupted.

"What's going in here?" My principal, Dr. Rose, stood in the doorway to my classroom, puzzled over the applause.

Jennifer shot out of her seat, raising a hand. "Dr. Rose, Mrs. McLaughlin talked to her missing sister," she reported.

"That's great news, Brooke. Is she okay?"

"I don't know," I replied. "Beverly's in an unidentified camp in the desert. She found a satellite phone and called me."

"Okay. Good. Continue on, class."

As far as teaching was concerned, I was finished. I waited out the bell and students moved into the hall for their next class.

As soon as the room emptied, I shut the door and phoned Becca. "I heard from Beverly!" I spurted when she answered.

"Where is she?"

"Somewhere near the Libyan border, she thinks."

"She thinks? What does that mean, Brooke?"

"Beverly isn't sure where she is. She thinks a refugee camp with a lot of other people," I explained. "She has food."

"Why hasn't she called one of us before?"

"She couldn't," I said. "She found a satellite phone outside her tent. She wants me to contact the Embassy in Egypt and give them the number registered on my cell phone. She hopes they can track the owner and find out where the camp is located."

"Great!" Becca exclaimed. "If Bev leaves her phone on, the authorities can use the Global Positioning System to locate her."

"Wait, the phone has to be on?"

"Yes . . ."

"She probably turned it off to save on the battery."

A moment of silence passed between us.

"There's another issue, Brooke."

"What?" Could anything be worse?

"Are you aware there's fighting and bloodshed in Libya?"

"No, but Beverly didn't sound afraid," I reported. "She indicated she had access to food, water and shelter."

"Well, at least she won't starve until we find her."

"There's another issue," I said. "Beverly doesn't know that Terah and his family were killed during in the church bombing."

"And you didn't tell her." Becca concluded.

"No, she has enough on her plate."

"Okay, the authorities can figure out the unknowns," Becca said. "This is a huge breakthrough, Brooke! Beverly's alive."

"How can I get the embassy's number in Egypt?"

"I'll phone Gary. He knows people in Washington. He'll get the number and call you," Becca hurriedly said. "Keep praying."

I ended the call, thanking God for protecting my sister.

36

GOOD NEWS CATAPULTED my spirits to Cloud Nine. By the time I arrived home with the boys Tuesday afternoon, I had fully embraced optimism. We would find Beverly and bring her home.

Benny and Jamie snacked on fruit then ventured out to the shed to work on a new model plane. They took their toy racecars with them. At least the cars weren't running around the house without batteries. And gratefully, the spirits had left Benny alone for over a week. Humming as I worked, I prepped for supper.

Gary phoned at 5:00 p.m. He'd spoken with the secretary of the American ambassador to Egypt and obtained an email address where I could send the phone number Beverly used to call me, hoping someone could track down its owner. I went straight to my computer and forwarded the information then texted Jeremy to share my good news. He replied back with hallelujahs to God.

Running out of steam, I fixed myself a cup of herbal tea and went into the living room where I kicked back in the recliner and read my Bible. There was so much for which to be thankful. And much prayer still needed for both Willard Jacobs and my sister. They would need God's guidance to maneuver through their trials.

Especially when Beverly learned that her husband for seven months had died with his parents during the church explosion. She would come home broken, sad, and traumatized from the hostage experience. However, I knew Beverly's fervent faith would revitalize her determination to serve God in the future.

In the blessed moment, I was at rest in my spirit.

Our family ate supper when Jeremy came home at six o'clock and we did all the usual things before bedtime. All the while, the indwelling Holy Spirit exploded inside of me with great comfort.

Lying in my bed that night, I easily fell asleep. It was not my job to kick out our ghosts or solve Alice Jacob's murder. In all ways, during all trials, God is faithful. He never forsakes us.

* * *

Wednesday morning cracked dawn and suffused the eastern horizon with magnificent color. I opened my eyes.

What would happen today?

As I made breakfast for my family, I hummed a gospel tune with the radio, realizing Willard needed my help if he beat the charge of Murder One. And I would need God's guidance.

Otherwise, I had no power to alter the outcome.

On schedule, we all left the house around eight. During my lunch break at school, my cell phone vibrated. I didn't recognize the caller, but why not see who was interested in contacting me?

Ah ha, I was never one to shun a mystery.

"Hello," I hurriedly said.

"Is this Brooke McLaughlin?"

It was a female voice I didn't recognize.

"Is this in regard to my sister?"

"No, it's about Alice Jacobs."

The caller had my full attention.

"To whom am I speaking, and how may I help you?"

"Topeka is my handle," the caller replied. "I never give out my real name. Privacy, you know," she said with a false laugh.

"Okay, how are you connected to Alice?" I inquired.

"I have some information that might interest you," Topeka said. "Alice and I are often in the same online chatroom."

"How do you know Alice?" I asked.

"We were once neighbors," Topeka explained. "I knew her handle was Tigress and we kept in touch after she moved."

"Okay, what is your point? I don't have long to talk."

"Well, as you probably know, a number of people visit a chatroom at the same time," Topeka said. "A woman using the handle Blade told me that the Tigress was seeing her husband."

"What does that mean?" I asked.

"Apparently, Tigress met Blade's husband in the chatroom and they connected on FACEBOOK," Topeka replied. "They later met at a restaurant in Las Vegas during a business thing."

My pulse leaped. Willard had mentioned Alice's Las Vegas connection. And he'd accused Alice of having an affair.

"Are you saying Alice had an affair?" I asked.

"Oh, I don't know if it was a full-fledged sexual fling or they just met up as friends," Topeka offered.

"Okay . . . where is all this leading?"

"Well, Blade found out Taurus was talking to Tigress, and she was fit to be tied," Topeka said. "She told me to warn Tigress to stop harassing her husband or she'd personally stop her."

"What did you take that to mean?" I asked.

"Nothing at the time," Topeka replied. "Then when I heard on CNN that Alice Jacobs had been brutally murdered, I began questioning if Blade had carried out her threat."

Topeka's news was shocking. This was a lead Detective Bennett could sink his teeth into. "If I give you the number of the detective investigating Alice's death, will you call him?"

"No way, I just thought someone should know."

"How did you get my name and number?"

"You were mentioned in an article I read," Tepeka replied. "Your church secretary gave me your cell number."

So much for privacy. . . I'd have a talk with Janice about giving our cell phone numbers to people outside our congregation.

"What do you expect me to do with this information?"

"Just tell the detective in charge of the case what I said," Topeka replied. "Maybe he will investigate Blade. I'd sure hate for the wrong person to go to prison. It doesn't ring true."

"I agree, and I will pass on the information," I promised. "But Topeka, that doesn't mean that Detective Bennett won't track you down himself for a statement." I fell silent.

"Look, my husband forbade me to become involved. I'm just a good citizen reporting what I know. Okay?"

I understood. Jeremy felt the same way about me.

"Okay, I'll do what I can. But I have no guarantees," I truthfully said. "Detective Bennett is a race engine on steroids."

"Thank you for being so honest, Brooke. I know you are a pastor's wife and will do the right thing. That's why I called you."

My cell phone lost Topeka's call.

I stood there, stunned. Topeka must have used a payphone or a prepaid burner. I had no way to call her back. Someone more techie than I would need to trace Topeka's call.

After lunch, I completed my afternoon classes and picked up Jamie at kindergarten. At Benny's elementary school, I lined up behind a number of vehicles waiting for my turn to get him.

Jamie was squirmy and wanted a lollypop. I retrieved one from the glove compartment and passed it over the back seat.

Fifteen minutes later, Benny was in the car.

"Mom, can we go to church tonight?" Benny asked.

"Is there some special reason you want to go?" I returned.

"Yeah, I met a new guy at school. His family is going to visit our church tonight," Benny revealed. "He's so cool and wants to play on our school soccer team this spring."

"Good news, buddy. I'd like to meet your friend's parents."

We drove out of the school parking lot and went straight to Burger King for sandwiches. Jeremy was fetching Sam from high school and they were going directly to church. Following Wednesday evening's Bible study, Jeremy had a staff meeting.

Afterwards, the Mary-Martha women's circle was serving them pizza and soft drinks. I thought it would do Sam good to be around people after so many hours alone at the house.

The boys and I were at the church by 5:30 p.m. Anxious to tell Jeremy about what I'd learned from Topeka's phone call, I didn't need his permission to talk to Detective Bennett about Blade's threats. But I preferred Jeremy know ahead of time in case my news meant my being more involved with the case.

I found Jer in his office about to head off to Bible study.

"Hi, Brooke . . ." he pecked me on the cheek. "How was your day?" He waved me to the cushioned chair in his office.

"Interesting," I said and shut the door. "Yours . . .?"

"Busy," he replied. "Dr. Simpson called late this afternoon."

My eyes widened with interest.

"He wants to talk with both of us tomorrow at his office."

"Is this about Sam's report?"

"I presume so, but didn't ask for details." He glanced at his watch. "We'll continue this conversation when we get home."

"Wait, I need to tell you something."

"Not now, Brooke, I'm running late for Bible study."

I stepped into the hall and felt weak in the knees. Too much was happening at once. I was emotionally on overload.

The Bible Study finished at seven and the staff meeting followed. Benny's friend from his class did not come. Of course, he was disappointed. Plans change, I reminded Benny. It was likely he had a good reason for not coming. Talk to him tomorrow, find out and plan another time to get together.

My reasoning seemed to pacify Benny. Back at the house, I sent him and Jamie upstairs to their bedrooms to dress for bed.

A minute later, I heard Benny's videogame turn on.

I was hanging clothes in my bedroom closet when I heard Jeremy walk in the bathroom from the hall entrance. The commode promptly flushed. Though annoying, I didn't comment as I joined him in the bathroom. "Hi, how did Sam do?"

"Great! He's a born communicator. Our staff adores him."

I sat down at the vanity stool and stared at my image in the mirror. Jeremy stood behind me, a frown emanating in his face.

I turned around to face him. "Is everything at church okay?"

"It's not that." He shrugged.

"Then, what is it about?" I turned around on the stool and snagged a tissue to remove my lipstick and makeup.

"What do you think is wrong with Sam?" He glared at me through the mirror. I turned around to face him again.

"He's rundown, I presume."

A couple seconds passed as we stared at one another.

"Like I said earlier, Dr. Simpson wants to meet with us to discuss Sam's test results," Jer said. "He wants Bill to be present."

"Does this mean Sam's condition is serious?"

"Brooke, you know as much as I do."

So this was a family conference with the patient's father, mother and step-father. Something was dreadfully wrong with our beloved Sam. "Will Sam be with us?" I thought to ask.

"No," Jer replied. "We're meeting at Dr. Simpson's office at noon tomorrow so you can come. Bill said the time was fine."

I thought my heart would drop out of my chest as I faced the mirror again. Jeremy did not miss the fear in my expression.

"Brooke, we shouldn't assume the worst."

"I already have." I jerked a breath. "I can't lose my son."

"Don't jump to conclusions when you haven't heard what Dr. Simpson has to say," Jeremy warned.

I nodded, denying a barrage of tears. Suddenly, if Willard went to prison for murdering Alice didn't seem so important to me anymore. Call it selfish, call it denial. That was how I felt.

Just when I was happy, at peace that Beverly would be found and brought home safely, another crisis loomed before me.

Dear God, how much more can our family endure?

37

THE WEE HOURS of Thursday was a waking nightmare for me. Sleepless in our haunted house, I laid in bed staring up at the white ceiling while listening to creaks and pops within the four walls. I couldn't prevent Gibby's family from creeping around.

Let them scream, appear, rattle the rafters, whatever, I refused to be intimidated. I would never figure out why *they* lingered among the living. Maybe Gibby had treaded on holy ground when he purchased this plot of land and built this beautiful abode. Who was I to answer those questions?

Hadn't volumes of books been written on the subject of the supernatural, films produced to scare the pants off people? In the movie, *The Haunting in Connecticut*, no one lived in peace in that house. Malicious spirits actively appeared, overturned furniture, and tore up things in fits of anger. Even as the house burned to the ground, corpses tumbled out of the walls. A mortician had once owned the house and operated his business in the basement.

I once assumed that storyline was fiction, but now I wasn't so sure. All I knew was I wanted out of this house. I wanted to be free of *them*. I wanted to leave and not take with me sick, disturbed, and frightened children. If God was not ready to cleanse this house of *them*, then cleanse my family of fear.

I dragged myself through Thursday morning's routine, mentioning nothing to Sam regarding our scheduled conference with Dr. Simpson. At 11:50 a.m., when my last class of the morning ended, I signed out at the front desk and drove over to the clinic. Jeremy and Bill's vehicles were parked out front.

I exited my Malibu and entered through the front door.

As anticipated, I was shown to the conference room. Jeremy and Bill stopped talking. Silence overwhelmed me as I took a seat.

"Okay, what's the bad news?" I blabbered like a goon.

The astute doctor cleared his throat. "Sam's report shows he has a form of leukemia." He made eye contact. "He needs to see an oncologist and undergo treatments as soon as possible."

"Cancer . . .?" I gasped, grabbing Jeremy's hand for support.

"Will you recommend an oncologist?" Bill asked.

"Deborah Clooney is well qualified to treat the disease," Dr. Simpson replied. "She works out of Vanderbilt Hospital in Nashville. I can set an appointment with her for Sam before you leave today. Or give you a list of oncologists to choose from."

"Are there different types of blood cancers?" Bill inquired.

"Yes." Dr. Simpson handed him a set of stapled paper. "This article lists the most commonly diagnosed types of cancers and explains in lay terms how they differently affect patients."

I denied my tears, crumbling inside. *Why my Sam, God?*

"I know this is a shock," Dr. Simpson continued, "but Sam's leukemia is treatable when diagnosed in its early stages."

I breathed a sigh of relief. "So you believe Sam will heal with treatments?" I grasped at threads of hope.

"To be honest, a lot depends on his immune system."

"If Sam has a fully charged immune system," Bill said.

"Yes, Sam can better fight the disease while receiving chemo," Dr. Simpson revealed. Bill nodded at me, satisfied.

Dr. Simpson said, "When you counsel with Dr. Clooney, she'll explain the procedure in detail. Sam needs to be present."

I looked at Jeremy then Bill. We seemed in agreement that Dr. Clooney would be the oncologist who treated Sam.

We talked a few more minutes then left the office.

The three of us stood in the parking lot. The air was chilly, not unbearable. The March sky was royal blue dotted with puffy-white drifting clouds. It was a nice day, considering our unrest.

Today was a turning point in all of our lives. As parents, we could no longer assume Sam would graduate high school, attend college, live and work without assistance, or even marry. We were now a family of special needs. I had no idea what that entailed.

But I'd learn. "Bill, do you want to be the one to tell Sam?"

"How would you feel about that?" Bill queried Jeremy as he stepped away, lit a cigarette, inhaled then blew out smoke.

"Whatever you and Brooke decide is good for me."

Brother Mac was compliant. I knew Sam trusted his dad to always be honest with him. Not that I would actually lie, but delivering such news would be difficult. I deferred the task to Bill.

"All right, Brooke, if that's what you believe is best," Bill said.

"When will you tell him?" I asked.

"Tomorrow," Bill replied. "I'll pick up Sam from school, take him out to supper and let him spend the night with me in Nashville. We'll talk Saturday morning then I'll bring him home."

For me to face him, I shuddered at the thought.

"Thanks, I'm far too emotional about Sam's illness to have a rational discussion." We walked to our respective vehicles.

I sat in my Malibu, absorbing the awful news. The idea of Sam enduring cancer was terrifying. How would he take the news? And how could this happen to our noble Christian son?

Sam had never once taken a drink of alcohol or experimented with illegal drugs to my knowledge. Just starting out in life, he was devoted to Christ's ministry. Intelligent, gentle, and kind . . . I thought to myself. Then I remembered my conversation with Topeka regarding Blade and her mystery husband.

I rang Jeremy's cell as I drove.

"Brooke . . .?" He answered on the second ring.

"Jeremy!" I rasped. "We've been so busy dealing with Sam's illness I failed to tell you about a phone call I received at school regarding Alice Jacob's death." My eyes erratically blinked.

"From Detective Bennett . . .?"

"No, not him," I replied. "The caller was a woman who claimed she'd been in an internet chatroom speaking with Alice."

"Slow down, honey, you're talking too fast."

I heard his motor silence. "I'm back at the church, Brooke. Can we talk about this at home?" The SUV door slammed.

"No, Jer, we can't! Topeka gave me a lead."

"What kind of name is Topeka?"

"It's a fake name she uses in a chatroom," I explained.

"This seems like a long conversation. Can't we talk about this another time? I need to concentrate on organizing my Bible Study material for Wednesday evening," Jeremy said.

"Wait, Jer! One more thing, I promise!"

"Okay, but only one then I need to work."

"Topeka spoke with a woman in the same chatroom who threatened Alice. Maybe Blade murdered Alice out of jealousy."

"Brooke, sweetheart, I know you mean well."

I cringed, feeling a sermon coming on.

"Honey, is this the right time to become more involved in Willard's case? Right when we need to concentrate on Sam."

"Wait, Jeremy! There is no right time for any of this!" I countered. "This is important and may save Willard's life."

"Okay, I'm in my office now and the door is closed. Tell me what you learned from the call." The silence said I was onstage.

"Topeka said that Blade's husband was seeing Alice."

"What does that mean? She was having an affair?"

"Topeka didn't know for sure, but Blade thought her husband was having an affair with Tigress. Blade threatened to stop Tigress if she didn't stop harassing Taurus." I paused.

"Jer, if that's true, infidelity is motive for murder."

"Who is Taurus?" Jeremy inquired.

"Blade's husband's handle," I replied.

"And you believe this nameless woman, Topeka?"

"I don't know if anything she told me is true," I admitted. "But doesn't it seem odd that Alice's computer was wiped clean?"

"I don't have an opinion, Brooke, based on the fact there is no proof that anything Topeka said is true. One thing I do know, Detective Bennett would classify this as meddling."

"I didn't call Topeka, she called me," I pointed out.

"I hope you're not headed for trouble."

"When I talked with Willard that Wednesday night at the church, he told me he was positive Alice met up with a man while attending a work-related convention in Las Vegas. Topeka's news supports his testimony. I have to let Detective Bennett know."

"Well, I suppose the right thing to do is to tell Detective Bennett what Topeka said and let him handle it from there."

"I wanted you to know before I went to see him."

"So now you've told me . . ."

My confession left me feeling less than content.

I returned to school in time for my second afternoon class. I didn't feel good about the way Jeremy and I parted ways. Apparently, he was handling the news of Sam's illness differently than I was, showing no visible outrage at the unfairness.

Throw in my passion to help Willard Jacobs, and the future was a deplorable tangle of unknowns. I needed God's grace to get me through whatever was coming in the next months. I needed to be strong for Sam. And Sam needed God's help.

Setting personal issues aside, I checked the class role and proceeded to teach French. After my last class at 2:50, I phoned Jeremy at church and asked him to pick up all three of the boys.

When the final bell for the school day sounded, I drove over to the police station. "Is Detective Bennett in?" I inquired.

"Do you have an appointment?"

"No, tell him it's Brooke McLaughlin and I have information pertaining to Willard Jacobs' case." I took a seat and waited.

Ten minutes later, Bennett hooked a finger at me. I trailed him down the hall to his private office. He seemed his usual, nasty self with little interest in why I was there.

"What is it this time?" He rudely asked.

"I recently learned something interesting," I said.

"Don't waste my time, Mrs. McLaughlin." He sat down at his desk and drilled holes through me with his piercing blue eyes.

"Trust me, Detective Bennett, you need to hear this."

I plopped my big purse on a vacant chair then told him about the phone call I'd received from Topeka, and how Blade had threatened to punish Alice. When I'd finished, he stared out the window. After a minute, I cleared my throat to gain his attention.

"Detective Bennett, I'm not trying to interfere with your investigation. Maybe you can use this information to help clear Willard's name. He's a decent, honest man, and so was Alice."

Humph. Bennett rotated his chair toward me, lacing his bulky hands over his muscular torso. "That's pretty interesting."

"Maybe you can trace Topeka's call and talk to her?"

Instantly, he stood up, shoved his chair back and held out his calloused left hand. "Let me see your phone, Brooke."

So now I'm Brooke? Did we just cross a threshold?

"Keep it for as long as you need." I handed it over. "I'll purchase a prepaid at Wal-Mart on my way home."

"Mrs. McLaughlin," Bennett said. "You're full of surprises."

I didn't know how to respond to his comment.

"In case you're right, I'll check it out," he said.

"Thanks. I know Alice would thank you if she could."

I left the precinct feeling pretty good that I'd done my civic duty. The rest was up to Detective Bennett to figure out how Blade was involved with Alice's death, or if she was. With that done, I needed to direct my energy toward Sam, find some way to help him cope with what lay ahead of him, which made me think of Paul of Tarsus and how much he had suffered for Christ.

It was a given that Sam's path would prove more difficult than other healthy teens. Perhaps God would later use his experience to glorify His Son Jesus. I am not a prophet. I am a wife and a mom, desperately trying to grasp onto faith.

38

I WADED THROUGH Friday in a fog. After school, Bill picked up Sam and drove him to his house in Nashville. The rest of us spent a quiet evening at home, enduring a fitful heavy rainfall. We ate too much pizza, watched a family-friendly comedy flick on TV then went to bed early. I was glad to put this workweek behind.

Saturday arrived and Jeremy took Benny to soccer practice at ten. With a little pleading, Jamie accompanied them.

So it was just me alone in the house.

"Did any of you do this to my son?" I called out from the hallway. "If this is part of your mischief to scare us, I want you to know you're wasting your precious energy on this family."

I paused for a response. None offered.

"Oh, you should know we are one for all and all for one! Not even death can separate us from God. Do you hear me?"

When no disturbances occurred I decided *they* got the message and began running the vacuum over the scattered rugs.

Then I heard the washing machine switch on. That was one of *their* favorite ploys, turning on electrical devices. I switched off the vacuum and went into the laundry room to turn off the machine. Less than enthusiastic, I resumed my household duties.

Jeremy and the boys arrived home at one o'clock for lunch. A pot roast bubbled in the slow cooker. I served mashed potatoes and butter beans with the meat, stuffing my stomach as a ploy to comfort my psyche as I watched the minutes and hours tick away.

I could think of nothing but Sam. How would he handle the fact that he had leukemia? I stared at the land phone but it didn't ring. Jamie fell asleep for an afternoon nap and Jeremy drifted off in the living room with a basketball game loudly blaring.

I used the spare time to review my next week's lesson plans. I'd already spoken to Dr. Rose about hiring a substitute teacher to fulfill my duties while I accompanied Sam to see Dr. Clooney.

Bill came into the house with Sam a little after four p.m.

"Hi, Mom," Sam nonchalantly greeted me as he slung his parka on the banister post. "Where's everybody?"

"Around," I replied, studying his demeanor.

"Dad told me." He turned soft hazel eyes on me.

I nodded. "Are you okay?"

"Yeah, I think so. Dad let me read the medical article about the kinds of leukemia people get. I seem to have the friendly kind." He offered a faint smile. "Well, almost."

I chuckled. Leave it to Sam to find humor in horrible situations. "I'm glad, son." I hugged him tightly. "Thanks for telling him, Bill. Do you have time for a cup of coffee?"

"No, I'm meeting some friends for dinner tonight."

Bill pulled Sam into an embrace. "Hang in there, son, your mom and I will be there every step of the way to make sure that oncologist does her job." He caught my eye with that same empathetic look that first drew me to him. Bill was a good guy and a fantastic dad. We were just too young and impulsive to be married. In my reverie, Jeremy came down the stairs.

"Hi, Bill." They shook hands.

"Hey, Sam, you doing okay . . .?"

"Yeah, I'm good."

We talked to Bill for awhile then said our goodbyes. He agreed to meet us at Dr. Clooney's office for Sam's appointment.

"I should know the date and time by Monday," I told him.

"Whenever, I won't have a problem taking off work under the circumstances," Bill said. "Twenty-four hours notice is fine."

"I'll call you as soon as we hear," I said.

"Keep me posted." Bill went out the door.

"He's a nice guy," Brother Mac commented.

"Yeah, I guess we were a little young to work out our shaky marriage. But, at least, we got Sam out of the deal," I said.

"Well, I'm glad you included me in your bigger picture."

"Me, too, Jeremy," I piped. "I love you and our boys."

Becca phoned after supper and sensed my reluctance to freely talk. "What's wrong, Brooke, you don't sound right."

"It's Sam. . ." I allowed myself to cry for the first time.

Cloistered in my bedroom closet with the phone glued to my ear, I sank to my knees and told Becca about Sam's cancer. She was shocked and empathetic, offering kind words of comfort.

"As if worrying about Beverly isn't enough of a trauma . . ."

"Sam is handling the news better than either me or Jeremy," I told Becca. "But you phoned me for a reason. Is it about Beverly? Did you hear from the American embassy in Egypt?"

"No, but I heard from my London contact," Becca said. "The UN peacekeepers, mostly the French, have checked several camps in the countries bordering Egypt and no one has seen a white girl. Among the dark-skinned Middle Easterners, people would notice. But they tell me, smaller campsites often move."

"Has Beverly used the phone she found again?" I asked.

"The London ambassador tried, but got no answer."

That wasn't good news. "Maybe the battery died," I said.

"Or someone took the phone from her," Becca speculated. "We can't know for sure. Beverly may not have cell service."

"It's a satellite phone. Service is all over the globe."

"Well, the good news is that the peacekeepers are still trying to find our baby sister. Beverly's call to you solidified the idea she's still alive. We just need to pray for her safety. And, of course, Gary and I will pray for Sam's healing," she added.

"Thank you, Becca. It's great having a big sister like you."

* * *

Sunday's services went off as scheduled. We agreed not to tell our congregation about Sam's condition until we knew more.

219

Brother Mac's sermon was about love and compassion for one's neighbor. No individual had a right to judge another's plight.

The day passed in a normal fashion, thank God.

Monday morning, our family left the house and resumed our weekly responsibilities. A March ice storm was forecast for later in the day, which meant our county and city schools would likely be closed tomorrow with icy county roads becoming impassable.

Dr. Clooney's nurse called me at school before the morning was out and told me Sam's appointment was set for next Thursday at 9:30 a.m. Bill and I would be there with Sam, I confirmed.

"What about Sam's health records?" I asked.

"Dr. Simpson sent them electronically," Chloe replied. "Mrs. McLaughlin, we'll take good care of your son. You need to trust us to do our job, and when Sam is home, help him follow our prescribed regiment. Will you do that? It'll be a great help."

"I will do the best I can, Chloe."

After school, Sam rode with me to pick up Benny and Jamie.

"Mom," he said, "do you think chemo will be hard?" It was a reasonable question and I owed him an honest answer.

"Sam, what I know about cancer I could list on five fingers. Talk to Dr. Clooney, she's the expert in treating cancer and I trust her judgment." I stared at my troubled son. "You'll be fine."

He nodded. "Thanks, Mom. I'm sure I will."

Even more than trusting the oncologist with Sam's treatment, I trusted God. Ultimately, He would give Sam the strength to overcome this terrible disease. "Sam, God loves you very much."

"I know, Mom. I'll be fine."

My brave son . . .

39

AS ANTICIPATED, SCHOOL was dismissed on Tuesday and again on Wednesday due to icy weather. Too many school days missed and summer break would be delayed. Teachers looked forward to summer almost as much as the kids. The time off was a blessing.

Due to the brilliant sunlight, the atmosphere warmed up on late Wednesday and melted the countryside's icy glaze; sparkling ice palaces began to lose their luster. Water rippled across our yard's barren ground in rivulets. Broken tree limbs sprawled across the ground like wounded soldiers. Red cardinals flitted from post to pillar, the only sign of the coming spring when they would build their nests and give birth to the next generation.

School buses resumed their regular routes on Thursday. I phoned Dr. Rose and reminded her I was taking a personal day. She assured me the substitute she'd found would do a good job.

"Just take good care of Sam for all of us," Dr. Rose said.

Jeremy, Sam and I showed up early at the Nashville Vanderbilt Oncology Clinic where Dr. Clooney practiced. We rode the elevator up to the fourth floor in the high-rise brick building with a convenient overpass to the hospital proper.

Bill was already seated in the waiting room, fiddling with his Bic lighter like he desperately needed a smoke. We greeted him and filled seats with matching green cushions while Sam crossed the room and sat in a chair next to his dad. As they quietly talked, my mind drifted aimlessly to avoid thinking about cancer.

Inadvertently, I surveyed the waiting room. The décor provided a picturesque setting for its clientele. Modern lamps perched on several tables scattered about the room. Colorful pictures hugged beige walls, featuring photographs of restful streams and wooded hills. Several floor bins were loaded with current magazines on various subjects begging to be read by spouses, family members, cancer patients, and their friends.

The interior decorator had gone to a great deal of trouble to make Dr. Clooney's patients and guests feel at home, but the results failed miserably. Nobody was happy to be here. If I had been wearing a seventies' mood ring, it would have turned black. The Grim Reaper might soon show up. Then I heard soft music.

Go figure. I released a profound sigh.

A woman not much older than me shuffled out a door from the back of the office. Her complexion was pale as sweet milk and she wore a headscarf. A ghostly image, she'd lost all of her hair. She looked haunted. I hated that word. Why think that?

A man close to her age, a husband or good friend, gently guided the patient through the waiting room and into the hall. The poor woman was living proof of what chemo did to you.

I felt sorry for her and wanted to cry. I caught Sam's eye and knew her appearance had frightened him, too. I could only imagine how he was feeling, a teen cursed with the disease.

I didn't have time to dwell on the future effects of cancer on my son because the receptionist called Sam's name.

Jeremy nodded for us to go on, he'd wait.

Bill and I leaped to our feet and followed Sam.

Led by a young nurse in full white uniform, we went through a door and down a long hallway and into a private patient's room.

I filled a chair to wait while Sam hopped on the examination table. Bill leaned against the wall, pensive and likely waiting for the next shoe to drop, so to speak. My gaze wandered.

A built-in desk supporting a laptop and a Kleenex box was in one corner of the room. A plastic dispenser of surgical gloves was attached to the wall. I presumed the other tools of trade were inside the metal drawers. An antiseptic odor permeated the air.

Shortly, an attractive woman entered the room, appearing much too young to be a specialist. Her jet black hair shimmered in the light with red highlights—suggesting she'd inherited the genetics of either Latino or American Indian parents.

Bill came off the wall and I stood up to greet her.

"Good morning, folks." Deborah Clooney's engaging caramel eyes fell on our sick son. "Are you Samuel?"

Sam nodded, grasping the sides of the examination table.

"I'm Dr. Clooney." She shook his hand then turned to face Bill and me. "I presume you are Sam's parents?"

"We are," we replied in unison—which reminded me of our marriage vows except then we had said "I do" separately.

I was more nervous than Bill, nearly giddy with apprehension. Before I could ask my first question, Dr. Clooney asked us to step out of the room while she examined Sam. From the expression on my shy son's face, I knew he was embarrassed to undress in front of a female doctor. While many teens his age were sexually active, he had taken a vow of chastity until he married.

"What do you think?" I whispered to Bill as we waited in the fluorescent-lit hallway during Sam's examination.

"What do you mean?"

"Dr. Clooney is awfully young," I pointed out.

"Either that or we're getting awfully old," he teased.

I smiled. Bill was skilled at diffusing awkward situations. That's why he was so successful working with Tennessee politicians. Time ticked off as we waited. It wasn't long before we were invited back inside the room. I prepared for bad news.

"As expected, Sam's glands are swollen," Dr. Clooney announced. "After reviewing his blood work sent over by Dr. Simpson, it appears he's in the early stages of Hodgkin's."

I locked eyes with Bill. *Is that the good or bad kind?*

"Sam's condition will be treated aggressively with regular infusions of chemicals to wash the blood. The most commonly used one in the US is a four-drug combination called ABVD.

I had no clue, my gaze on Sam who was intently listening.

"I'd list the chemicals involved, but it would be meaningless to you." Dr. Clooney paused. "All you need to know is that the medicine attacks the cancer, but at the same time wipes out white blood cells. So we monitor Sam's blood count closely."

"Will you elaborate a little more," Bill requested.

"Okay, red blood cells carry oxygen to the body, but the white cells fight off infections," Dr. Clooney explained. "We are a fine-tuned organism requiring all parts to work in unison."

"How will the meds make Sam feel?" I inquired.

"He'll be lethargic, sleepy, apathetic—with all the symptoms of low blood syndrome," Dr. Clooney replied. "He may develop mouth sores, nausea, and vomit at times. Too few blood platelets causes bruising of the skin, even nose bleeds. Sam will be sick."

The silence in the office was overwhelming. After eyeing us, Dr. Clooney continued. "I know you're upset that Sam is sick, but the only way to help him get well is to treat the Hodgkin's."

Bill and I both nodded.

"Sam will begin losing his hair in approximately three weeks after his startup treatment. I recommend a barber shave his head before that happens. Shedding hair can prove traumatic."

"All my hair is coming out?" Sam spoke up for the first time.

"It will grow back, Sam, even thicker," Dr. Clooney said.

I heaved a breath. This was not supposed to happen to any of my children. We are God-fearing people, in the ministry of extolling Jesus Christ. Why, God? Why Sam? Help me cope.

"Does he need to be on a specific diet?" Bill asked.

"No," Dr. Clooney replied, "but he should be careful not to eat spicy foods. Taking a one-a-day vitamin can be helpful and, of course, plenty of rest. If Sam's white count drops dramatically, he'll be treated at the hospital. She paused. "Any questions . . .?"

Her gaze swung between me and Bill.

"Wow, this is a lot to take in." I trembled inside.

"Will Sam be able to attend public school?" Bill asked.

Dr. Clooney looked at me and said, "Mrs. McLaughlin, you might consider homeschooling Sam during his treatments." She touched Sam's shoulder. "I'm sure your teachers will cooperate and email your assignments. That way you can rest more often."

Sam nodded, his face washing out even whiter. He was my social kid. He loved being around friends. "That won't be a problem," I uttered, agreeing with Dr. Clooney it was best.

"Sam?" Dr. Clooney gained his attention. "You won't be alone in your studies. Tennessee has a program whereby homebound students can receive assistance from online qualified instructors. Your mom can Google available programs since she teaches school and can't be home with you during the day."

It was all good information and much appreciated.

"When will Sam get his first treatment?" Bill spoke up.

"Today, if you're in agreement," Dr. Clooney replied.

"How long are the treatments?" I queried.

"Up to three hours. Leave Sam in our care. Go have a cup of coffee, shop a bit, get lunch and be back here . . ." she glanced at her wristwatch, "by, oh say, 1:30 p.m.? We like to observe our patients for thirty minutes before they leave us."

I nodded my consent then glanced over at Bill.

"Do either of you have questions?" Dr. Clooney asked again.

"Not now," I replied, "maybe later."

"Would you like to see the room where Sam will receive chemo?" Dr. Clooney asked. We both nodded.

The treatment room was larger than the room where Sam was examined. Located three doors down the hall was a lab. I peeked inside and spied a technician in a white coat analyzing blood samples and entering the information on her computer program.

Bill and Sam were already inside the treatment room when I came back. Three people of various ages were seated in padded recliners, each hooked up to an IV drip with the chemical wash.

"Why are the patients so calm?" I quietly inquired.

"Benadryl mixed in the chemo cocktail," the oncologist replied. "Since it takes hours to slowly infuse the meds, lying perfectly still is necessary so we try to make the process easier."

"Will I be sick today?" Sam suddenly asked.

"Patients react in different ways. I'll give you a prescription to minimize nausea," Dr. Clooney said. "In a few days your body will ache, much like the onset of influenza. Those symptoms will subside, but by then you'll be due for another treatment."

Sam's eyes dropped to the floor.

"I'm sorry Sam, chemo won't be pleasant."

He nodded, his upper lip slightly quivering.

I asked Sam if he was okay with being left alone during his treatment. He said he'd be fine and would call me on his cell if he had a problem. Our son was a trooper and I was proud of him.

Dr. Clooney may have looked too young to practice medicine but she had a professional manner that put all of us at ease.

Jeremy and I climbed in Bill's SUV with him, satisfied that Sam would get the best available treatment. With prayer and medical help, he would get well in time. And later, all this would seem like a bad dream. Bill dropped us off at Starbucks while he drove over to his office to check on some impending work issues.

I was sipping on a hazelnut latte when Jer asked, "How did it go with Sam?" He was drinking his coffee black.

I detailed our conversation with Dr. Clooney best as I could recall. "We need to be back at the clinic by one thirty to get him."

He nodded. "I have to go back to the church."

"Will you get Benny and Jamie after school?"

He nodded and finished off his coffee, his gaze drifting to the chalkboard for specialties. "Are you hungry?"

"I could use a snack." I suddenly felt famished.

Jeremy ordered fattening pastries for both of us. We had a plan. Sam had a plan. And I prayed God had a plan for all of us.

40

SIX DAYS LATER, Sam was beginning to feel the effects of the chemo so I arranged for him to receive online instruction through the Tennessee Educational Association. Routinely taking Tylenol to minimize pain, he was lethargic much of the time.

To boost Sam's immunity, I purchased flavored health shakes loaded with multivitamins. Due to the mild nausea, he had little appetite for solid foods. I discovered Sam loved cold green grapes and stopped by the grocery store every other day after school to make sure the crisper drawer was loaded with fresh fruit.

Jeremy was staying at the church for the Wednesday evening Bible study and would not be home for hours. Home from school with the boys, I collapsed on the sofa in the living room.

With a roaring fire glowing at my feet, I opened my Bible to a Psalm penned by King David, a man who understood persecution and illness. Having seemingly committed unforgivable sins, God had still called him a man after His own heart. Christians often identified with David's weaknesses, such as I did at the moment.

"All have sinned and fallen short of the glory of God," I recalled the New Testament scripture. Except for God's grace and mercy, people of faith like me would feel constant defeat.

About to read Psalm 91, my cell phone dinged. I retrieved it from my sweater pocket and saw it was my sister Becca calling.

"Tell me you have good news!" I spurted.

"I do!" she exclaimed. "They've found Beverly."

"How—when?" Questions assaulted my splintered thoughts.

"It's hard to believe but our sister staggered into a hospital in Cairo, Egypt and asked for medical help," Becca revealed.

"What about her captors?" I asked.

"Evidently, she found a way to escape."

"How did she get from Libya to Cairo?" I questioned.

"I don't know the details, Brooke—just got the call ten minutes ago. As we speak, Beverly's being flown in an army plane back to London then driven to the American Embassy."

"That's great news!" My spirit lifted thanks to God.

"Yes, it is. How's Sam doing with the chemo?"

"He feels poorly—hasn't lost his hair yet," I replied.

"I'm so sorry he has to go through all this . . ."

What Becca didn't know was "all this" involved more than just cancer. We all had been terrorized by our resident spirits.

"Are you still there?" Becca queried.

"Yes, I'm just really tired. I feel like I'm wading through the hours, trying to appear optimistic. My dreams at night take me down scary paths." I sighed. "Sam is too young to face death."

"Do you want me to come for a visit?" Becca asked.

"Spring break would be better, when I have time to visit."

We talked a few more minutes about Sam then speculated on how Beverly would react to her kidnapping episode. Had anyone told her Terah died with his parents in the church bombing? We needed to work out the logistics of bringing our baby sister home to American soil, but until we knew more our plans were on hold.

"I should call Gary now and tell him the good news," Becca said. "When I hear from London again, I'll call you."

"Thank you, Becca, for all you've done in finding Beverly."

Our conversation over, I was pocketing my phone when I noticed Sam standing in the doorway. "Are you okay?" I asked.

"Who was that?" Sam asked.

"It was your Aunt Becca. Your Aunt Beverly walked into a Cairo, Egypt hospital yesterday," I said. "She's en route to a London hospital via a military plane where she'll be examined."

"That's great news, Mom. I'm so happy for you."

"You didn't answer me, Sam. How to you feel?"

"I'm making it, Mom." He stepped into the living room and crashed in a chair. At a closer glance, I noticed his complexion was even paler. His dull hazel eyes reflected his discomfort, his joints obviously aching. It was beyond my comprehension how a person so young like Sam bravely faced an illness like cancer.

If it were me, I'd be terrified. I am terrified because he's my sick son. Surely, God had a miracle waiting for Sam.

"Were you able to complete your homework?" I asked.

"Yeah," he said. "A few kids from school called me today."

"Did you tell them you were sick?"

"They already knew." He shrugged.

"Yeah, it's the school grapevine in full force."

He smiled. "My friends said they'll pray for me."

"That was kind of them," I noted. Cancer sometimes scared people away, fearing it was contagious though no proof existed.

"It's pretty lonely not being able to attend school."

"I know, Sam. Chemo won't last forever," I pointed out. "Meanwhile, you must rest and avoid public settings."

"Like, I can't fight off a cold," Sam said.

"Yeah, like that."

Fortunately, the spiritual activity in our house had diminished in the last month. Only a few bumps in the night, and my washing machine kicking on by itself, indicated that they were still active. After Sam had a snack, he went back to bed.

When Jeremy came home around eight thirty, I told him about Beverly. We rejoiced together. In bed that night, I asked God again to cleanse our home from evil spirits, considering if they were lost souls trapped between earth and wherever God was sending them. Some people believed demonic spirits manifested themselves as deceased human beings. I didn't pretend to know.

Whatever, whoever they were, I prayed that God would command them to leave us alone! My last thought of the day.

* * *

Saturday arrived and Becca phoned mid-morning. She'd received a call from the American Embassy in London. Our sister was scheduled to fly American Airlines into Atlanta, Georgia.

"When . . .?" I was beside myself, so excited.

"Gary and I are picking her up at the Atlanta International Airport tomorrow around noon. Do you want to be there?"

"Of course, I want to be there!"

"You'll need to be at the airport by noon," Becca said. "I'll text you the flight number and gate and we'll meet you there."

"Jamie and Benny can go with Jeremy to church tomorrow and Sam will be fine at home." I calculated the drive would take four and a half hours. "I'll take off work on Monday, and drive home later in the day. I want time to visit with Beverly."

"Great!" Becca said as I envisioned us seated at a table in a fine restaurant, having a nice meal somewhere then spending the night at a downtown Atlanta hotel before we parted ways.

Where is home for Beverly now?

"Has Bev been told that Terah's deceased?" I asked.

"I guess we'll find out tomorrow."

"Okay, see you in Atlanta soon."

Becca ended the call. I stood motionless, a silly smile on my face. "I assume that was good news." Jeremy observed my antics.

"Great news, in fact, Beverly's flying to Atlanta tomorrow. Becca and I plan to meet her plane—if it's okay with you."

Jeremy hugged me. "Of course, I'll hold down the fort."

I clung to him tightly. "Now if Sam could just get well."

"Solve one problem at a time, sweetheart," Brother Mac advised. "Too much at once can overload your mind, make you nervous, and steal your rest. One day at a time, remember?"

"Tell me about it!" I actually laughed.

As Jeremy glanced at his watch, I realized it was past time to feed the children their lunch. "Would you check on Benny and Jamie? I swear they must be building the next flight to Mars."

"Sam's illness bothers them more than they're letting on," Jeremy said. "Play is an escape from reality. Games challenge our intellect and take our minds off the mundane processes of life. It's a way of coping with boredom as well as fear."

"How did you get so smart?" I poked him in the chest.

"What's for lunch, Mom?"

I turned around and spied Sam standing at the bottom of the staircase. "What are you hungry for?" I asked.

He shrugged. *Anything . . .*

"I can warm a can of soup, make you a sandwich, or cut up some fresh fruit—your choice, Sam." I waited.

He stood loosely in his pajamas, trying to decide. "Warm soup with some fresh fruit cut up in yogurt sounds reasonable."

"Good choice!" Jeremy hugged him.

The three of us walked down the hall toward the back of the house. Sam entered the kitchen with me while Jeremy exited the backdoor to fetch the younger boys from the shed.

"Who was on the phone?" Sam asked, plopping down in a chair at the table. "You seem happy, Mom."

"I am. It was my sister, Becca. She received news your Aunt Beverly is returning to America tomorrow."

I removed a can of cream soup from the cabinet and snagged some fixings from the fridge to make the rest of us sandwiches. Benny and Jamie would turn up noses at the soup. Ham and cheese, lots of it between bread smothered in Mayo for them.

Then I ripped open a package of green grapes.

"Is she okay—I mean after being kidnapped?" Sam asked.

"We don't know the whole story yet," I replied. "Apparently, Beverly left the family's Coptic church just before a terrorist bomb exploded then wandered into some kind of refugee camp. She phoned me once then I lost contact. Next thing we heard, she was in Cairo, Egypt, at a hospital seeking medical help."

"Is she coming here?" Sam asked.

"Not right away, I'm getting up early in the morning and driving to the Atlanta airport to meet your Aunt Becca." I handed Sam a bowl of washed grapes while I warmed his soup.

"Will you be okay while I'm away?" I looked at my Sam.

"Don't worry about me, Mom, I'll be fine."

Fine was a word you said when things were almost okay. I knew things were not okay with Sam, but he was making it day by day. He'd been in church all of his life. He knew the power of prayer and faith. I trusted he would figure out how to handle all this. If anyone knew what *this* was . . . my thoughts drifted.

41

AT AMERICAN AIRLINES Gate 21 by 11:45 a.m., I did not see Gary or Becca. Probably en route from downtown, I prayed they weren't stuck in Atlanta eight-lane traffic. I found a seat at the gate facing the plate-glass window and watched the arriving planes. I offered a grateful prayer that Beverly was coming home.

Before I realized it, I had dozed off in my chair. Time had ceased to exist until I felt a warm hand on my shoulder.

Jesus, is it You? I slowly opened my eyes.

"Sorry to wake you, little sister."

I sat up, sloughing off sleep. Gary and Becca stood in front of me. "I can't believe I fell asleep praying." I laughed then stood up to greet them properly. "What time is it?"

"12:20," Gary replied. "Beverly's flight is running late."

Standing to stretch my stiff body, my stomach grumbled loudly for nourishment. "Sorry, I ate early this morning."

"I can remedy that . . ." Gary retrieved a white Subway sack from his backpack and handed it to me. "Your sister made me buy this for you." He smiled as I unveiled my lunch.

"You're the best, Gary!" I gorged on pita bread with roast beef and veggie trimmings. "Umm . . ."

"I see the huge double-decker plane pulling up to the gate." Becca pointed through the window. "It must be Beverly's flight."

I shaded my eyes with a hand to shield the sun's glare.

"Doesn't Bev need to go through a security check?" I asked.

"American Airlines has all that worked out," Gary said.

"We'll know soon." Through the opening to the Jetway, I spied the weary faces of passengers strolling out in waves.

Young children looked like battered soldiers dragging their suitcases behind them as they trailed their parents. The double-decker 747 Boeing carried up to five hundred passengers, so the deplaning took some time. We waited patiently as passengers for later flights filled the seats in the area around us. Conversations and audio announcements were loud but I felt blessed to be in the midst of the confluence. When Bev didn't come out with the flow, I feared she'd missed her flight. Then I spied a flock of blond hair tucked under a colorful knitted cap. Our sister came into view, still pencil-thin but with a pooch in her stomach.

"It's her!" I exclaimed to Becca.

"I see her!" Becca ran over and grabbed our baby sister first.

Their tongues wagged for a good two minutes before Becca let Beverly go and I hugged her. Gary stood idly by watching.

"As you can see, Brooke, I'm pregnant," Bev announced.

Stunned, my tongue lollygagging, I didn't know whether to congratulate her or say I was sorry. She was carrying a dead man's baby she would likely raise alone. "Welcome home," I managed.

"Let's talk about everything when we get back to the hotel." Gary wisely intervened. "I suppose you have baggage we need to collect," he said to Beverly, ushering her out of the pandemonium.

We joined the flow of terminal traffic toward BAGGAGE. I carried Beverly's small case of personal items, debating with myself over how best to relate to her. We reached a bank of elevators, boarded one and ascended two floors to the main level.

Using the crosswalk, we exited the main terminal and entered the short-term parking garage where Gary located his silver gray Cadillac. "What about my bags?" Beverly asked Gary.

"I'll get them," he said. "You girls take the Cadillac and go back to the hotel. Give me your receipt for luggage, Beverly."

"What about my car?" I asked.

"I'll drive your Malibu to the hotel. Keys, please . . . go on, girls! Have a good sisterly visit, I'll catch up with ya'll later."

Becca opened her mouth to protest as I handed over keys.

"Don't argue, love, I'm the man of the house."

For once, I kept mine shut. Gary was right. In Beverly's delicate condition, she didn't need to walk the distance required to reach BAGGAGE. I watched him trot away with purpose.

"Is he always this bossy?" I teased Becca.

She waved a hand. "He sometimes has good ideas so why bother challenging him?" She remotely popped the locks.

Once settled in the four-door sedan, Becca drove us straight to a Starbuck's where we ordered specialty coffees.

"Are you hungry, Bev?" Becca inquired.

"Actually, I feel a little queasy."

"When did you last eat?" I asked.

"I'm not sure, time change messed up my bio systems. Unfortunately, I've passed a little blood."

"Do you want an ER doctor to take a look?" Becca asked.

"No, I just need to lie down and rest," she replied.

"Okay, let's go back to the hotel," Becca advised.

We piled into the Cadillac and drove toward town. On our way to the Hyatt, I phoned Jeremy. It was nearly two p.m.

"Beverly made it okay," I told him. "How was the service?"

I listened to an upbeat report. Many church members had shown up and prayed for Willard Jacobs. Nobody could fathom he was guilty of cold-blooded murder. I certainly couldn't.

"Surely, the truth will surface," Jeremy said.

"Hopefully . . ." the trial had officially commenced the second Monday in April. At some point I'd be summoned to testify. Only God could put the right words in my mouth.

"We're on our way to the Hyatt Hotel in midtown Atlanta," I informed Jer. "Beverly's not feeling well, she's pregnant."

"Is she okay with that? I mean considering . . ."

I understood Jeremy's concern. Raising a child alone would not come easy after having the freedom to transverse the planet.

"Actually," I whispered, "we haven't had the opportunity to discuss Terah. Beverly's exhausted and sleeping in the backseat."

"Where's Gary?"

"He's getting Bev's luggage and driving my car to the hotel."

"Gary's a good guy," Jeremy said, "Johnny on the spot."

"Yes he is, very thoughtful. How's Sam doing?"

"Took his meds at lunchtime and went back to bed. I found clumps of his hair in the shower stall," he reported.

"We need to get him to a barber this week," I said.

He agreed.

"Are Benny and Jamie behaving?" What I really wanted to know was if the old hag had been haggling Benny.

"Are you kiddin'? With Mama away, the mice will play," he teased. "Don't worry I have everything under control. We're going to play a serious game of Battle this afternoon."

Cards, I knew he meant. "And when you get beat, what's next?" I envisioned an afternoon of frolicking.

"I'll think of something, just enjoy your visit with your sisters and come home. We miss you." Jeremy fell silent.

"Hugs and kisses." I ended the call.

"Are Jeremy and the children doing all right?" Becca asked from the driver's seat, glancing back at our sleeping sister.

"They don't even miss me." I laughed.

We rode in silence for awhile.

The gray leather interior of Gary's Cadillac smelled new. It came equipped with all the bells and whistles modern technology offered. He made a fantastic salary working as an architect at a major Birmingham firm. They were financially set for life.

Seeing Becca was barren, I prayed that Beverly's pregnancy would not upset her. Early on, a psychiatrist had helped her deal with her inability to have children. Sisters can rejoice together but they can also experience jealousy. It was the same for a church congregation. Those gifted with many talents were often envied.

Vehicles of all descriptions moved from lane to lane in the hectic eight-lane traffic like they were surfing. It took us an hour to reach the Hyatt Hotel. Bev rallied as Becca pulled into the high-rise parking lot, found a space and turned off the motor.

"Sorry I fell asleep," Beverly apologized. "Did I miss anything?" Our blue-eyed sister sluggishly got out of the car.

We took the elevator up to the eleventh floor. Becca had key cards to adjoining rooms. I didn't realize how tired I was until I spied a queen bed with fluffy pillows begging me to submit.

"I need a shower." Beverly traipsed into the bathroom.

Becca perched on the end of a queen and flipped on the TV. "Just checking the weather conditions tomorrow," she announced.

Crashing on the other queen, I heard the shower running full force and hoped our baby sister had saved some hot water for me.

I yawned as I listened to the weatherman's report. Before I knew it I had drifted off to sleep. When I woke up thirty minutes later Beverly and Becca were seated at the round table talking about her experiences. Now it was my time to apologize.

"Come over and join us, sleepyhead!" Becca waved me over.

"I can't believe I fell asleep. Give me a sec."

I pattered into the bathroom to freshen up with splashes of cold water. One look in the mirror and I wished I hadn't. I was a wreck, my long sprayed hair in disarray, no lipstick to speak of.

"So that's when I decided I had to escape the camp," Beverly was saying to Becca when I returned to the room.

"Does she know?" I looked at Becca, referencing Terah.

"Yes, the American ambassador in London told her."

Beverly looked at me, sadness in her gaze.

I'm so sorry, my lips moved but no sound came out.

"Copts are brave people, Brooke. They face persecution all the time, even death at the hand of radical Muslims. Terah would want me to go on, especially now that I'm carrying his child."

I just didn't know how to respond. I could never be so brave if I lost Jeremy. He was a part of me, a soul mate. If he died I would be one of his lost sheep wandering in a wilderness.

"A missionary from Alexandria convinced Beverly's captives to let her go since she was pregnant," Becca said. "A Christian pastor drove her to Cairo, Egypt." I learned the shorter version.

"When I'm better, I'm writing a book," Beverly said. "People should learn about the persecuted church in the Middle East."

I nodded; grateful our bold little world traveler didn't die during the church explosion that killed seventy people.

We girls sat around the table, talking about our early days as children. We laughed. And we cried. And we giggled.

Gary arrived around 4 p.m. and informed us that he'd reserved a table for four in the hotel restaurant for six o'clock. Becca went with Gary to their room and rested until it was time to go down to the restaurant. We met in the hall as planned.

Our orders were promptly taken. I selected the rare prime rib with a loaded baked potato and a Caesar salad. Gary had the same, but Becca and Beverly went for the grilled fish served with low-cal veggies. We all ate until we could hold no more then ordered coffees with slices of raspberry cheesecake.

When the bill arrived, Gary snagged it against my protest.

We talked a little while longer then went upstairs to our respective rooms. Beverly was about to drop, coping with the time change and her precarious pregnancy. After being hyped for days, I crashed early, too. God is so good was my last thought.

42

I WAS HOME BY three p.m. Monday. I found Sam in the kitchen warming a can of Chicken Noodle Soup. I noticed he'd lost weight and wondered what I could do to help improve his diet.

"Hi, Sam. . ." I gave him a hug and felt his bony ribs crush against my chest. He'd always been on the slim side but now . . .

"Mom, you're home!" He smiled. "How are my aunts?"

"Wonderful! Beverly's expecting a baby." I held my son at arm's length. "Soup again for lunch . . .?" No amount of money could replace the love I spied tucked away in Sam's crooked grin.

"Yeah, it's an easy fix." He spooned soup to test its warmth then filled a big bowl and opened a box of crackers. "Does Dad know you're back?" He walked to the table with his food.

"I phoned him as I crossed the Tennessee-Georgia border." I removed my sweater. "Are you feeling any better today?"

"Yeah, I guess." He slurped his soup. "Got up this morning feeling like I'd live. . ." he meant it to be humorous.

Not so much . . . "That's good, I'm glad."

I washed out the coffee carafe with hot water, filled it to the brim with cold water then loaded the basket with strong Columbian. Seconds later, I heard hissing and bubbling sounds.

"How's online school going?"

"I downloaded my assignments for the week." Sam opened another pack of crackers, slurping on his soup with purpose.

"Now that you're hungry, I want you to eat more solid foods, Sam. How does a steak with a loaded potato sound?"

He grinned. "I think I can handle that."

"Good. Did Benny and Jamie behave themselves?" I added cream to my coffee and took a seat across from Sam at the table.

He looked at me like I'd struck him. "What?"

Sam shook his head, lips quivering slightly.

"Sam! It's not tattling if you tell me the truth."

"Then why does it feel like tattling?"

"Point well taken," I replied, aware I would get a report from Jeremy before the day was out. "I need to unpack my bag."

I left Sam to his own devises.

During the afternoon, I reviewed my lesson plans for the week. Starting Tuesday, I'd resume my maddening routine. But knowing Sam was better and my sister Beverly was safe, made me feel better about life. God works all things out for the good of those who love Him. If God is for us, who can be against us?

Jeremy and the two boys were home by 4:30.

We had a steak and baked potato supper at six, and the evening hours merged into routine as we closed down the day.

After Benny completed his homework, I sent Jamie up to take a shower and put on his PJs. My almost-seventeen-year-old Sam was on no set schedule, sleeping often. His bedroom light was sometimes on until the wee hours of the morning since he enjoyed reading. I was so glad he'd eaten well at suppertime.

"How did the boys behave while I was away?" I brushed my long locks of blond hair, peering in the bathroom mirror at the dark circles under my eyes. Jeremy was already dressed for bed.

"Sam was a jewel, very helpful with Benny and Jamie."

"Helpful is not an answer." I turned around and faced him. "Did something bad happen you're not telling me?"

"You know, Brooke," Jeremy professed, "the older you get the more beautiful you become." He smiled through the mirror.

"That's still not an answer." I resumed moving my makeup.

"Okay." He wrapped his arms around me as I sat before the mirror. "You want honesty? Benny had a terrible episode Sunday night. Came downstairs screaming that the old woman was in his room and he never wanted to sleep in his bed again. I told him to bunk in with Sam on a pallet. What else could I do, Brooke?"

My eyes were wide and engaged. "You're teasing, right?"

He shook his head. "I wish."

"Jeremy, I've had enough. Get us out of this house!"

"You want me to quit my job at the church?"

"Promise me you'll pray for a new assignment."

"You know I can't do that, Brooke. But I will pray that God's will is accomplished in our family's lives, and that our Savior Jesus will meet all our needs. That's the best I can do."

I sighed. "I guess I can't ask for more."

* * *

Wednesday, a week later, Sam had a second chemo treatment that left him with the same flu symptoms he'd experienced before. By then his head was bald and his eyebrows were thinning.

One evening at supper, he asked if he could get a gold earring. Although we objected to piercing, we made an exception.

It was already the third week of April. If I could only hold out till summer, Sam would be finished with chemo and our family would be in a better place. Although Jeremy refused to pray for a new assignment, I did. God forgive me if it was a sin.

Unfortunately, Jamie was exhibiting signs of hyperactivity.

Is it *them*? I wondered. Our youngest constantly fought with Benny, far from his usual behavior. Always the easy-going child, we took him to see a pediatrician in Nashville for a psychiatric evaluation and he was put on medication to calm him down.

In the days that followed, Jamie became wild, uncontrollable, and couldn't sit still or concentrate if I left off his meds. His kindergarten teacher had trouble keeping order with him around.

To gain attention, he sometimes got on his knees and barked like a dog. I wondered if he had an environmental sensitivity to the house. I'd read where children needed fortified bedrooms to protect them from electrical impulses. He was traumatized.

Friday, during my lunch break at school, I went over to the historic county courthouse to sit in on the deliberations and learned that the opposing attorneys were finished with their summations. A number of people had gathered in the galley.

Spectators stood as Honorable Judge Daniel Hartford entered a rear door and approached the lectern. He rapped his gavel to signal court was in session. Since Willard had pleaded innocent to murdering his wife Alice, it was up to his defense attorney to prove it. Seated near the back of the packed courtroom, I noted many of our parishioners were present to prayerfully support him.

On the second pew behind the District Attorney's table sat Alice's sister, Elise Jackson. Next to her was Anthony Barnes, Alice's son. Detective Clay Bennett was also present, looking as smug as ever. I wanted desperately to speak to him concerning the internet lead I gave him over a month ago. I had no choice but to watch the legal proceedings and pray the truth came out.

The D.A. representing the people of the county stood up and approached the jury. He artfully laid out his case against Willard for Murder-One. Willard's DNA was on the knife. He had no alibi between 3:45 and 5:15 p.m. when he reported finding Alice dead in their master bath tub with sliced wrists. Although Willard had called 911 to report Alice's suicide, the jury should not assume he was innocent. This was a heinous crime of passion, possibly driven by jealousy or rage. Willard Jacobs had murdered his wife in cold blood and should be held accountable for his crime.

Wow, even I felt convinced.

After Willard's defense attorney rebutted D.A. Ray Peterson's remarks, the judge told Peterson to call his first witness. Dr. Galynn Wynn, a forensic specialist, took the stand and reported that she'd examined Alice Jacob's body for DNA evidence and the knife used to end her life. I only heard part of Dr. Wynn's testimony, realizing my first afternoon class was starting soon.

Quietly exiting the courtroom, I drove back to school and checked in at the office. "There's someone here to see you."

"Who?"

Our secretary Gladys pointed through the glass window at a man seated in a room adjoining the principal's office. I glared through the glass insert but didn't recognize the gentleman.

He stood as I opened the door and entered the room.

"Are you Brooke McLaughlin?"

"Yes," I replied.

"Consider yourself served." He handed me an official-sealed document and started for the door. "Wait, sir. What is this?"

He turned around and looked at me. "Just read the document, Mrs. McLaughlin, it's self-explanatory."

Shakily, I tore away the seal and began reading the doc. I had been summoned by the prosecuting attorney, scheduled to appear in court on next Thursday—which meant I'd likely be absent from school on Friday, too. I was badly shaken by the summons.

Gladys stepped into the room. "What was that all about?"

"I'm being summoned as a witness for the prosecution in Willard Jacob's murder trial," I returned.

Nervous hands flew to her face, pale green eyes wide with comprehension. "You're a witness against Willard Jacobs?"

I nodded it was true.

"Doesn't he go to your church?"

"Yes." Her horror reflected my inner fear.

"What are you going to do, Brooke?"

"My civic duty," I replied, hoping a cross-exam would afford me the opportunity to tell what I'd learned about the mysterious wife of the man Alice met on FACEBOOK and hooked up with in Las Vegas. Having no knowledge if Alice was engaged in a sexual affair, Willard's accusation that her wounds were self-inflicted struck a chord with me. Was she after a lucrative divorce settlement as Willard suggested? If only I knew the man's name.

43

WEDNESDAY, THE FIRST week in May, the day before I was scheduled to testify in court for the prosecution, Jeremy accompanied Sam to Nashville for his fourth chemo treatment.

They were already back by the time I arrived home after school with Benny and Jamie. "How was the treatment, son?"

"Same 'ol," Sam replied, removing a jug of Cranberry juice from the fridge. The injections always left him thirsty.

"Did you see anyone at the office you knew?"

"Mom, it's not a social club. They pump Benadryl into your veins until you're comatose. Nobody wants to talk about cancer. We just listen to a TV drone on and on and on."

I regretted asking my question, incapable of sharing in Sam's pain. As a Chinese philosopher might proclaim, it is his path.

I stood in the kitchen staring out the bay window at the white and red buds popping out on tree limbs, realizing the kitchen landline was ringing. Like a zombie, I reached for the phone.

"Yes?" I peeped.

"Brooke, is that you? I can barely hear you."

Every ounce of me became alert. "Is Beverly okay?"

"Yes," Becca replied. "I left several messages but you haven't returned my calls. What's going on?"

"It's been a crazy week. Sam had a treatment today, plus I've been summoned to testify in court tomorrow by the prosecution." I reminded Becca that Willard was a member of our church.

"I'm so sorry, Brooke. Beverly is anxious to see you. She's asked me to drive her over. Would you rather we didn't come?"

"No, I'd love to see both of you." I did a quick mental check regarding our family schedules. "Let me get back to you after this weekend. Sam will be too sick to be around visitors," I explained.

"Okay, I'll tell Bev you'll let us know when it's convenient."

"Hey, remind our sis she can call me anytime. She doesn't need permission from anyone." I knew I'd sounded too curt.

"I understand how you must feel, but Beverly views me more like a mother figure. Terah's death has finally hit her."

"I'm sorry for my comment, don't tell Bev."

"Actually, Brooke, I'm worried about her mental state."

"Does she need professional help?"

"Our pastor has talked to her and they've prayed together, but I think she blames God for taking Terah away from her."

"I understand her sentiments." We hadn't been able to cope with our haunting guests. Yet, God hadn't intervened.

"Beverly feels guilty for not dying with him."

"That's insane! What about the baby she's carrying?"

"My sentiments exactly, so I keep reminding her that Terah would be happy to know he has a son to carry on his legacy."

Sometimes I wished I would think before speaking.

"I've been trying to locate Terah's relatives to see if Bev inherited any portion of his estate. Our baby sister is flat broke."

"Not to mention lonely and despondent," I added.

Broke? Human beings were all broken in some fashion, and in dire need of God's grace. "Please tell Beverly we'll work out a time for her to visit. Meanwhile, she can call me and we'll talk."

"Okay," Becca let out a slow breath, "I'll tell her."

I ended the call and faced Jeremy. "Beverly's depressed."

"Join the world," Brother Mac quipped.

* * *

Thursday came and I was at court fifteen minutes early. A few minutes before nine a.m. the jury filed in, their faces somber.

Judge Daniel Hartford barreled through a rear door in his polyester black robe, his horn-rimmed glasses perched low on his bulbous nose, partially hiding his dark secretive eyes. A large man, he was a scary site and I could only imagine Willard's plight.

The bailiff called the court into session with a hear ye, hear ye spiel he'd memorized to fulfill his legal duties. The female clerk clicked away on her computer. "Call your next witness, Mr. Peterson," Judge Hartford announced in a booming base voice.

"I call to the stand, Mrs. Brooke McLaughlin."

District Attorney Ray Peterson's piercing green eyes struck me like lightning. Approaching middle-age, he had a full head of Clairol-enhanced blond hair and a tanning-bed skin tone. I tentatively rose from the bench where I sat and unsteadily walked to the front of the courtroom where I would be sworn in.

"I do," I agreed to tell the truth and took a seat on the stage in front of a microphone. All spectator eyes were on me.

"State your name please," the D.A. instructed.

"Anna Brooke McLaughlin."

Peterson took a moment to peruse the audience, then the jury, before looking me square in the eyes. "Mrs. McLaughlin, you were the last person to see Alice Willard alive, is that correct?"

"We had coffee and visited early afternoon before she went home," I replied. What I didn't say was understood.

"Please answer yes or no." A half smile tore at his thin lips.

"I don't know if Alice spoke or saw anyone else," I returned.

"Mrs. McLaughlin . . ." Judge Hartford intervened. "Please answer the D.A.'s questions with a yes or no."

"I apologize, Judge, I'm new at this."

Someone in the audience chuckled at my response and two of the jurors snickered. I felt entirely stupid.

"My answer is yes. I may have been the last person to see Alice Jacobs alive before she died." I was as concise as possible.

"Now. . ." the D.A. moved on, "according to your testimony recorded by Detective Clay Bennett in January, you observed bruises on Alice Jacobs face when you met her at the Coffee Shack for lunch on the day of her death. Is that correct?"

"Yes."

"Did Alice tell you that her husband Willard struck her?"

"Yes, she did. But Willard told me her wounds were self-inflicted," I added before I thought.

"Objection!!" Peterson shouted. "Instruct the witness to answer the question and not add information to her response."

"Sustained!" Hartford rapped his gavel. "The court secretary is instructed to strike Mrs. McLaughlin's last remark from the record." He told the jury to disregard my comment.

"But what if what Willard said is the truth?" I cried out.

The ensuing response to my outburst disrupted court proceedings for the next five minutes. From the look on Judge Hartford's face, I thought he might cuff and toss me in jail.

"I'm sorry," I said, digging myself into deeper trouble.

"Sidebar," Judge Hartford barked, motioning for Willard's attorney and the D.A. to approach the bench.

I overheard the judge's comment: *I realize Mrs. McLaughlin is a hostile witness, Mr. Peterson, but if she continues in this manner I will hold her in contempt of court.* Every word stung like a wasp.

"Yes, Your Honor," the D.A. responded. "Please bear with me, Mrs. McLaughlin has testimony critical to the prosecution."

"Are you certain you want to continue with this witness?"

"Yes, Your Honor, I am."

Waving the two attorneys to their tables, Judge Hartford turned to me. "You heard what was said, Mrs. McLaughlin. Do you want to be in contempt of court, pay a fine or go to jail?"

"No, sir, I don't."

"Then behave yourself and answer the questions. When Mr. Jacobs' attorney cross-exams, you will have the opportunity to tell the jury what you know. Is that satisfactory?"

"It's more than fair, Your Honor."

So we were back to the questions again, which I answered as truthfully as I recalled, suppressing remarks that would favor Willard's innocence. Only God knew the real truth.

When court adjourned for lunch I felt exhausted. I was guilty of nothing but information, yet I felt the weight of being tried and tested. My integrity was on the line with the jurors. They would hear both sides of the story then decide which one was true. Willard Jacobs' life depended on the jury's honest and fair conclusions. So I began to pray for the twelve jurors.

Since I had a substitute for the day, I left the courthouse and went straight over to the church. Jeremy had ordered sandwiches sent in for the staff. I found everyone in the fellowship hall. My shepherd husband glanced up when I entered the room.

"Brooke!" He walked over to me.

"How did court go?" he asked in a low voice.

"It went." I plopped my big gold purse on a side table and walked over to the counter to help myself to some coffee. I did not want to discuss the trial, in fact I had been forbidden to do so.

"What's left to eat?" I asked.

"Lucky for you, there's one sandwich left."

"Yeah, lucky me!" I tore into the lunch sack.

44

FRIDAY, AT SCHOOL, my French class students bombarded me with questions about the trial. Sworn to silence by the court, I promptly took the fifth, advising them to read the newspapers.

Halfheartedly, I maneuvered through my morning classes, ate little for lunch, anxious to end the day and get home with the boys. Sam had questions, which I answered without answering.

Saturday morning, Jeremy took Benny to his soccer practice while I cleaned the house. Beverly phoned midmorning to talk about her feelings and we both cried over Terah's death.

"He was a great guy, Bev." I agreed with my sister.

"I know, I just have to decide how to live the rest of my life without him. I have his son to think about now."

Since I was a witness in a murder trial, neither of us thought it was the time for a visit. Maybe early June would be better. School would be out for summer and Sam finished with chemo.

* * *

Monday, our family resumed work and school routines. Sam was suffering from muscle cramps and nosebleeds and stayed in bed. I felt sorry for him but had no remedy other than the meds Dr. Clooney prescribed. Jeremy phoned me at school during my lunch break and asked if I'd seen the local morning paper.

I went straight to the office and snagged one from the pamphlet bin. There was a lengthy article on the trial. As I read about the material facts, even I could believe Willard was guilty.

But I also knew the twelve jurors did not yet have all the facts necessary to effectively evaluate his guilt or innocence. When the defense had its turn, we'd see. And I'd do my best to help.

A week went by and we were halfway through May. No ghostly appearances, thank you, Jesus! Sam was recouping from his last chemo treatment. After talking to a few other teenage cancer patients over the internet his mood noticeably improved.

Other young people had survived their cancers. They had remarkable stories and Sam embraced hope. So I rejoiced.

When the sun broke through the rainclouds the next morning, moisture clinging to leaves deposited glitter in the trees. A bright day signaled warmer spring weather was inching closer.

I was notified by mail to be present in court on Friday, the third week in May. Willard's trial had lasted far longer than anyone anticipated. All I knew was what I read in the newspaper. I informed my principal that I would need a substitute that day.

* * *

The day arrived I was to testify in court. I was at the county courthouse half an hour before court proceedings were scheduled to begin. I sat on a pew with a few other spectators, praying for the truth to surface. Shortly before nine, a side door opened.

Willard was led into the courtroom by two burley guards. Wearing a blue spring suit with a striped tie and polished black dress shoes, he'd cleaned up nicely. Attorney Harold Vanguard, III, born and bred in New Orleans, was his new defense attorney. The Cajun was seated at the table with Willard, quietly talking.

Craning my head to get a better view of Attorney Vanguard, I noted he had the polished appearance of a professional French gambler—which made me wonder how a Tennessee jury made up of mostly Christians would view him. Wearing a black-and-white pinstripe suit with a white shirt and red bowtie, Vanguard's shiny black hair was slicked back like a porcupine's. The word "dandy" came to mind. *Oh, Willard, I wish you'd chosen somebody else.*

The court secretary took her seat, her electronic devices poised to record the court proceedings. Then the jurors filled their stadium seats and the bailiff called court into session.

"All rise." Judge Hartford entered the courtroom and hurried to the lectern, promptly rapping his gavel as he was seated.

I was the first witness to be interviewed. Having been sworn in earlier, I took a seat on the stage and stared into the eyes of the New Orleans dandy. I was actually surprised to see a speck of kindness in his black eyes. "Mrs. McLaughlin, try to relax."

I took in a huge breath and did my best.

"You and your husband, Reverend Jeremy McLaughlin, spoke to the defendant about his wife's death. I believe you testified earlier that he came to the church office. Is that correct?"

"Yes, sir, that's correct."

"Now, Mrs. McLaughlin, would you tell the jurors what Willard told you about his wife on the day you met with him?"

Mr. Vanguard took a moment to peruse the jurors to be sure they were attentive. He certainly had my attention and I knew this was my moment to shine. I gathered my thoughts and launched.

"Willard told us he thought Alice was having an affair. They were friends on FACEBOOK and got together while she was in Las Vegas on a work trip," I explained. "He said Alice wanted a divorce. He also claimed he never struck Alice, that her wounds were self-inflicted." I paused, wondering if I'd said too much.

"Did Willard say why Alice inflicted the wounds?"

"Yes, he'd signed a prenuptial agreement that basically said in the event he ever abused Alice and she filed for a divorce, there would be financial compensation." I fell silent.

Spectator comments erupted. Unhappy with the disruption, the Judge Hartford rapped his gavel, said, "Order in the court!!"

Vanguard cleared his throat then asked, "Did Willard explain why Alice wanted that clause included in their prenuptial?"

"Yes, he did. Alice was previously married to a man who physically abused her. She was apprehensive to marry again without some protection. Love is not always enough."

At that, the spectators and jury laughed.

"Alice wanted to be compensated for pain and suffering if Willard ever treated her badly," I told Attorney Vanguard.

"At some later date, Mrs. McLaughlin, you went to see Detective Clay Bennett with some additional information concerning Alice's death. Is that correct?"

"Yes." I collected my thoughts. "I received a phone call from a woman who claimed there was a threat issued against Alice's life by someone she was talking to in an online chatroom."

"Over the internet," Vanguard clarified for the jury.

"Yes," I answered. "Topeka, her fake internet name, told me over the phone that the wife of the man Alice was seeing had threatened Alice. If she didn't stop harassing her husband, Blade herself would stop Alice." I heard gasps in the courtroom.

"Order in the courtroom!" the judge called out.

"Thank you, Mrs. McLaughlin, that will be all for now."

Vanguard then addressed Judge Hartford. "I reserve the right to recall this witness at a later date."

"So noted," Hartford responded.

As I took a seat in the courtroom Vanguard called a woman to the stand. Martha Kinsley was the person who phoned me.

After revealing she was Topeka, my caller, Martha confessed she did not know Blade's real name, or if Tigress, Alice Jacobs, was engaged in a sexual affair with Blade's husband. However, Blade had threatened to stop Alice from talking to her husband.

When Martha stepped from the stand, Judge Hartford called for a lunch recess. Court would resume at one p.m.

I had a Subway down the street and was back at the courthouse by 12:45, feeling Willard was gaining positive ground. But his attorney still had a ways to go to prove his innocence.

The knife that slit Alice's wrists had Willard's fingerprints on it. He had both motive and the opportunity. Aware that Alice had a relationship with another man was a motive for murder.

If we knew the man's name, he could clear up the matter.

The next witness called was a coroner from Nevada.

Lionel Barker was sworn in and testified that in late December he embalmed a man who had died in a similar fashion to Alice Jacobs. The police had concluded that Henry Fairchild had committed suicide by slitting his own wrists.

Attorney Vanguard held up a sworn affidavit and waved it at the jury. "Here in my hands is sworn statement from the Sheriff of Lincoln County in the state of Nevada that Patricia Fairchild confessed to murdering her husband and admitted to taking the life of Alice Jacobs in exchange for a more lenient sentence."

Vanguard waited for the loud conversation in the courtroom to die down. All of Judge Hartford's rapping didn't silence them.

"Are we ready to proceed?" The judge was rattled.

"I am," Vanguard replied. "Patricia. Fairchild confessed she flew to Nashville on Tuesday, December 30 of last year and drove over to Alice Jacob's house to confront her. In a fit of rage, she murdered Alice in cold blood with a knife she'd found in the garage. Using surgical gloves, she left no DNA evidence."

The court was in disarray, reporters scurrying in and out of the doors despite police presence. I was elated over the news.

"Order in the court!" Judge Hartford rapped several times.

"Furthermore," Vanguard continued, "the Lincoln County sheriff's department verified that Patricia Fairchild worked as a forensic scientist for a Las Vegas laboratory. She had both the knowledge and skill to pull off a perfect crime. . .

"Dr. Fairchild confessed to hiring a detective to follow her husband Henry when she suspected he was having an affair. Presently, she's being held for trial on Murder One in a Spring County Jail. In lieu of this evidence, I request a dismissal by this court, and that Willard Dean Jacobs be cleared of all charges."

The dandy had done a dandy job, I thought.

"Hand me that document," Judge Hartford told Vanguard.

After carefully reading the sworn statement, the judge declared the case dismissed, excused the jury, and instructed the guards to release the prisoner. Reporters' cameras flashed all over the courtroom as applause broke out. The smile on Willard's face was priceless. I knew he loved Alice, and he grieved her death.

To be accused of her murder was an unbearable burden to an innocent man. To think Willard might have spent his life behind bars was unthinkable. But, now he was a free man.

45

FLOWERING GRASSES DOTTED the green grassy hills behind our house with color. Summer was upon us and I'd yet to invite my sisters for a visit. Sam was better but still subject to infections.

June emerged, exuding its charm and giving birth to darker greenery covering the countryside. Primroses were in full bloom and I was all about spring cleaning while quoting Bible scripture to discourage our unwanted guests. I invited my sisters for a visit.

Becca drove Beverly from Atlanta to our house for a three day sisterly visit the second week in June. We had a great time shopping in town and reliving childhood adventures. I learned Bev purchased a cottage in Stone Mountain and joined a church.

Sam was almost finished with chemotherapy and his white blood count was currently stable. After six treatments, he had been evaluated by the oncology staff at Vanderbilt University.

While my sisters were with me, I received the report.

Sam's Hodgkin's was in remission. Dr. Clooney would continue checking his blood every three months up to a year. If the cancer did not return, she would see him every six months. After one year of being cancer free, checkups would occur yearly.

Sam's spirits soared as his hair grew back. I told my sisters goodbye and promised to visit them soon. Meanwhile, Jeffrey was asked by the Bishop if he'd like to pastor a mid-city historic church in Chattanooga. He came home with the news, smiling.

"What did you tell them?" I quietly asked.

"Yes!" He swung me around in circles. "I told them yes!"

We gathered the family in the living room and shared our good news. We had been in our house for nearly four years. These had been the most trying times of our marriage. Our family had witnessed paranormal events and somehow coped, realizing that ghosts were something no human would ever comprehend.

I didn't pretend to know how it was possible for disembodied spirits to actively interfere with the living. Whether these ghosts were lost human souls trying to avoid damnation, or demons emulating people who had violently died in the house, Jesus only knew. For a pastor's wife, a mother of three boys, or a skilled teacher, deciphering the truth was way above my paygrade.

In my own way, I told Gibby goodbye and admonished him to please rest in peace. That was what I intended to do.

With Sam on the mend, our family looked to a better future with less aggravation. July thirty-one, we moved out of the house and put it on the market. In time, it sold to a retired couple.

I stood outside the house one last time and sighed.

Now be nice, Gibby, I quipped as I drove away.

A Note from the Minister's Wife

The publication of this book was delayed because I had difficulty reading it at first. My children did not come away from our haunted house without psychological problems but we're coping as a family. Realizing that paranormal activity is a reality and that quantitative evil exists in the world gives me a greater appreciation of God's goodness and grace toward humankind. I left that house wiser about conquering my fears and overcoming challenges. I've also learned that life as a Christian doesn't mean freedom from pain and suffering. As human beings, we experience illnesses, unknowns and hardships, just like unbelievers. But we have something valuable as Christians: faith that God is always faithful.

About the Author

M. Sue Alexander is the author of the *Resurrection Dawn 2014* Christian-fiction series and other independent novels. In her Res Dawn twelve-novel series she depicts a time in American history when secular thought is in conflict with Christianity in social, political and religious venues. Heroin Victoria Tempest is learning that practicing her Christian faith is difficult while she solves her attorney-husband's murder, a twenty-five-year-old cold case.

M. Sue lives on a farm in Middle Tennessee with her husband. She had three grown married children and six grandkids who all love to visit the farm. View Sue's website at www.resdawn.net for more information on her novels sold on Amazon Books as print-on-demand paperback novels or download copies on e-readers.

www.ingramcontent.com/pod-product-compliance
Lightning Source LLC
Chambersburg PA
CBHW071255250626
47159CB00004B/1191